Critical praise for *The Spartan*

Harrison has accomplished the difficult feat of incorporating a powerful spiritual idea in a sexually provocative entertainment — because he knows that male love makes brothers of us all.
—The Advocate

An athlete's-eye view of an important part of our past.
—Gay Community News

In the tradition of Mary Renault's *Last of the Wine*, Don Harrison, with the writer's brush, has painted a vivid portrait of the splendor that was ancient Greece, and the glory of her Olympian champions... a reading experience that is pure pleasure.
—This Month in Mississipi

Illustrated by the author

The
SPARTAN

Don Harrison

Boston • Alyson Publications, Inc.

First published by Alyson Publications, Inc., Boston, Massachusetts, as a paper-back original.

First edition, first printing: June 1982
Second printing: September 1983

ISBN 0 932870 20 1

*to my friend
Jim Wylie*

❦ 1 ❧

"Pin him! Take him down, Pantarkes!"

Cleon's words were a blur. As easily as if he were taking a melon from market, Milo drew my head under his strong arm, squashing my ears, cutting off sound. He dug his feet into the soft sand to secure his hold on me. Hoping to trip him I whipped my legs around and dug my fist into his belly. With my other hand I reached up his back, trying to grab his hair. Still I couldn't free myself. I thrashed around, helpless; the pain inside my skull was becoming too much to bear. Shit. I reached down and gave Milo's dangling balls a firm downward yank. With a scream he released me, then he fell over into the sand, doubled up, his hands and arms between his legs.

"Damn you, Pantarkes!" Milo's teeth were clenched, his face contorted with pain. "That's not fair, grabbing the balls, and you know it. I'll tell the trainer."

"Don't be a sissy, Milo. Where's your Spartan courage? Did you see anything, Cleon?" Cleon, waiting beside the sand-pit for his turn to wrestle, shook his head.

"I didn't see anything. The trainer is over there with the young runners. He didn't see anything either." Near the columns a bearded man, his back to the wrestling pit, watched as several noisy adolescent boys prepared to run the length of the colonnaded palaestra.

"It's my word against yours, Milo. Get up, you big stupid oaf. I've got a wrestling match with Cleon. We can't wrestle with you flopping around in the sand-pit." Milo sneered as he slowly got to his feet, his

7

hand clutching his genitals, and hobbled off in the direction of the trainer.

"He might cause trouble for you, Pantarkes," Cleon said as he jumped into the pit. "His father is an Ephor of Sparta, you know." I backed up, my hands and arms held in front of me, slightly bent from the waist in the wrestling stance.

"I know. Milo's a slob even if his father is a big man in Sparta. Nobody likes Milo. But he's strong as an ox, and grabbing his balls was the only way I could break his grip. Shouldn't have, I know, but..." I watched Cleon take his stance. I liked Cleon. He was near my own age of sixteen and was my height and weight. The hot afternoon sun glistened off his oiled body. Hours of training in the palaestra had broadened his shoulders, and the fibers of his muscular triceps quivered with tension as he made ready for the match. We circled, our legs and feet tense, ready to take the brunt of a fall.

I grabbed Cleon's forearms and moved in. Eye to eye, we watched one another carefully, each anticipating the other's move. Quickly, we were at each other. Breaking, rushing in, grabbing Cleon around the chest; our legs and feet tangled. He braced his forearm against my chest, trying to throw me backwards. I held on to his slippery skin, and my hands locked together in the small of his back. I squeezed with all my strength. Cleon groaned, arching backwards, trying to pull away. His sweat made his oiled skin even slipperier. My skin was sandy after an afternoon of wrestling, the sand sticking to the olive oil, and he was able to push me away with a heave, breaking my grip to send me back into the soft sand with a thud. Quickly he fell on top of me, holding my shoulders down, pressing his advantage. I squirmed but he held me, the hot sand of the pit biting into my back. I raised my index finger in surrender. Cleon rolled over, laughing, sweat pouring off his brown sunburnt body. He pulled off his headband; wiped his brow, and tossed the hair from his dark eyes. He gasped for breath.

"It's about time to call it quits. The sun's hot." Cleon brushed the sand off his strong flat belly and from the thin line of black hair that traveled up from his thick, wiry pubic hairs. "I've got sand in my balls." We got up.

"Me too," I said, brushing the hot sand from my legs and genitals. "It's best we scrape down. I'm getting hungry." I threw my arm around Cleon's shoulder and we headed for the other side of the palaestra. The loutron, the room set aside for scraping and washing the body after exercise, was almost empty because most of the athletes had gone home. We grabbed the bronze strigils from their hooks on

8

the dirty whitewashed wall and had begun scraping the oil, sweat and dust from our bodies, when an attendant came in.

"Want a bath?" he said, indicating several large water jars standing against the wall.

"We're pretty dirty... yeah. Have you seen Timon, my pedagog? The old helot went down to market to get some stuff for supper."

"He's back. He's sitting with the others out in the sun. Want me to call him?"

"No. Let him set. Those old bones need the warmth." The attendant went to the wall and picked up the big jugs as Cleon and I sat down on the bathing slab. Returning, the attendant poured the tepid water over us. The water felt good as it washed the remaining grains of gritty sand from our hair and bodies. "Think you slaves would clean up the latrine once in a while. The place smells."

"Up my ass. If you want it cleaned, you do it." The old slave gave me a mean look as he threw us a towel and went off to get our tunics. We got up, briskly rubbing the rough towel over our wet bodies. The slave returned. "That'll be three obols."

"Three! Yesterday it was only one."

"The price just went up for you," the slave said as he put our clothing down on a bench. I dug into my purse and found the three small bronze coins. The attendant grabbed them with his gnarled hand and walked away.

"I don't think he liked your remark about the latrine."

"To Hades with him. I should report his insolence." We put on our tunics, our broad-rimmed sun hats and our sandals. As we started out of the palaestra, we were halted by the trainer. From the scowl on his face I could see that he was angry.

"What in the shit are you doing with those sandals on? Take them off. You know they're forbidden. A soldier's feet must be hard for marching. What's this I hear from Milo? He says you grabbed his balls, Pantarkes. You know that's forbidden. You know the rules: no gouging the eyes, no biting, no ball-grabbing. Could get you kicked out of school or worse!" The lean trainer spoke with a harsh edge, as if to emphasize his warning.

"Milo's a big stupid oaf. Always whining. In all of Sparta there's no one more stupid." Cleon and I bent down to remove the offending sandals.

"He could get your ass for this. He says he's hurt. His father's slaves carried him home. His father is an Ephor of Sparta and you know what that means."

"Yeah, yeah, I know. A beating at the temple if he goes against me. I've tasted the lash before. It was nothing. I didn't mean to do it. I'm sorry." And I was sorry, too. Everyone knows the power of the Ephors and the dreaded Krypteia.

"Just stay out of his way. If Milo is seriously hurt... just stay away from him." The trainer's voice had lost a bit of its edge. He wasn't a bad guy and I thought he had my interests at heart. I knew he disliked the whining Milo as much as anybody.

"I plan to do just that." Cleon and I walked out of the cool colonnade, into the hot dusty portals of the big palaestra. Sitting on a low bench in front of the shabby building were several old men. I saw Timon, my pedagog. Timon had been responsible for my care for as long as I could remember. Since he was a helot and a non-person no one kept track of his age, but he must have been near to sixty. Old Timon sat with his white hair and beard bobbing up and down, snoring loudly, a sack of groceries at his feet. It was lucky for him that a thief hadn't made off with it, but it's said that the gods protect drunks and old men. I smiled. "Better go wake up the old man.... to Hades with a soldier's calloused feet, these rocks are hot. I'm putting my sandals back on." Cleon and I bent down. "Be careful going home, Cleon. If you see anybody, take them off. It could be a crack-down." Cleon waved as we parted and he walked away down the dusty street for home.

There is a saying: All Hellenes fear the Spartan, but the only thing the Spartan fears is another Spartan. And it's true. You never know when one of those Dorian bastards will try to get you for violating one of their stupid rules. You learn to be careful. I went over to Timon and shook him. "Wake up, old man, it's time to go home." Timon nodded; his eyes opened and he looked up at me.

"Pantarkes, my boy. I must have fallen asleep waiting for you. The sun's hot and warms me. Help me up. Seems every year the stiffness in my joints becomes more painful." I took his hand and slowly Timon gained his feet.

"Here, let me help you with the sack."

"The vegetables don't look good. I've asked your father to start a garden, but he says it's too much trouble. We'd always have fresh things." The old man got his walking stick and we started down the hot street toward home. Summers are a bad time in Sparta; winter too, as a matter of fact. We go from blistering heat to bitter cold. Sparta is a stern place, even grim. Our only claim to fame is the temple of Artemis Orthia, that terrible goddess, her altar clotted with dried blood. Sparta, unlike other cities I've heard of, has no walls. Our warriors are our only walls, as the saying goes.

My father's house was on the other side of town and was a long walk, made even slower by the stiff-jointed Timon. The sun was setting as we reached our house, a low-walled building, some parts of mudbrick and some of stone. I opened the wooden gate, allowing Timon to go in first. The courtyard is small, planted with several ancient fig trees. We entered the main room, the megaron, with its large circular hearth. As usual my father's three great Laconian mastiff hounds set up a noisy bark to greet us, nearly knocking us to the floor with their big paws. My father was at the table going over his accounts as we entered. He looked up.

"Pantarkes, Timon, you're back. How's school?" he asked with warmth.

"Fine. Had some good matches. I was thrown several times though."

"You've got young bones. You can take it."

"Where's brother?"

"Outside playing. Call him in, it's time for supper." Father went back to his books; Timon went to the kitchen; I went outside to look for my brother Damon, who was nearly fourteen years of age, and was fond of playing in the hills around the house. I called his name, which echoed around in the growing darkness. Soon he came trotting like a young puppy down from the hills, dirty as usual. Damon was big and strong for his age and something of a neighborhood bully. He would often pick on boys older and bigger than himself, sometimes with unfortunate results: a black eye or a bloody nose. You grow up tough in Sparta.

He carried a short spear and something was flung over his shoulder. He held it out as he approached. "Look, I've caught a hare. There'll be some meat in the soup tonight," he said, proud of his catch. Arm in arm we went back into the house. Timon had lit the oil lamps and the pleasant aroma of cooking filled the air. Damon took the hare to Timon in the kitchen where it was cleaned and thrown into the cooking pot.

I worried about my father. His health was never good. He was a wine merchant and business was sometimes good, sometimes bad. Rough seas had sunk several merchant ships in recent years, sending the cargo of wine to the bottom. Some of the soil in our vineyards had turned saline and our crops had diminished over the years. Now we

11

had to count our obols and drachmas. When my mother died three years earlier we had been able to afford only a small grave marker, though it was of the finest marble. Her grave goods were only a leaky old iron pot and her weaving stuff. It was all we could afford.

Our family had farmed in Sparta as long as anyone can remember and once had much property — that is, until the Dorians came and took it all away. Our family was reduced to being mere perioikoi, freemen with few rights, really no better off than the slave-helots. But we survived as best as we could. I thought of this while I watched my father at his ledgers. At last Timon brought the soup pot and we ate our supper.

Father has always insisted that my brother and I learn to read and write, skills which receive little attention at school, since the goal of Sparta is to produce the perfect warrior and a soldier doesn't have to be literate. So after supper, Timon, Damon and I read from faded papyrus scrolls the words of Homer and Hesiod. Sometimes I would play the pipes or strum on an old four-stringed kithara, but oil for the lamps is expensive so we usually went to bed early.

My brother and I shared an upstairs bedroom. I lay in bed staring up into the darkness, waiting for sleep and listening to my brother's deep breathing. Visions of the gold-bearded Aristion passed pleasantly through my sleepy head. Aristion, the Olympic runner. Such a fine, handsome man; all of the young athletes had a case of puppy-love for Aristion. To have won victories at Olympia... Aristion... I drifted into sleep to the sound of hoof beats far away.

Snap. Thud. Boom. I was in bed. I was young, a boy. The sound of horses. Clop. Clop. Pounding. I heard my father screaming. I fought the horror of the dream, trying to wake up. Dimly reality returned, but the sound or horses remained. I could hear the thundering hoofs of horses coming down the road. I waited for the noise to pass our house. The shouts of men filled the night air. Torchlight flickered off the ceiling of the bedroom. My heart froze. A trickle of sweat ran down my backbone. There was a pounding on the courtyard gate. I got up, wrapped the sheets around me, and went downstairs. The hounds set up a loud barking and they were at my heels as I went through the house, stumbling, cracking my knee against father's table in the darkness. I opened the gate and for a moment the torchlight blinded me. Gradually a figure emerged. I thought that it must be a daemon from deepest Hades come to take my soul, so frightening was the sight. Whatever it was wore a long cloak, a crested helmet, and held a sword, which it had used to pound on the door. It spoke. "I seek the

12

house of Panyasis, the perioikoi wine dealer." I froze. This was no daemon from Hades, but it might as well have been. I recognized the thick gutteral voice of the Persian, henchman of the Ephor and of the Krypteia, the dreaded secret police. Had they come for my father? What had we done?

"I am Panyasis, the wine dealer." Father had arrived, followed by Timon. "What do you want?"

"I seek the boy, Pantarkes."

"I am he." I spoke up, my voice quivering with fear. Wordlessly the Persian and his guards strode in. Their heavy hobnailed boots clunked on the stone floor of the house. We followed in their iron-like wake, like little mice being fed to a huge snake. They turned suddenly on their heels, facing us.

"What do you want?" Father's voice was timorous, not really wanting to hear the answer. "What do you want with my son?"

"Shut up! We've only words with the boy." The five torch-bearing men, their heads covered by bronze and crested helmets with only small eyeslits for vision, loomed like underworld monsters. Their leader, the Persian, spoke like a foreigner and was difficult to understand. All Hellenes hate the Persians, that's why this man was given the name, but he could have been any sort of barbarian, Egyptian, Mede, or anything. I stepped forward, ready to take whatever came my way.

"I am Pantarkes."

"A complaint has been made against you by Milo, the son of the Ephor of the second district. You injured him today while wrestling. He is in great pain and his scrotum is swollen. His father is much angered."

"I didn't mean to hurt him —" My words were broken off.

"The injury was made by a perioikoi to a person of high rank. The Ephor calls for your death."

"No!" My father cried out, falling to his knees in fear and dread. I backed away towards the door. Should I make a break for it? They would never catch me in the hills.

"Stop! You'll never get away. Seize him!" The four guards grabbed me, holding me fast. "While the Ephor calls for your death, there was one who spoke up for you. Why he did, I cannot understand. He suggested that since this dispute started in the wrestling ring, it should end there. Milo challenges you to a grudge-fight. A pankration, with no rules. You'll meet him in two days. If you run away a proxy will be selected, perhaps the sandal-wearing Cleon." The five bearers of evil

13

news clanked out of the house with no more words. The sounds of their swift horses faded out of hearing.

"What's this all about, son?" I told Father of the events of the former afternoon. "You've made a serious enemy. Can you win against this Milo?"

"I don't know. A no-holds-barred pankration against someone older and stronger. Milo is a champion wrestler. The Ephor wants my death one way or the other. One thing is certain, you can never trust a Spartan. Only the trainer knew about our wearing sandals, and he told. Who can you trust in this place?"

"You seem to have a friend, the one who spoke up for you. Do you know who that might be?"

"I don't know, might be anybody. As far as I know I've no friends in high places."

"We should have escaped years ago. When you were a child they came like they did tonight and took me away; they accused me of selling watered wine to the garrison. I was there for months before I was found guiltless by the Gerousia, the council of elders. That stinking jail."

"Yes, I remember the night they came. We were terrified."

"Escape, son. Seek the protection of the Thebans at Messene. Certainly the Ephor means for you to die at the hands of his son. Go to Messene, for my sake. I couldn't take your death, after the death of your beloved mother. You're strong, strong and vital. Find a life somewhere else. I love you and Damon more than anything. Escape, son, while there's still time."

I was deeply moved by my father's words. He had never before expressed his feelings to me in such a way. I had always taken his love and protection for granted, not thinking about it. I embraced my father for the first time in years, feeling great love for him. "I cannot leave you. I must stay. We're the true Spartans, not the Dorian invaders. It's us against them." I mustered every bit of courage I had. "I must face Milo, though he may kill me. That's the true Spartan way. He'll never defeat me. I'm a better wrestler than he is. You'll see." My words were empty boasting. Crawling deep in the pit of my belly was raw fear. I didn't stand a chance against the brute power of Milo and I knew it.

"I know you will, son."

"Besides, if I bolt, Cleon will have to fight Milo and that would be unfair."

Dawn came. I had not been able to sleep and I watched the still, sleeping form of Damon. He had inherited mother's fair complexion and his blond hair framed his innocent face as the early light filled the little room. Gradually he stirred from his sleep and sat up, scratching himself and wiping the sleep from his eyes. "Pantarkes, you're awake. I thought I heard a pounding last night. It was probably a dream."

"It was no dream. The Persian showed up. I've been challenged to a grudge-fight at the palaestra for breaking the rules. You know these Dorian bastards and their rules."

"Can you beat the guy?"

"Yeah, nothing to worry about."

"Nobody can beat my big brother at anything. He's the best." Damon gave a wide grin that warmed my heart.

"Come on, get out of bed. The goats have to be milked and the cow fed. I can smell fresh bread."

After the chores and the morning meal, Timon and I set out for the palaestra. Already the garrisons and barracks of the famed Spartan warriors were alive. Men and boys were on the field practicing the soldier's arts: sword and shield, javelin tossing, and marching to the harsh commands of the drill instructor. Girls are not exempt from military training: strong mothers bear strong sons. Only the strong survive in Sparta, the weak are taken to the throwing place and tossed out onto the sharp rocks — the grim place is a favorite hunt of wild beasts. Timon and I watched for a while, then moved on down the road.

I looked down at the palaestra with fresh eyes that morning. It was the place of my downfall. The trainer, whom I had thought to be my friend, I now looked upon as an enemy. Timon went to market and I went inside to strip. Cleon ran up to me. "Pantarkes... I heard... it's all over the palaestra. A grudge fight with Milo. Oh, Pantarkes, what will you do?"

"Fight him. It's the only thing I can do."

"You can't stand up against that big lout. They found out about our wearing sandals. I've got a beating coming up. The Persian was at my house last night."

"Mine too. Scared the shit out of all of us. Don't trust the trainer, he's the one who told the police."

"I figured that out. I saw him, he didn't say a word. I left my sandals home this morning."

"Me too. Well, Cleon, we'll just have to face our punishment. How many lashes will you get?"

"Ten."

15

"Oh, Cleon, that's terrible. Five is the usual number. Can you stand it?"

"I don't know. With any luck I'll pass out before the final lash. Shit."

"Oh, come on, let's have a match. It'll take our minds off our troubles." We stripped and entered the columned palaestra, which was filled with naked athletes, men and boys grunting, straining and sweating. The boxers' hands were wrapped with himantes, soft ox-hide strips to strengthen the wrists and to steady the fingers. They pounded each other with mighty blows. Jumpers, with metal weights in their hands, practiced their art, the length of each jump carefully measured. On the far side of the building hefty men practiced throwing the discus.

We went over to the wrestling pit, but it was full and it would be some time before we got our chance. We watched for a while as the young men grappled with each other; nervously looking for an opening; grabbing; eyeing a weakness or quirk that would give them an edge; seizing a chance to move in; throwing for a fall; getting the pin.

Different men have different builds that determine what sport they are best suited for. Runners and jumpers are lean; their body sinewy, flat, all bone and muscle. Others, like myself, are stronger, more filled out, with big chests, arms and legs. With a build like mine, I could have taken up the discus or boxing, but I've always liked the feeling of man against man, the raw strength of muscle power. Besides, there is an element of sensuousness in wrestling. I like feeling another man's strength against me; my strength against him. More than one time my cock had gotten hard in the ring and several times I even had an orgasm, once with Cleon and he with me. We laughed and took a bath.

We walked around, watching the athletes. I stopped and leaned against the plaster wall, a grimy wall made dirty by generations of sweaty and oiled bodies leaning against it, while Cleon wandered off to the smelly latrine. There was a cheer. The athletes in the yard all stopped and looked toward the entrance of the palaestra. My heart dropped into my belly. It was Aristion, the Olympic champion, Sparta's favorite son and hero and the object of many crushes. I daydreamed about him often, myself. Hellas has many famous kings, warriors and philosophers, but not one of our citizens is more honored than those who have competed and won in the Games. As a youthful runner, Aristion had taken victories at Nemea, Isthmus, and Delphi, and at eighteen and at twenty-two years of age, had taken

16

victories in the famous Games at Olympia. Statues were raised to honor his name, odes were composed celebrating his victories and Sparta had given him gold to last a lifetime.

The crowd cleared away. Aristion stood alone in the bright morning sunlight. He saw me and started my way, grinning. My heart, which was already in my belly, fell down to my big toe. "Pantarkes, my friend," he said, extending his hand in greeting. What can I say? I almost fainted as he touched me.

"Aris... Aristion?" My voice quivered as his intense blue eyes caught mine. The sun glanced over his gold-bronze hair and beard, his lean frame clothed in a tunic of finest wool, his headband of spun gold, his feat shod in sandals of finest leather.

"I want to talk to you, Pantarkes. Let's go over there." He pointed to a quiet spot beneath the shaded colonnade. "I've watched you in the wrestling pit, you have great skill." He spoke softly as we walked. "You know the decision of the Ephor? I was there when he called for your death. It was a hasty and stupid decision. The Ephor is a stupid man, just like his son, but he loves his son and was very angry. It was all I could do to save your life. I thought with your skill you would have an easy victory over Milo. A pankration was the best I could do. An Olympian does have some power, but in this case, not enough." Aristion took hold of my arm. I could feel tenderness there in his light grip. Tears came to my eyes. I looked away, not wanting him to see them. We stopped.

"Why do you turn away?" he said, taking my chin with his hand, turning my head. "What? Tears? Pantarkes? Why is this?" His voice was a whisper. All sounds and all visions faded as I looked at this man of perfect beauty. I was silent for a moment, stunned. Aristion had saved me from the Ephor's vengeance, I realized. He brushed away my tears.

"I... I'm scared as all hell. Milo's a full hand higher than me, and heavier. I'll never win."

"Pantarkes, my young lad, you can take Milo any day."

"I can't. He's too big for me."

"You've got something that he hasn't got... a head on your shoulders. Use your brains. Guile and cunning have been known to topple the biggest men. Outsmart him and the victory will be yours."

"I hadn't thought of that. He's stupid and can't see very well."

"A true victor realizes his assets and makes the most of them."

"That's true." Cleon had walked over and stood watching us. "Cleon, you know Aristion?" I asked, noticing my friend. Cleon

17

gulped. "Cleon is a much better wrestler than I. He threw me yesterday."

"We all know of Cleon's skill." The Olympian extended his hand in greeting as Cleon blushed. "My young athletes, my friends, I must go. It seems that I must take a bride, now that I approach my thirtieth year. No more the running fields or the palaestra, but only domestic chores. A role I'll be unaccustomed to playing." He turned to me. "Be of stout heart, Pantarkes. The gods are always with the better man." He took me by the shoulders and smiled, kissing me. "You're in my thoughts, beloved friend." With that, he turned and walked away down the colonnade.

"A true Homoioi," Cleon said with awe.

"Yes," I replied, "an equal to the greatest."

The day of the match arrived. Father, Damon and old Timon walked with me to the palaestra, which was crowded with spectators, each betting on the outcome. Grudge-fights are always popular, especially if they concern the high and the low. The aristocratic Dorians were lined up on one side of the big square and the lesser perioikoi on the other. The nature of the contest, that it was a pankration, heightened the excitement. A pankration, "all-strength" as it's called, is dangerous. A poke in the eye, a torn muscle, or a savage bite can disable a man for life.

At the far end of the palaestra the Ephor sat on a throne-like chair, with other high officials. The Persian and his henchmen stood nearby in case the mob got out of control, for there is great hatred between the classes and riots are not unknown. Aristion stood behind the Ephor, who with studied disconcern was eating grapes. He was richly dressed in a gold embroidered himation; his lean face, lined with middle-age, was framed with flowing silver hair.

The trainer stood in the center of the square, leaning on his forked-stick, his only task to watch for the raised hand of surrender. I walked out into the morning sunlight followed by Timon, and from the other side Milo appeared, followed by his pedagog. We were to wrestle on the hard-packed earth. I ignored Milo, not even looking at him. While his heart may race with fear, an athlete never shows it. I removed my tunic, giving it to Timon. Standing naked, I was ready to be anointed with olive oil, which Timon poured from the small clay jar tied around his wrist. Oiling the body makes a hold more difficult and gives a sheen to the body, and as it is a gift from the gods, it clothes our naked selves with magical protection.

Oiled and ready for the match, I turned this way and that, letting the sunlight play over my burnished skin. Milo did the same, but as I happily noted, with less applause. I kissed the air, sending a prayer to the Immortal Hermes, patron of the palaestra and protector of wrestlers.

We took the stance; the trainer raised his stick; we moved in, dancing around for a while, looking for a hold. Milo grabbed for me; I moved aside; he fell, then got up with a grunt. I avoided his grip, but I couldn't keep that up forever, or I would forfeit the fight for showing cowardice. Taking the offensive, I lunged at him; he moved away, just as I knew he would. I grabbed his upper leg as I passed by and jerked him around. His squinty pig-eyes looked surprised. He reached out for me, trying to get a hold on my hair; I ducked, moving away. With my arms around his leg I butted my head into his belly, hoping he would fall backwards. He hopped around on one leg. Then, he locked his fists together and brought them down on my back, knocking out my wind.

Pelted by his blows, I quickly released my hold, grabbing his fists, swinging him around. I released him; he fell backwards with a heavy thud. I jumped on top of him but his raised knee hit my lower belly. A sharp pain shot through me. He grabbed my hand, but my forearm was held hard against his throat. Something cracked. For a moment, the searing pain in my hand made me forget all else. Then I recovered. Bracing my toes into the hard earth I brought all my strength into my forearm, pressing his throat. He gasped, grunted, tried to gain a breath. I pressed harder. The pain in my hand was worse, but I saw his stupid face turning purple.

"Surrender, you shit! Raise your arm. I've got you," I screamed. Milo's head turned this way and that as he fought the hold. Minutes went by, they could have been hours. The trainer moved in, expecting Milo to surrender. I applied more pressure. Suddenly there was no resistance. Milo went limp beneath me. His tongue rolled out, a trickle of blood oozed from his lips, his eyes were glazed over. He stopped breathing. His arm fell away from the hold he had on my hand.

"Surrender, you stupid shit!" I again screamed into the purple pig face. The blood streaked onto my arm.

"Milo is dead. You've killed him."

"No!" I grabbed his arm with my good hand, trying to raise it, but it fell to the earth in a dusty plop. He was dead.

Someone shouted. The crowd was talking, getting noisy, wondering what had happened. I stood up and looked down on Milo's body. I had won a fight that could have cost me my life and I should have been pleased. But I felt no joy. The trainer announced Milo's death. There were cheers of anger and of joy: anger from the nobles; joy from the others on seeing one of the hated Dorians go down in defeat.

"Seize Pantarkes!" The Ephor, one fist raised, was pointing the finger of his other hand at me. Beside him the black-clad Persian had drawn his great sword and was coming toward me. My hand and wrist throbbed. Timon gasped with fear, looking at me with big eyes. I looked at him, at my father and brother, who were coming out onto the square.

The Persian, the angry mob... I stood there for only a moment, then I turned and ran for the entrance of the palaestra, running with raw fear from the scene of my victory. I ran out of the portals and down the street, going I knew not where, hopping on one foot and then the other, trying to avoid the sharp stones and the people on the street. I was running out of breath. I must stop or burst. Around a corner was an open door and I rushed in, running full speed into a young girl. She must have just returned from the fountain house; her carefully-balanced jug fell to the ground, shattering and spilling the water. She fell forward as I grabbed her around the neck. "Don't scream! Don't say anything or I'll choke the life out of you," I gasped. She froze. I grabbed the edge of her himation and stuffed it in her mouth, then untied the cord from around her waist and bound her hands as best I could. "Now sit down. I won't hurt you... I'm sorry about the jar." She must have thought the naked boy who so rudely entered the house quite mad.

I caught my breath as I silently closed the door. Loud shouts came from outside. My mind buzzed in circles. What had happened to my father, brother and Timon? What should I do? Go back? Escape? I remembered Father's words about the Theban-held city of Messene, a good two days journey. A place of refuge. The Ephor might seek vengeance against my family. They would escape and join me at Messene. I had to be on my way. The owners of the house might return at any moment. I would go to Messene and ask the Thebans for protection.

The decision made, I had to quickly find clothes and a weapon. I scurried around the house, finding an old cloak and a rusty sword and scabbard. I took some bread and cheese, and was on my way. "I'm sorry, but your masters will be returning soon, and they will untie you." The girl mumbled through the cloth, but I was out the door. Carefully, street by street, I made my way out of Sparta and into the foothills of the Taygetus Mountains. Halfway up the rugged pathway I turned, looking for the last time at the Lacedaemonian plain and Sparta, my home. The five villages looked so small from so high up. Sending a prayer to the gods, I reverently asked them to watch over my family and I turned away, not knowing what lay ahead.or if I would ever see Sparta or my beloved family again.

❧ 2 ❧

"Yeah, he's a Spartan," the hoplite said, noting the faint scars left on my back. "Can always tell a Spartan — by his whip marks."

I faced a dark-bearded man. A bronze cuirass encased his chest and back, greaves covered the front of his lower legs, a cape of wool covered his shoulders, his helmet lay on the table next to him. He sat on the edge of the table looking at me with sharp eyes. From his bearing I assumed him to be the strategos of Messene. "So what did you do, boy? Sneeze at the wrong time? Don't see how you Spartans put up with all the crap. No, don't tell me. I don't want to know why you escaped. You've had military training?"

"I served my time," I replied.

"Very soon there'll be no Spartans left. They can't have any more than about three thousand men under arms, now, down there. Give them a taste of freedom and they never go back. But give me a hard-trained Spartan man any day. They're stupid as hell, but they can follow an order."

"Yes, sir."

"Sparta's nothing now. We Thebans saw to that. There's more serious problems now, with King Phillip and his barbarous Macedonians breathing down the Hellenes' necks. Looks like war up there. What about you, boy, want to be a soldier for Thebes?"

I thought for a moment. Since the age of seven I'd spent many long days learning the soldier's art, but the profession never held much appeal for me. "I hadn't thought about being a soldier."

"It's not a bad life for a young man like yourself. You'll get a fancy

23

uniform, three-squares a day, good pay, a chance to travel and lots of women."

"I don't know, might give it a try."

"Tell you what, why don't you rest up, get your hand taken care of and we'll talk later. Think about it, all right?"

"Yes sir, I'll think about it." The hoplite showed me an empty bed in the soldier's common dormitory, pointed out the latrine, and took me to a physician.

"Lucky for you the hand wasn't broken, but only strained. The swelling should go down soon. A warm water bath might help," the physician said. He turned my hand around. It was still a painful reminder of that terrible day in the palaestra. As I lounged around the walled town for the next several days I watched the hoplites go about their duties. After the stern and rigid life at Sparta, the lack of firm discipline surprised me. The soldiers were a jovial bunch, much given to drinking wine and chasing the local whores. I was approached several times, but turned them down. I still carried thoughts of Aristion around in my head.

The relaxed life at Messene changed abruptly one day. Drums, trumpets and banners announced the arrival of the strategos of Messene. His men were called to formation in the great courtyard of the town. I went down to watch. The dark-bearded man, now dressed in full military gear (and looking very sharp, I thought) loudly announced that a group of people called the Macedonians were on the march. Three-quarters of the Messene garrison was to return to Thebes; they were to pack their gear and move out the next day, taking a galley back to their city. The formation was dismissed, with much shouting and running about. The strategos saw me sitting on the steps and came over.

"Well, lad, what's it to be? You can't stay here forever without earning your keep. If you don't want to be a soldier, we can send you down to work in the kitchens or clean the latrines. No work, no food."

The thought of having to clean the latrines for the rest of my life had no appeal. It was the work of a helot, not a Spartan. There was a certain flash, a bravado about being a soldier, and I sensed a chance for adventure in the life of a soldier. "I've thought about what you said, sir. I think I would like to be a soldier."

"No thinking about it, boy, either you are or you're not. What's it to be? Will you fight for Thebes?" The strategos spoke with harshness, not wanting to spend time on a foolish boy.

24

"I'll fight."

"Good. I thought you might, the kitchen's no place for a fine-looking boy like you. The cooks have strange vices, besides. Come along, we'll get you fitted up and you can march out tomorrow." He called one of his guards, indicating that I was to go along. I followed the guard deep into bowels of the central fort, to the armory where the weapons of war are kept.

"A new recruit," the guard said, "get him fitted up." The keeper of the armory looked up from his desk and came over, mumbling about too much work to do. The stone walls of the big room were lined with spears, swords and shields, body armor, and all sorts of implements of war. The keeper looked me up and down.

"We're low on stuff right now, but I'll see what I can find. Follow me," he said. "Here try this on." He handed me a cuirass consisting of many layers of linen glued together into a stiff shirt, the lower part slit so that the wearer could bend over.

"That fits pretty well. A little tight in the chest, but you can get better stuff when you get to Thebes," he said. He found a plain bronze helmet and a pair of greaves. "What do you want to be? Swordsman? You're heavy in the chest, strong arms . . . the spear's the thing for you." He grabbed a javelin from its place and gave it to me. I was no stranger to that weapon: the long wooden shaft felt familiar in my hands. I found the balancing point near the center of the shaft, taking the imaginary aim with the bronze tip. "I see that you know the javelin," the keeper said.

"I've used it. A Spartan is brought up with a spear in his hand." The keeper recorded my name and place of birth in the records and I officially became a Theban warrior, declaring my allegiance to serve that city for five years. Even so, I had little idea where in Hellas the city of Thebes might be, except it was somewhere in the North, near Athens. Uncomfortable in the tight-fitting stiff shirt, the heavy helmet and greaves, javelin in hand, I marched upstairs into the courtyard. I now looked like everyone else, yet I felt strange and a little silly. The general saw me.

"What do we have here? There was a little Spartan boy here before, but he's gone. In his place is a Spartan man. You look good, Pantarkes. You'll be a good soldier!" He gave me a firm slap on the back. I grinned. I felt a little better about my new role in life.

"There's something I want to talk to you about. I left Sparta in a hurry, leaving my father and brother behind. I don't know what happened to them. I fear for their safety. I thought they might follow me to Messene, but. . . if they should arrive, tell them where I've gone. Please. My father's name is Panyasis, my brother is called Damon and there's an old helot, Timon. If they should come here. . . tell them."

The strategos promised to keep a watch for them. At dawn the five hundred men mustered in the courtyard, then marched out beneath the massive fortified gateway of Messene. We headed south to the seacoast and the port town of Pharae, where we boarded a big, sleek trireme. The warship pulled out of bay. I had never been to sea before and I spent most of the time with my head over the side, puking. Rough waters, howling winds and puking is all I can remember of the long voyage to Thebes.

There's a line saying: If a Hellene has no enemy, he'll go out and find one. Fighting is the main occupation in Hellas. Spartan against Athenian, Athenian against Persian, Theban against Spartan. At this time in our history the Thebans stood on top of the heap of warriors, but their power was threatened by Macedonia and its King, Phillip. All this I was to learn later. As I marched into the city of Thebes that early fall day, my legs shaky from the voyage, I had little idea where I was or who I was to fight.

Thebes, on the Boeotian plains, is not a large city, but it has all the amenities common to any Hellenic city: the Agora with its merchants, the strategion holding the military garrisons, civic buildings, a temple, theaters, and a stadium for sports. We marched to the strategion and quartered. Most of the hoplites were native Thebans and were greeted by their families, but I stood apart, watching. I was alone in this strange place. I walked over to the common mess-hall but there were few men there, outsiders like myself or forgotten mercenaries mostly talking amongst themselves in their native tongues. I went back to my bunk to rest.

The next day, my new life as a soldier was to begin in earnest. The loud and nasty voice of our syntagmatarch bellowed through the dormitory. The brutish-looking drillmaster beat against the foot of my bed with the edge of his sword scaring the devil out of me. The men around me seemed to be instantly awake and on their feet. After the morning meal of wheaten porridge, we ran onto the training field to muster and to practice that torturous invention: the phalanx.

In my boyhood days a unit of only thirty-six men had formed a phalanx, but here it was made of an entire syntagma of two hundred and fifty-six men, arranged into sixteen columns of sixteen men each. Each man carried a shield and a sarissa, a pike nearly fifteen feet long.

26

Somewhere near the middle of this mass of men I was to take my position. Here is the problem: the men ahead of you, behind you, and to either side, are each no more than a foot away. Our shields were locked, our hands carried the unwieldly pikes. In this close order we marched backward, forward, and sideways.

The first day was chaos, as men stepped on each other, banged each other over the heads with the long pikes, rammed each other with the shields. The syntagmatarch and his many assistants ran around screaming and yelling at us. Fighting broke out: the Theban infantry, flustered, pelted each other with blows. In desperation we were broken up into smaller units of eight to twelve men, which seemed to work. We raised and lowered the pikes with some ease, moving this way and that. Slowly I learned to stay out of the way of the hoplite in front of me, and I learned to lower my pike without banging him on the shoulder. "Right turn. Left turn. Raise. Lower," the commands were given briskly, sharply, by the drillmasters. Day after day we drilled and with time we came together as a cohesive fighting unit.

Later an Athenian battalion and an Athenian orator, the middle-aged Demosthenes, arrived in Thebes to seek an alliance between the two cities against King Phillip of Macedon. From what I heard, Demosthenes greatly feared Phillip and often spoke out against him, saying that Phillip sought the conquest of all Hellas. Other Hellenes were favorable to Phillip and would welcome his armies. This had split our country into many factions, some for the king and some against him. Meanwhile his armies moved slowly southward, threatening an invasion although no one knew Phillip's exact plans. Of course, this all means very little to a soldier; decisions are made at the top, gradually filtering down the chain of command to the lowest ranks.

The autumn air was chilly; great flights of migrating birds were crossing the Boeotian sky. In the three months since I had fled Sparta life had become a constant source of new experiences. I made several new friends, who taught me much about my adopted city. Besides going to the palaestra to wrestle, I went to the theater to watch plays. The Spartans would never allow such frivolity! I visited the library, which is a shrine to the great lyric poet Pindar, a native son and pride of the city. His odes to the athletes at the Games fill many large scrolls. His house is carefully preserved and visited by all. Inspired, I tried to write a poem or two, but I doubt if Pindar will have much competition from me. I also took up lessons on the kithara. It had interested me in Sparta but there such things as writing poetry or plunking away at the kithara are frowned upon as unmanly. Here they are encouraged as a mark of a well-rounded man.

On my days off I'd head for the stoa, where I could listen to the philosophers argue about the world and its conditions, of the heavens and the nature of the gods, and of the striving for excellence. Some of their ideas disturbed my thoughts. Several philosophers even professed no faith in the gods, doubting their existence! To speak against the gods seemed to me the highest form of hubris, and I secretly hoped Zeus would throw a thunderbolt at these so-called lovers of wisdom. Some said that life itself had no meaning, that it was best not to have been born at all. Others harangued against our loose morals, saying that we were doomed by our depravity. It was all very confusing, unaccustomed as I was to thinking at all, having learned only to follow orders from my superiors. I went back to the palaestra and the training field where life is more simple.

> Snow on muffled wings,
> long, silent death brings.
> Waiting at the walled place,
> longing for a warm, familiar face.

My little poem reflected my mood as winter closed in upon the Boeotian plains. We would huddle around the dormitory braziers, trying to keep warm, talking about more pleasant times. My thoughts returned to Sparta, to my mother's cheery face, warm kitchen odors, my rough-and-tumble brother playing with the dogs. Many days, wrapped in my wool cloak, I would go to the city gates to stare at the few people coming in, hoping for a sign of recognition. One by one they passed me by and I gave up looking.

In the middle of the winter the strategos called us to the grain bins. The bins were to be closed, the precious grain confiscated for the use of the military. The citizens would have to forage as best they could. Riots broke out, but the citizens were no match for the sharp spears of the hoplites. Many civilians starved as winter dragged on. We were sent into the hills to cut firewood, but as the earth became denuded, our trips grew longer. And there was guard duty. The Macedonians must have been in the same fix; they were raiding the small farms around the town of Chaeronea, some twenty miles west of Thebes.

One frosty morning our syntagma lined us up, our breath white in the chill air, shivering in our military gear. We were about to begin a month of patrol duty, the syntagmatarch announced. We tromped off in the light snowfall, hoping the Macedonians had moved on and were no longer in our area.

The second day out we split into units of sixteen men, and were told to fan out. Our unit went north toward the hills, following a rocky pathway through the low scrub. Something ahead flashed in the weak winter sun. It was the tip of a javelin. We could hear men talking. "Hurry along. We'll get back to camp in time to carve these goats for supper." We ducked as a dozen armed men appeared, shoving a herd of goats along with the butt ends of their short javelins. Our leader raised his spear and rose, charging into the surprised men. Before they could turn their javelins around, the tip of my javelin caught a man in his gut, and I ran him through. He fell backwards, the shaft abruptly aiming at the sky, nearly knocking me over.

The frightened goats ran this way and that. One billy lowered his sharp horns and crashed into my belly, knocking the wind out as I fell to the ground. My left arm and shield crashed against the rocks and my helmet flew off, the strap broken. Between the flying hooves of the goats, I saw a man running toward me, his javelin thrust out. I scrambled up on all fours and tried to crawl away, backwards. I picked up my helmet, and threw it at him; he swerved, giving me just time to get to my feet, but he was on me, his javelin caught the edge of my cape. Then he stumbled, the tip of his javelin ran into the frost-hard earth. I grabbed the edge of his cape as he fell, and yanked him up, then with a swift kick to his groin I brought him down on his back, kicking at the snow. I pulled the upright javelin from the ground and aimed its tip at his throat.

"No! Don't kill me!" he shouted. His helmet had fallen from his head, and I could see that he was only a boy, younger than I. His blond curls stuck to his forehead. His wide blue eyes looked up at me. "Please, don't."

I'd never seen a barbaric Macedonian before. He didn't look much different from us civilized Hellenes. I hesitated, I didn't really want to kill a boy. I raised my javelin slightly. Quick as a weasel he grabbed the shaft from my relaxed hands and sharply kicked my greaves, knocking me backwards. He sprang up, aiming the javelin at my belly. "Die, you stupid bastard," he snarled, his innocent looks replaced by a hard grimace. I backed away, raising my shield. He jabbed at me, I parried this way and that. He ran at me. I blocked his javelin and our shields crashed together. I grabbed at his face and I tried to push him away, but the tip of his javelin caught my leg, gashing my calf. I pushed even harder, giving the tip of his nose a vicious twist. He yelled. I tried to poke his eyes with my fingers. As he backed away, I brought my wrestling skill to bear. I tried to trip him, catching the back of his leg with the tip of my boot and pushing against him with my shield arm.

We stood together locked in battle for several moments, then finally he fell backwards, with me on top of him. The javelin, caught between our bodies, broke in two. I grabbed the short tip and brought the sharp bronze down; the polished metal flashed in the sun before it sank into the boy's throat. His brief scream pierced the cold air. Gurgling, rasping, blood rushing from his gaping wound onto the white red, he thrashed his arms around in agony. A moment later the handsome boy was dead.

I got up with pains of my own, covered with my blood as well as his. I rubbed a handful of snow around my leg wound, then looked around for my fellow hoplites. They were finishing private battles of their own. Soon all the Macedonians had fled or were dead. We rounded up the goats and continued on our way, reaching Chaeronea before dark the next day. Chaeronea is a small town, important only because it lies beside a major road to the north. Forty miles away is the pass of Thermopylae, where the brave Leonidas and the three hundred Spartans died against the Persians so long ago.

Chaeronea had become a military garrison, the townspeople pressed into serving the needs of the soldiers. Older women washed our clothes; younger women served other functions. An old warehouse had been converted into a dormitory, although we had no beds, only our woolen cloaks. My wound, while not serious, was cauterized to prevent infection. Held down by my fellows, a bit in my mouth so I could not bite my tongue off, they pressed the hot iron against my skin, sealing the wound. A true Spartan never flinches in pain, but I had been in Thebes too long. I let out a scream that must have aroused the entire town. They gave me a cup of wine which tasted like vinegar; I gulped it down, limped to my place, curled up in my cloak, and slept the night away.

With the Macedonians nosing around the region, the local farmers were brought into town along with their livestock. The place was chaotic. The slow-moving farmers were constantly under the feet of the soldiers who always acted in a hurry to get someplace, though more often than not their strutting, barking and growling served no purpose other than to look important.

"Up on your feet, you lazy turds." I opened my sleepy eyes. The

30

hoplites around me slowly stirred, crawling out of their cloaks or piles of straw. Here and there, through the wooden rafters of the warehouse, hazy sunlight filtered through the chinks of the roof. I heard a loud banging. It was the syntagmatarch beating the broadside of his heavy sword against the wooden stanchions as he lumbered down the wide central aisle of the big room.

"On your feet, off your butts." Our syntagmatarch, Kratos by name, was the biggest, meanest son of a bitch I had ever met in my young life. His temper would put to shame the three-headed Cerberus, guardian of deepest Hades. Well over six and one-half hands high, with a powerful and massive physique that would pale even mighty Herakles, Kratos towered over the rest of us like a great colossus. Kratos liked three things: drinking, whoring and boulder-throwing. At the training field he had a large collection of rocks, each marked with his name and the weight of each stone. I could barely lift the smallest, but Kratos could lift the largest with ease. Sometimes we would all gather to watch him exercise — his sweating, his groaning, his heaving, were awesome to see as the naked giant, holding a great boulder, would lift his huge arms overhead and fling the stone, the ground trembling as it landed. We all hated Kratos, but would have followed him to faraway Persia if he had asked us, for we grudgingly admired him. "Up, Pantarkes, you've had enough rest. Your wound should've healed by now."

"Yes sir." I looked up at Kratos. His face was a scarred battleground. His nose had been broken in some ancient fight, his left ear was missing, his teeth were yellow and broken.

"You're on guard duty. Watch those filthy farmers, we've had some trouble with them."

The guard mustered before the big wooden building, each man armed with spear and shield. We were watched by the gaunt, shaggy farmers and the villagers as we marched down the wet street to the corral. The cows, goats, sheep and pigs had been seized by Kratos for military use, and the town was tense with resentment and hatred. Hungry eyes followed us all the way and a large crowd now stood around the corral. The smell had reached us from some distance away, and as we neared the corral we could hear the mooing, bleating and bellowing of the caged animals.

The guards who we came to replace moved out and we took their places, our backs to the corral, making a circle of spears around the pen. Fear kept the mob at a distance. A gang of bold and dirty boys gathered around me, giving me the finger, waving their crotches obscenely. I ignored them. An hour passed, then some hoplites came, opened the gates and dragged away an old mangy cow. The mob pointed to the cow as if it were made of gold. They raised their pitchforks, made threats and jeered at us. The boys found a wet pile of cowshit, picked some up, and threw it. A smelly glob landed on my cuirass, oozing down into my tunic. This was too much! I clouted the boy on the head with the butt end of my spear. He fell to the ground, then scrambled away with a bloody head, screaming. The mob gasped and began picking up shit, offal and garbage, pelting us with the smelly stuff. We raised our shields.

"Better go and get Kratos," someone shouted, and a guard ran away down the street. We defended ourselves as best we could, standing our ground. Several members of the mob caught a spear in the gut when they got too close to us, and rapidly the earth was becoming a mire of blood and muck. Soon we heard battle-cries and the heavy clunk of armed men as the mighty Kratos, with his guard, came running down the street. They plowed into the mob with drawn swords, stabbing this way and that. When he reached the corral Kratos let out a battle scream. With sword and spear, more muscle than mind, he was, as we all were, nothing but an efficient killing machine.

Under orders to try to avoid bloodshed Kratos limited our rations, sharing our food with the farmers and villagers. We were left hungry but were glad to see the killing end. These people were of our own blood and we disliked killing our own kind. Better we should save our energy for the Macedonians.

Thirty or forty Macedonians had been captured lingering, and were now waiting in a make-shift prison to be taken back to Thebes, where they would be held for ransom or exchanged for our own prisoners. The prison, a wine-cellar that had been set with heavy wooden bars, held the silent warriors. Now without their claws, they paced the room like captured lions, becalmed but ready to spring at the slightest chance.

A fellow hoplite and I arrived for guard duty late one night. There was the sound of loud snoring, sneezing and coughing, for the stone floor was cold and even the straw and their cloaks could not keep out the damp of winter. With nothing else to do we spent the night playing dice, watching for a lucky number to appear on the little ivory cubes. After a while I noticed an old man squatting on his haunches, watching us from the prison, his gnarled face catching the torchlight through the bars. He seemed to enjoy the game, cheering when a lucky throw came up, groaning when it was unlucky. I was losing more often than not. "Better check those dice, lad, looks like they're fixed." He spoke in a strange dialect.

"These dice are straight. Is that bastard accusing me of cheating?" My friend's voice was edged with anger.

"You do seem to be winning more than I am. Let me see those dice." He handed them over, but they looked all right to me.

"Here, lad, let me see. In my time I've seen lots of loaded dice." He thrust his hand through the bars. I hesitated, having learned not to trust the enemy. "What can I do? I'm an old man, no match for a young lad like yourself." I gave him the dice. He turned them around, shaking them, looking at them carefully. "There's a trick of boring a tiny hole in the side, filling it with shot, making a winning throw a certainty." He threw the dice. "I guess I'm wrong. Looks like a case of just plain bad luck for you, lad." He gave back the dice.

"You're Macedonian?" I asked, making idle conversation.

"Yes, from Pella."

"Pella?"

"The chief city of Macedonia, the capital."

"Where's that?"

"Far to the north, at least two months of marching away. You, where are you from?"

"Sparta. Ever heard of Sparta?"

"Sparta... that's where they let their women run around naked in front of the men, even lock them up together so they'll fuck. Ha, that sounds like the place I'd like to go." The old man sucked on his gums, making clicking sounds, pleased with the vision in his head.

"Do they really do that?" my friend asked.

"Yes. Sparta needs warriors. The offspring is raised by the state, there's no shame in it." I turned to the old man. "Too late for you. Old men like you are driven out when they've served their time."

"I've had my days. True, I'm old, but I can remember how it was. I'll retire soon, go back to Pella and die, too old to fight, but I can steal goats and carry slop buckets."

"How long have you been a soldier?"

"All my life, near to fifty years I've given, first to Phillip's father, then to Phillip, marching in his armies. That was long ago. He's come a long way since then. Now all of Hellas trembles before him. He'll take the Thebans in one great big chomp if they oppose him."

"You think there'll be war?"

"Phillip will take Hellas, either by bargaining or by war."

"He's a barbarian, an outsider, not a true Hellene at all."

33

"I wouldn't call him a barbarian to his face, not unless I wanted a sword through my gullet. He fancies the Hellenes and their fine culture. His palace up at Pella is filled with mosaic floors, fluted columns and gold fittings. He has poets, artists, and even a fancy philosopher to teach his son to think like a proper Hellenic gentleman. Aye, there's no end of his love for the Hellenes."

"He has a son?"

"Yes. Alexander should be about eighteen by now. It's been a long time since I served as a palace guard. Phillip was a man to behold in those days, full of energy, ready to do anything, fighting and whoring. His wife is crazy you know, a sorceress. She and her snakes can work the darkest magic. Everyone's scared of her and her spells. She adores Alexander. One time she denied Phillip's paternity, saying the boy was sired by a god. If you wear the royal purple you can say anything no matter how looney. To my way of thinking the she-bitch means to do in Phillip and put Alexander on the throne. . . if she can. Her son just might have been sired by a god, he's handsome enough. Never liked him, arrogant and stuffy, if you know what I mean. He stays his distance from us common folk, runs around with his "Companions" and his lover, Hephaestion. Phillip never lost his common touch or his feeling for the people, I'll give that much to him."

"I don't see how he can win with Thebes and Athens standing in his way."

"From what I've seen the Hellenes have grown soft, lost their will to fight. The Macedonians are rugged mountain men, not used to the effete city ways. Phillip's not lost a battle yet and he'll not lose this one. Got anything to eat?"

"Food's getting short," I said. "Maybe I can find something in my sack." I searched and gave the old man some stale bread.

He broke off a piece. "It's hard to eat with only three teeth. How long have you lads been in the army?"

"Not very long, less than a year. That goes for both of us," I said.

"Like it?"

"Oh, not very well. I want to do something else with my life besides kill people, I don't know just what. If things had been different I would have taken over my father's wine business at Sparta, but I can't go back there now."

"Why not?"

"I killed a man."

"No harm in that, I've killed many in my time."

34

"The man I killed was the son of a high official and that makes a difference."

"Aye, that can make a difference. It's not good to hobnob with the high because they can turn against you in a moment. It's them that has the power, to raise up or cast down anyone they like. Life's like those dice, a game of chance. At times you win, other times you lose."

A loud noise came from the top of the staircase. It was our change of guard. Two men bounded down the stairs, followed by a woman carrying a cooking pot.

"It's time to feed the animals. Get those Macedonians up for their morning feeding," one of the new arrivals said. My fellow and I were dismissed and went up into the cold.

Kratos had already aroused the dormitory with his banging, standing in the middle of the big room barking commands. There was an extra edge of roughness to his voice and as I passed, the smell of rancid wine stung my nostrils. "Pantarkes, where have you been? Out whoring?"

I looked up. "No, guarding the prisoners. I haven't had any sleep."

"You'll get no sleep today. It's time to move out of this dump. Our replacements will arrive soon. I want you to stand guard. We're going to clean the town out when we go, we've been too nice with those shitty farmers. Get on down to the corral in case of trouble."

"But I haven't had any sleep and no food. . . ." Kratos grabbed my cloak, pulling me up with his left hand so he could shout in my face, his strong wine-soaked breath souring the air. With his right hand he pressed the tip of his sword into my gut.

"Listen to me you little shit, don't give me any back talk. You'll do as I say, or else!" He dropped me, swung me around, and with a hard kick to my backside sent me sprawling across the floor. I could tell it was going to be a bad day. Kratos' temper, never the best, grew even worse if he had been drinking. I was lucky he hadn't run me through, as he had others. I rose with as much dignity as I could, while the entire dormitory looked on, and I hurried to the corral.

The day passed without incident. Fortunately for us, the farmers of Chaeronea didn't know they were about to lose their cows, sheep and goats. Spring was arriving in full force and I stood in a drenching rain that day. Great rolls of thunder crossed the sky. The dark clouds flashed with lightning. I was tired, miserable. . . . I would be glad to see the last of this dismal little town. I cursed the Fates who spin out the thread of life. What thread were they spinning for me, and when might they cut that thread? Perhaps I would have a short life, full of glory, as had Achilles and his lover Patroclus, their lives recorded by the Immortal Homer. Or would I end up like the old man in the jail, haggard, toothless, waiting for my thread to be cut? Such grim thoughts passed through my mind that day as I stood soaked with rain, guarding a bunch of cows, in the middle of nowhere. At last some hoplites came to relieve us. We tromped back to the dormitory, mud and grime covering our boots and greaves. I borrowed a dry cape, snuggled in a pile of straw and fell asleep.

A loud yell awoke me. There was screaming and much commotion. I poked my head out of my cloak: there, standing by the doorway was Kratos. The light from the glowing brazier caught his face, it was an ugly face, contorted by anger. Kratos weaved around in a drunken stupor, staggering against the wooden stanchions, lurching, stepping on sleeping men. A loud banging and the sound of angry voices came from outside. The villagers were crying for food and for Kratos' skin. "Enough of rape and stealing our food!" The sound of the villagers' bitter voices rose up from around the building. They began to force the door open with pitchforks, clubs, or rusty spears. "Get that raping bastard Kratos!"

The sleeping soldiers were on their feet, grabbing for weapons as Kratos lurched against the door, but even his strength was not enough to hold back the mob. The door gave and Kratos backed away, stumbling and watching through bleary eyes as villagers dressed in tattered rags, their faces contorted with blind rage, stood for a moment on the fallen door.

"That's him, the one who raped my little girl!" a villager cried. As he waved his pitchfork his face glowed red from the torchlight and the braziers. With a wild growl the villager charged into the room toward Kratos, who stood fumbling for his sword. The rest of the soldiers and I had found our weapons, but we would stand little chance against the hate-filled mob that now filled the room. They paid little attention to us, merely pushing us aside as they made for Kratos who now stood in the middle of the room. He had managed to draw out his sword and raised it above his head, but his arm wobbled and looked as if it might fall.

The villagers stopped, awed by the huge bulk and the fearsome strength of Kratos. They formed a ring around him, shaking their weapons. Kratos growled and snarled like a caged beast, and swung out with his sword. Raising his massive head, he bellowed out epithets: the villagers were pigs fit only for slop and their women were fit only for rape. There was no stopping the mob now. Pure rage possessed them, and in a collective scream they came at Kratos. I watched as in a fitful dream. Someone tipped a brazier over on the floor. The hot coals scattered, catching the dry straw, and we grabbed our cloaks to try to put out the flames, but it was of little use. The flames leaped from straw to straw, soon lighting the wooden floor and the stanchions.

"Get out of here! The whole building is going up! Try to get those bastards off Kratos!" someone yelled. We pulled at the villagers, but the men of Chaeronea were blind to the danger, wanting only to pull their victim to the floor. They grabbed at his legs, arms, only to be thrown off as Kratos struggled against them. A spear flashed; Kratos roared in pain. By now the heat was intense, flames shot up the stanchions, catching the overhead beams. We ran. As I reached the doorway I turned for a last look. Kratos was kneeling, his hands at his chest, his body bathed in fire. The villagers ran out as the stanchions gave way and the roof fell in, covering Kratos with a sea of fire. Kratos died in a funeral pyre of his own making. Several days later our replacements arrived and we marched back to Thebes.

The Kore, beloved Persephone, to Hades taken,
Mother Demeter, great of grief, bitterly shaken
grim Winter brings. No leaves. No flowers.
Now Kore, released, in bright array, fragrant bowers
New life, new hope, young lambs through verdant meadows run.

So went my salute to spring after the grim winter. Of the four seasons none is sweeter than spring, which finally came to the plains of Boeotia. Shoots of greenery surrounded me as I ran to the palaestra. I was in bad shape. Meager rations had made me thin and gaunt. My muscles were stiff from lack of exercise, my skin pale from sunless skies. I filled my lungs with the sweet, bright air of spring as I ran jubilantly down the path.

The Theban palaestra is very beautiful, not at all like the plain building at Sparta. It's built of pure white marble with fluted columns, and elegant capitals. The roof is of red tile and the architectural parts brightly painted. On three sides, beneath the portico, are splashing fountains, with lion-head spouts of greenish bronze. On the north side stands an enshrined multicolored image of Herakles, and a circle of fragrant incense floats up from an altar left by his priests at the morning service. (Herakles, hero and demi-god, was conceived here in Thebes by the Immortal Zeus and the mortal Alcmene.) The great colonnaded square is the pride of Thebes.

I was almost ashamed of my peaked condition as I stripped for exercise, but as I looked around I saw no one in much better shape; we all looked like plucked chickens ready for the stew pot, fish-belly white to a man. But it was good to strip away my tunic and to stand naked, the warm sun on my skin. I stretched this way and that, soaking up the warmth. I greeted old friends as they, too, made ready for exercise.

When I had arrived in Thebes last fall my reception had been much different. Anxious to begin my wrestling after that wretched sea trip, I had barged in like a smart-ass ready to take on all comers, wanting to show the sissy Thebans a thing or two about wrestling. Soon my challenge was accepted by a boy about my age. We took the stance and in a minute I had pinned the boy, cuffed his ears, and bloodied his nose. As he raised his finger in defeat I heard a loud twang and felt a string of sharp pain across my back. Angrily I got up and looked around.

"What's this you're doing, beside mauling this poor boy?"

"I'm wrestling," I replied.

"Wrestling? What kind of wrestling is that, pray tell?"

"Spartan wrestling," I answered with a note of defiance.

"Oh, that kind." The massive man, his trainer's stick in hand, a crown of golden leaves circling his bald head, looked down at me with scorn on his round face. "I thought as much. Go for the throat, the groin, the eyes or nose, anything for a fall. Yes, I recognize the variety. Get up, please. You're forbidden to wrestle here again. If you want to wrestle go join a pack of wild wolves, they'll be more in your league. Away with you, now!"

"What?" I was astounded. Aggressive wrestling was much admired at Sparta. "You can't do that. I love wrestling and have trained for many years. Please don't send me away."

"I can send you away because I'm the trainer in this palaestra. I'm responsible for my men. You've nearly maimed one of my best students with your rough ways and I wish to see no more of you."

"Please wait. I didn't mean to hurt him, that's the way I've been taught." The man stood for a moment looking me over. He walked around me, tapping his stick here and there on my body.

"You've good muscle structure, good skin tone. Can you read and write?" he asked. I nodded.

"Shows you have some brains, anyway. You can stay for a while, but no more challenges. Go and join the boys." He pointed to a group of noisy boys some years my junior. "They're beginners, you are a beginner, and you will begin at the beginning." It gauled me to join the beardless boys, since I stood tall over them. (At that time I was trying to grow a beard, wishing to look older and more manly. I was very proud of it, though I confess the hairs were skimpy and the color much lighter than my normal light brown hair. My beard was bright yellow. One day someone asked if I was growing cheese mold on my face. I shaved it off, hoping the beard would thicken and darken with age.)

I joined the little boys. I learned that the imperious man, Melesias by name, had been a three-time wrestling champion at the Pythian Games at Delphi, sanctuary of Apollo. His victories entitled him to wear the golden crown of laurel leaves. I was ashamed of my hubris.

I *did* have a lot to learn. Here the techniques of wrestling were much different, with an emphasis on balance, leverage and agility rather than on brute strength. The Thebans admire harmony, each part of the body moving in graceful coordination with the other. Our exercises were accompanied by young men playing flutes, thus making our movement more rhythmical. The basic program of the palaestra focused on three elements: the body, the mind and the spirit. It strove to balance and blend these three elements through exercise, learning, and above all, through service to the Immortals who give us life.

All these things were new to me and changed my way of thinking about myself. There is an inscription over the entrance to the palaestra, taken from Homer. It is the words of a father to his son, who was departing for the Trojan war: "Always be the best and excel over others." The words stuck in my mind as I read them. I would be the best, but as I stood with the beardless boys I really didn't know how or what I would be best at doing.

I remained with the boys for several weeks. One day Melesias came over to me. "What's your name, boy?"

"Pantarkes, sir."

"Well, Pantarkes, you want to be a wrestler, eh?"

"Yes sir."

"You look strong, a good flat belly. A wrestler should be strong, but not fat. Your upper body looks weak, but that can be built up. You need a little more weight in the arms. You look like you've got courage and a will to fight. I'll give you a try-out, but no rough stuff, understand?" Melesias tapped the palm of his hand with his forked stick, the badge of his office, which I had already felt on my back.

"Come along, then. You'll do the orthopale, the upright wrestling, and if you get one throw out of three I'll take you on as a student."

I followed Melesias out into the great square to the sand pits. "I've selected this lad to be your opponent. You're about the same weight and height. One throw Pantarkes, all right?" I nodded, overjoyed at my chance, eager for the honor of being trained by a champion. My opponent and I took our stances. In orthopale the object is to remain on your feet while throwing your opponent to the ground or falling on top of him. Melesias watched carefully, prodding us with his stick, giving us instructions. My opponent got the first two falls and I began to worry about my chances. Determined to get one fall I moved in quickly, before my opponent had a chance to think. Legs and arms flew, our heads bobbed, but the slippery boy evaded me. We circled; I went in and our hands locked together. Using every ounce of strength I got a hold around his neck. His head was against my belly; his hands against my waist; he pushed against me trying to break my hold. I heaved, throwing him up over me through the air, onto his back behind me. I had gotten my throw, and with a wide smile I turned to Melesias.

"Good throw, Pantarkes, a hold on high, the best one that I've ever seen. I think you may have some talent, after all. We'll begin training tomorrow."

My joy was difficult to put into words. I made my way to one of the fountains to wash the sand away. My opponent came over, slapped me on the back and thanked me for a good match. But due to the lateness of the season, I had very little chance then to train.

Now spring had arrived and I looked forward to starting again. Melesias had about twenty students that spring. Some had not survived the winter. Others, like myself, bore wounds from our scuffles with the Macedonians. Some were missing an eye or an ear. One poor fellow had lost an arm and sat disheartened on the sidelines. Melesias talked him into changing his sport and the one-armed fellow became an accomplished discus thrower. We began each day with calisthenics, moving our bodies to the rhythm of the flutes, warming up our muscles, getting our psyche in tune for the day's workout. Then we proceeded with the halterobolta, weight-training with halteres to build up the muscles. The bronze or stone weights, of various sizes, we held while we exercised, building our arm and shoulder muscles.

One day as I ran around the training field I noticed Kratos' rock pile, now grown over with weeds. The unfortunate Kratos, with his massive build, had made a deep impression on me. I decided that if he could lift those boulders, so could I. I cleared the weeds away from the smallest rock, then with a heave and a grunt I lifted the thing up. Thoughts came to my mind of the wonderful Milo of Kroton who once carried a four-year-old heifer on his shoulders around the stadium of Olympia. Day after day I lifted those rocks, and gradually my arms grew in strength and I found new strength in my back and legs.

The palaestra, besides being a training school for athletics, was a kind of social club. I enjoyed the companionship of my fellows. There was lots of fooling around: ass-slapping, towel-snapping, water-throwing, cock-pinching, and general nonsense. Athletes are a hardy bunch. Our training is difficult and we like to blow off a little steam once in a while. Usually the colonnades are lined with onlookers, admiring the fine physiques of the athletes. All Hellenes have spent some time in the palaestra and follow sports with great passion and enthusiasm, cheering their favorites, booing the losers. Since I'd done nothing of note, of course, I had no following.

Then there are the others who come to the palaestra, the wolves, the boy-hounds, older men. . . the erastes, seeking romantic liaisons. The eromenos, boys like me of sixteen or seventeen, were the prey. Along with spring, Eros had arrived.

Eros of Aphrodite born. Young, winged God,
man pierced by his dreadful arrow is made mad.
Silly passion, relentless lust, strangely odd,
running here, running there in hot pursuit, somehow sad.
Awful God, cruel God, blinding men so they cannot see.
Oh dear Eros. . . when will you come for me?

Since the time Father Zeus took handsome Ganymede as his eromenos to serve as his cupbearer on Mount Olympus, the ritual of finding a lover has been governed by custom. The approach is made by the older man, the erastes. If he finds you interesting he will try to draw you aside in conversation; getting that far he may brush your face with his fingertips or touch your genitals and then give you the traditional love gift: a cockerel, a hare, a quail, a dog, a horse, even a stag, all leading to romantic involvement.

There's a great amount of arrogance on the part of the eromenos, for we know we hold the reins of the chariot. It's a game and you play hard to get, for the more difficult the prey is to get, the sweeter the conquest, though you have to be careful or the erastes will go on to

41

someone else. Or you may reject the erastes, who will then moon around for a while contemplating the spot where you've placed your genitals or ass, knowing that the spot has gotten a lot closer to you than he will. At times things get out of hand, as when an erastes won't give up his conquest and the eromenos will chase him away with a stick or a kithara. And those love gifts are always escaping the arms of the lovesick erastes. The place looks like a farmyard somehow gone wrong, as the roosters, rabbits, dogs and other beasts bolt here and there. Pandemonium breaks out as the anxious men and boys chase them around. You may find a rabbit has joined you in a wrestling match or a rooster has landed on your head, crowed and shit down your back. At times the palaestra is so chaotic that it closes until the annoying erastes have gone away, but they always come back. It's all very silly until Eros strikes you with one of his deadly barbs and then it's a different picture.

One day I lay on my belly in the sandpit. I had just been thrown, landing with a mouthful of sand, and I looked up to see three beautifully dressed men, two older and one younger, enter the palaestra. They wore golden cuirasses, bronze helmets with horsehair crests, and sword and scabbard hung at their side. Everyone stopped to look at them, and I thought I recognised one of the older men. Melesias ran over to the visitors, shaking their hands, smiling broadly. I thought they might be from another city making the rounds of Theban attractions. They talked for a while, then started across the palaestra.

Melesias introduced the members of his team all around and finally came over to me, where I still lay in the sand, trying to catch my breath. "Theagenes, this is one of my new students this year, he shows fine possibilities," Melesias said to one of the older men. "Theagenes... Pantarkes." I got up and brushed the sand away, slyly looking at the man with proper decorum. He reminded me of Aristion, but it was only because I wanted to see a familiar face so much. Theagenes was much older, his hair and beard shot through with silver. His was a soldier's face, lined, rugged and hard. I looked away, not wishing to give him any ideas.

"I hope you do well. Melesias is a fine teacher, the best in the city." He reached up and brushed his fingertips against my cheek. It was unexpected and I was too tired to think quickly or I would have caught his hand to show my disapproval. I blushed. He walked away with his friends. While pretending to brush the sand away I followed him out of the corner of my eye. He looked at me several times. After the men had left, Melesias came running over to me.

42

"Pantarkes, do you know who that was?"

"No."

"Theagenes, leader of the Sacred Band and one of the richest men in Thebes. You caught his eye, that's for sure."

"What do you think I am, a porne waving my ass at everybody for a drachma?"

"Oh no, Pantarkes. Theagenes is a man of the most honorable intentions and esteemed by all Thebans as a man of great valor and courage." Erastes and eromenos came running over to me, looking me up an down, as if trying to discover what a man of such high position had seen in me. I was embarrassed by their attentions. As I walked to the loutron, several erastes tried to grab me but I brushed their eager hands away. When I arrived at the palaestra the next day all eyes followed me as I stripped and oiled my body. I let them get their eyes full. I looked good; exercise had muscled my physique, the sun had darkened my skin, and with food now available my haggard look was gone. I am as vain as the next fellow and it was nice to be the center of attention in the games of Eros. Many vied for my attention, but I ignored them all, going about my business of learning to wrestle as best I could.

I kept an eye out for Theagenes and several days later he arrived. He wore a simple tunic and carried a short spear. While not handsome his body was muscular, lean, his chest covered with dark hair. He looked around for a while, then spotted me and came over. He knelt beside the wrestling pit to watch my partner and me practice throws. Everyone watched to see if I would accept his advances.

I managed to throw my opponent. Theagenes smiled. "Good throw, Pantarkes," he said as my opponent hit the sand. I looked at him, feeling the pressure on me: would I reply or would I reject him? I had nothing for or against Theagenes, and to tell the truth, his high position meant very little to me at that time.

"It'll do," I said without commitment.

"You show fine form. Have you thought of entering the panegyreis later on in the spring?"

"The festival? I might. Haven't thought about it much."

"You should. It's the big event of the year, the bringing in of the first fruits of the new year. I have some talent with the javelin and I always enter and I always win. Know the spear?"

"I should. I've had one in my hand since I was a child, never had much skill, though."

"Let's see what you can do, my spear against yours. All right?"

43

"All right." We got up and went to the training field, an area outside the palaestra used for running, javelin throwing and at times for chariot racing. I made the first throw, but it landed short. Theagenes took up his javelin, which was nothing but a pointed wooden stick, without a bronze tip. A leather thong was tied at the pole's center of gravity. He took the thong in his two fingers and, after a short run forward, he hurled it. The throw was the best I had ever seen: the javelin traveled up into the blue sky, almost out of sight, and finally came down some distance away. Onlookers cheered; Theagenes beamed; I was impressed. "That was really a very fine throw, sir . . . Theagenes." Blushing like a schoolboy Theagenes came over to take my hand into his, brushing my cheek with his fingertips. Eros had entered my life. Theagenes' spear had not hit the earth, but had hit my heart. The next day he gave me the same gift that Father Zeus had given Ganymede so long ago; a cockerel.

❧ 3 ❧

"And what, pray tell, do the Athenians call you, dear Demosthenes?"

"Batalos."

"An ass, a babbler, a prattler, unmanly and womanish in temper."

"And you, dear Theagenes, of manly figure and hairy chest, what about you and your Sacred Band, three hundred erastes and eromenos. You claim to be the elite backbone of the Theban army, proud and brave to the last man. I hear that the 'Sacred Band' is only an excuse to have one continuous orgy. Is it true, dear Theagenes, that you need three hundred men to satisfy you?"

"If a sword was permitted in this Assembly you would be a dead man, dear Demosthenes. Your Athenian fame as an orator means little here. You're nothing but a rabble-rouser, a babbler. I hear that the Athenians like you even less than we. They listen to Isocrates, who warns that the wily Persians are the enemy, not Phillip. The Macedonian king is our friend and plans no aggression against Thebes. As a matter of fact he was sent here in exile by his brother, Perdiccas, as a peace hostage, when he was sixteen. He spent four years here. He's our friend."

"Sixteen years old... just the right age. Did he spend those four years in your arms, dear Theagenes?"

"Oh, if I had my sword, dear Demosthenes, your head would leave your shoulders in an instant. Phillip was more of a guest than a hostage, and more interested in how we trained our armies than he was in romance. Besides, he cared only for women."

"Phillip, even then, was no fool. Why waste your time on eros when you can learn the arts of war? The result of his learning has been the conquest of all of Macedonia and now his 'learning' threatens all of Hellas."

"We have a treaty with Phillip and we have no wish to break it. It would seem that Phillip is against Athens, not Thebes. Has he not taken the Athenian-held cities of Maroneia, Methone and Abdera, the city of Olynthus, your ally? Has he not seized Athenian merchant ships and set seige to Byzantium? Did he not intervene when the sacrilegious Phocians took the sacred treasures from the temple of Apollo at Delphi, your enemies? We have a treaty of peace with Phillip and will not break it."

"You're fools. All of you are damn fools! He plans the conquest of Hellas and of Athens. He'll set up a slave state and our only purpose will be to serve the barbarous Macedonians. I've no wish to be a slave."

"You think and care only for your beloved Athens and little for Hellas."

"Athens *is* Hellas and don't you forget it. Will Thebes be remembered? Sparta? Corinth? Where else in all of Hellas does the torch of liberty and freedom burn so brightly? The eons will remember Pericles, Miltiades, Peisistratus, Socrates, Callicrates, Phidias and myself, after all of the rest of you have turned to dust."

"We may say that humility is not one of Demosthenes' greatest virtues. The famed orator speaks noble words of liberty and freedom. You speak out of both sides of your mouth, dear orator. Is it true you permit your eromenos, the handsome Aristarkhos, who sits yonder, to bugger you in the ass and to beat you up? Oh, unmanly Demosthenes, shame! How can we believe the words of this woman, who stands there with henna on his hair, rouge on his cheeks and khol on his eyes? You talk of war. War is sweet to those like you who have not tried it, but the experienced man is frightened to see it advancing. Would you fight in the Athenian army?"

"Against Phillip I would fight by myself. And you, Theagenes, do you bugger your dear eromenos? That beautiful wrestler you picked up at the palaestra? I hear you got him only by the toss of a javelin. Poor buggered Pantarkes. He should have held out for more than a scraggy rooster. Eros knows I have to pay Aristarkhos a high price for his favors, but you Thebans are so quaint and bucolic."

"One more word, dear Demosthenes and the sanctuary of this Assembly will be broken by my sword in your gut."

"Ha! Tell me, handsome Pantarkes, do you only let Theagenes stick his cock between your beautiful thighs? If that's all I pity you. It's not much fun . . . but heroic, I suppose. You ideal warriors are all the same; if you would only give up your odd ideas about who's going to be top-dog and stop worrying about 'womanly positions' you'd have lots more fun. Come over to my house sometime, beautiful Pantarkes and I'll lift my legs for you."

"This discussion seems to have sunk to a low level."

"My dear Theagenes, you started the mudslinging, not I. I'm not here to criticize your curious lovelife, but make a warning. I want this Assembly to listen to me now: Phillip means to have Hellas in his pocket or on the tip of his sword. To my way of thinking he means to resolve the question this year. This year Phillip will march on Hellas!"

"You told us that last year. I would leave the arts of prophesy to the oracles. Listen to me, men of Thebes. . . Demosthenes is an Athenian rabble-rouser and even his own city won't support him. I say we send him packing back to Athena's city. What's the vote?"

There was a loud chorus of "Yea's" from the crowd.

"That should tell you something. The 'Yea's' have it in a loud affirmative."

"So the vote is against me. What can I do? What can I say? I'm defeated. You're against me. Athens is against me. Perhaps I'm wrong. Phillip may be content to stay in Macedonia . . . but again he may not. Only time will tell."

I watched as Theagenes and Demosthenes argued from the stone seats of the Theban bouleuterion. Around me some six hundred council members had also sat listening. Now that the vote had gone against Demosthenes the council got up and left. Demosthenes walked out with a snort, his handsome eromenos at his side, and Theagenes climbed the tier of stairs to sit beside me. "I'm sorry that you were brought into this Pantarkes, but the old woman will sink to any level, no matter how low, to make a point. He's defeated now and won't bother Thebes again with his idle threats."

"Oh, that's all right. He seems to know everything about you. And you seem to know all about him."

"Paid informants and spies. The Thebans have them, the Athenians have them and Phillip has them. Spying is a brisk business for some who have no scruples and being spied upon is the price one has to pay if they are someone of importance. Now that you're with me, you've become important and an object of discussion. But enough of that. I thought today you'd like to come out to my estate and meet my sister. I want you to stay with us — the common dormitory is no place for you now. Would you like to do that?"

"Oh, yes."

"Come then and we'll be off." We left the bouleuterion and went to Theagenes' chariot. Slaves held the reins of the two fine milk-white stallions. We mounted the car from its open rear, then with a flick of the whip and at a fast gallop we sped out of the city into the surrounding farmlands. We drove up to a rambling villa and pulled into a paved courtyard. Slaves ran up to take the horses and arm in arm we entered the villa. We stood for a moment while slaves removed Theagenes' armor, then we sat while they took off our sandals and washed the dust from our feet. Theagenes directed one of the slaves to call his sister. The slave scurried to the rear of the house. Several minutes later a group of women and girls came running across the mosaic floors. Theagenes embraced an older, rather matronly-looking woman, then turned to me. "Pantarkes, I want you to meet my beloved sister, the lady Timokleia."

"Pantarkes. I've heard so much about you, now I can see what my brother sees in you. You're like a young god," she said as she held me. "These are my friends, my sisters. We follow Sappho, the poetess from the city of Mytilene on the isle of Lesbos. You've heard of her, I'm sure."

"My sister is such a great woman. She's saved many a girl from certain death, when they are exposed to the elements and wolves by parents who don't want them or are too poor to support them. She's turned the place into an orphanage for unwanted girls as Sappho did."

"Yes, I felt it my duty to my sisters to save those whom I could. Our customs are so cruel, so heartless, sometimes. Mothers now bring their baby girls to me, knowing that they'll be fed, clothed, taught skills that will make them appealing to a husband. Hellenes are hard on their women; we wash, we spin, we cook, and we must appear veiled on the street when we go out, not at all like the painted and perfumed hetairai who can go anywhere they like. Oh, I must sound bitter, but we're little more than slaves!"

"But things are changing, you can now sit in the Assembly with the men."

"Veiled, of course."

"Yes, but these things take time. You're free here, it's you who runs the estate and you can do anything you want."

"And I have — you're away so much with the army and your men. But it's time for lunch. It's such a beautiful day, let's eat in the open courtyard. Show Pantarkes around and I'll call the servants."

Theagenes' estate was large, with fruit trees, grain fields, groves of olive and fig trees, and livestock. His chief passion was breeding horses for chariot racing and we watched the mares and their foals romp across the meadows. His stablemaster showed us around, pointing out the best horses and explaining why they would someday win races. I knew nothing about horses and it was difficult for me to see the good points and the bad, since one horse looks so much like the other. The stablemaster asked if I'd ever driven a chariot. I confessed that I hadn't. So after lunch we returned to the stables and I got my first lesson on how to drive a chariot. It wasn't easy, but with Theagenes at my side the lesson was a pleasure. We drove out across the fields, the reins in my hand and Theagenes' arm around my waist. The chariot bounced along, the horses trotting at a slow pace, snorting the air, no doubt feeling my timidity.

"These are racing stallions, give them the whip, Pantarkes! Don't be afraid." Urged on, I snapped the reins and in an instant the stallions were at full gallop. We sped across the fields, the wind blowing against us. I couldn't hold on and gave the reins to Theagenes who liked the race and the speed and drove the chariot like a wild man. I clenched the edge of the chariot for dear life, watching the fields go by in a whirl of dust. It was exhilarating to go so fast, the chariot bouncing up and down, the warm wind hitting my face. At last Theagenes drew up before a big tree, and we jumped down and tied the sweating stallions to a low-hanging branch.

"Well, Pantarkes, you handle the horses very well. I don't think you're ready for the hippodrome quite yet, but given enough time . . . . do you love me, Pantarkes?"

"Yes, more than anything." My legs were still shaking from the bumpy ride and the question surprised me.

"It's been a long time since I've felt love for anyone, but I feel it for you. I want you to love me and to join me and the others in the Sacred Band. Each has taken sacred and binding vows to love one another and to die together if necessary. Do you think you love me enough?" Theagenes placed his hands on my shoulders, looking deep into my eyes as though searching for an answer to his question. I melted.

"Yes, Theagenes, I love you and would die for you." My emotions spun like the wheels of a chariot as he kissed me. He unfastened my tunic and his, and pressed our naked bodies together passionately.

"Come, Pantarkes, let's celebrate. This is the most joyful day of my life." With only the horses looking on we ran hand in hand through the fields of ripening grain, laughing and embracing like young colts. When we grew exhausted we collapsed into the tall greenery, Theagenes falling on top of me, our hard cocks against our bellies. His passion and wet kisses overcame me with wild desire and as eros took over there were no holds to our lovemaking. Filled with satisfaction, our love spent, we lay back looking up at the sky. He wove me a garland of wheat stalks and placed it on my head. "You've made me a satyr, lusty and insatiable. I can't get enough of you."

"I've never known eros like that. . . . I've never raised my legs to a man before."

"Eros knows there's no shame in that. I like my mouth on you, young satyr. Now lay back, my mouth hungers for you." I lay back looking at the sky, feeling Theagenes' mouth on mine. I hardly noticed the sky darkening, as thunder rolled from far away and lightning flashed. A light rain began to fall. Theagenes raised his head. "Even the gods celebrate our love with bright flashes and joyous thunder." He misread the omens: they were not of celebration, but of fateful doom.

Theagenes' patronage changed my life. I was driven to the palaestra each morning in a fine chariot and my fellow athletes praised my feats to high heaven — always with a note of envy in their voices. Theagenes gave me two slaves, one to carry around my oil jar and to oil my body before exercise, and another to massage my muscles before and after exercise. Being human I suppose I let all this attention go to my head. Some days I was an arrogant, boorish snob, walking around the palaestra like I owned the place. But I was becoming a good wrestler and I worked hard to perfect my style. I was developing a following, and my flying overhead throw was much admired.

One day Theagenes told me that he had arranged a symposia, a drinking party with some friends from the Sacred Band. They wanted to meet me and their approval was necessary before I could join the group. I was pleased and rushed home that evening. I was in a dither deciding what I would wear; I finally choose a himation of fine Egyptian linen for the party. Servants washed, perfumed and curled my hair into fashionable ringlets that fell around my shoulders. I was pleased with my looks as I examined myself in a polished bronze mirror, picking an ugly pimple from my cheek.

Theagenes' beautiful villa was aglow with the light from many oil lamps as his guests arrived for the feast. The erastai and eromenoi arrived arm in arm, and Theagenes introduced me to each one. Some of them would become good friends in time, others I would hardly get to know at all. Theagenes led us into a large room lined with high couches in which one could recline while eating. The center of the room was cleared for the hired entertainment. Servants removed our sandals, washed our feet and held basins and towels for washing our hands. Theagenes and I took our place on one of the pillowed couches, and the others did likewise. The caterer brought in the food: roast meat (a rarity in our land), fish, bread, onions, and garlic, all served on low tables.

After the food was cleared away it was time to choose a symposiarch, a toastmaster, who would decide the ration of wine to water and pace the party. I was given the post by a roll of dice; I decided to mix three parts of water with two of the syrupy wine. Keeping with tradition I proposed the first toasts to the Immortal Gods, the Heroes, and to Zeus Soter. We drank deeply of the rich red wine, and the party began. More toasts were made and the servants kept busy mixing the wine and water from a big krater on the floor. "Evoe, Dionysus, giver of wine," someone shouted. "Man's blessing, man's ruin."

"I'll take the blessing and not the ruin," I replied.

"What'll be the topic for tonight's party? We dedicated the last party to Dionysus and we all got drunk. Decide a theme, Pantarkes," Theagenes asked.

"A theme, beloved Theagenes? What will it be? Eros, of course." I was getting a bit dazed by the wine. I leaned back on my pillow, my head in Theagenes' lap. I looked up at him and he bent over to kiss my lips.

"Eros... a warrior's eros. I toast all the brave young men who have died with their lovers in battle and the others who have loved. Achilles and Patroclus, Pylades and Orestes, Harmodius and Aristogeiton, Solon and Peisistratus, Socrates and Alchibiades, Epaminondas and Pelopidas. Blessed Pelopidas. Do you know, Pantarkes, that he formed the first ranks of the Sacred Band? Did not they break the power of Sparta at Leuctra so many years ago? Epaminondas and Pelopidas broke the Spartan phalanx."

"Sparta... that seems so long ago. Was I ever there? It seems I've always been in your arms, Theagenes. A toast, then, to lovers." The mellowness of the wine was taking me over.

"Pantarkes, I love you so. We forget our guests... Where is the expensive entertainment? Call in the flute-players, the dancers, the acrobats, the jugglers." In a moment the center of the room was filled with excitement as the sweet high pipings of the flutes were heard and lithe boys tumbled across the floor, flip-flopping, head over heels, while dancers swayed in motion to the flute. Meanwhile a servant boy moved from guest to guest, refilling the wine cups with sieve and dipper. He seemed to like his task and several of the men made passes at him, grabbing his cock, but he gracefully moved away.

"This wine really goes through you. I've got to piss." Theagenes rose and walked over to a basin in the corner of the room. I followed him with my eyes but lost sight of him in the confusion. A young man came over and sat down beside me, nearly missing the edge of the couch as he sat.

"Evoe, Dionysus," he said, his words slurred. "By the Immortals, I'm getting drunk, but that's what parties are for, eh, Pantarkes? Well, how does it feel to be the eromenos of the great Theagenes? He made a play for me once, I could kick my ass ever since for turning him down. But I've got me a man now, a real man. Gives me a taste of the whip when my eyes wander, if you know what I mean." The youth looked at me; his was a nasty face, somehow obscene. He put his wine cup down and his hand shot up my himation, grabbing my genitals. I jerked away, spilling my wine down over his head.

"Get away, you're drunk," I said, but he was on me, the wine dripping on my belly from his wet hair. I tried to push him away as a big burly man came over and lifted the youth in his arms.

"You shitty snot, I told you not to play around. Just wait until I get you home." With that the big man hauled the kicking youth out of the room. I covered myself up just as Theagenes returned. "What was that all about?" he asked.

"Nothing. Eros with Dionysus sometimes makes us less than men."

"I propose a toast," someone said, "to Theagenes and Pantarkes. Their names will be known forever, along with the other warrior-lovers who are remembered today. Be with us, beautiful Pantarkes, take your place with us. The Sacred Band of Thebes welcomes you." There was a shout of approval.

"Now let's join together in a warrior's dance. Pipers and clappers beat a merry rhythm." We all got up from the couches and joined arms. The beat started slowly but picked up pace as we swung around, hopping, skipping, jumping to a drunken frenzy. Around and around we went, and I began getting dizzy, my head spinning as the dance became more frantic. Soon my belly was doing cart-wheels from the food and wine. I broke away, puked the whole thing up, and passed out on the floor.

"Better let him sleep it off...." The voices came to me from some far-away place, echoing around in my head, bumping off the sides of my skull. Gingerly I opened one eye, then closed it again as the harsh morning light flashed through my muddled and aching head.

"Poor Pantarkes, he really tied one on last night. Better let him sleep." When I finally woke it was late afternoon, much too late to go to the palaestra. I swung my legs over the edge of the couch. "Well, you finally woke up." It was Timokleia. "We thought we'd let you sleep. Want something to eat?"

"I don't think I could stand the sight of food. Where's Theagenes?"

"He left for town. He has some things to arrange for the spring festival. He says that you're to enter it."

"Yes, I want to compete in the wrestling contests."

"I am pleased you'll be with my brother in the Sacred Band. You've made him very happy."

"He's made me happy too. He's such an important man, with so many duties."

"Yes, that's true. He's rarely at home. You boys had a lot to celebrate last night, we could hear you upstairs — and what a mess to clean up! Some of the men are still sleeping it off. I hope they go home soon. It's time for spring cleaning; this room could use a white-washing and the hearth must be cleaned and rededicated to Hestia."

"I think I could use a cleaning myself. I got sick, got my new himation filthy. Yes, it was quite a party. I didn't mean to get so drunk, next time I'll drink the water without the wine."

"Have the servants warm you a bath." I started to leave, but she caught my arm. "Do you really love my brother?"

"Yes, I do." She let go of my arm and turned away.

"You're not the first. He's had other boys.... they wander on. He's always been unlucky in love. Sometimes wealth isn't enough. Faithless boys, empty-headed and fickle.... tossed about in a light breeze like the feather of a dove. Don't disappoint him, Pantarkes. He's not getting any younger, he's nearly forty now, getting gray... but he's still a boy, running around with his 'Sacred Band,' playing at war... so silly. The men of Hellas never grow up."

"Men are made for war."

"War! It leaves the cities in rubble, decimates families, children starve, crops go unharvested and women mourn. What good is it?"

"Spartan women are joyful to see their men go to war. Return with your shield or on it, they say. Our men wear cloaks of red so they will not show their blood."

"Spartan women are stupid fools!"

55

"No, they are proud women, proud of their soldiers!"

"Proud of what? Only of death and devastation. Go, boy, you annoy me, you smell of sour wine. Have your wars then, they bode nothing but evil." I walked away. I thought I'd become a Theban, but there was still some of Sparta in me.

As for all important occasions, seers and astrologers were consulted to decide a good day and correct time for my initiation. It was to be at the time of the next full moon, when the powers of good are the highest. The evening arrived; it was a warm spring night, the moon paling the star of Aphrodite in the west. Some two hundred men assembled for the march to the shrine and sepulcher of the eromenos of Herakles, the boy warrior Iolaos. His tomb lay a mile from the city in a sacred grove and in a gala processional we marched there. Priests of Herakles led two white sacrificial rams, their gilded curling horns glowing softly in the silver light of the moon. The rams were festooned with ribbons and garlands of flowers for the happy occasion. I was dressed in a simple tunic; I would receive my armor during the rite.

The tomb of Iolaos was made of softly glowing white marble. From above, the painted marble statue of the youth looked down on us with sad eyes as we entered the pine grove. The several priests prepared for the ceremony, incensing the altar and purifying it, chasing away any evil spirits that might lurk around, and laying twigs for the sacrificial fire, all the while muttering prayers to the Hero. For us it was a most sacred time, man and god united, sharing the meal of the sacrificed animal, but in the back of our minds there was a sense of forboding. It is never easy to know the will of the gods.

After the holy precinct had been cleansed of impurities, Theagenes and I knelt before the altar to receive the blessings of the priests. Hoplites brought my armor — a gift from Theagenes — and helped me to dress. The muscled cuirass was finely made of bronze, decorated with silver inset nipples and floral designs. In the center was an aegis of Herakles, his beard and hair inset with gold and silver. After it was buckled in place, lappets of leather were hung from the cuirass. The richly ornamented helmet bore a colorful horsehair crest. My greaves were strapped to my lower legs. The final gift was a bronze sword and a scabbard of enameled gold, with a bronze and leather shield, again embossed with the aegis of Herakles.

It was the proudest day of my life as I stood dressed in the beautiful armor, Theagenes at my side. We pledged our service to the gods, to the state and to each other, vowing to stand in battle or to fall in battle, each protecting the other from harm. We said our vows softly, then rose from the altar, joined forever in life and in death. So enraptured by the sacred moment were we that we hardly noticed the sudden chill in the night air or the sharp wind that gusted through the grove of trees.

The bearded, white-robed priests prepared the rams for sacrifice, first blessing them and pouring wine over their heads. The beasts stood quietly at first, but as the priest raised his golden hammer to stun them they became nervous, skitterish, tugging at their ropes. With a frantic bleat one of the rams broke its rope and bolted for the woods. Several men chased it but the ram was out of sight in a moment.

It was a fearsome time; had the Hero refused the sacrifice for some reason? Was it a bad omen? The rite stopped, the wind whistled through the trees, blowing the flames of the torches, and a mist began to form around the tomb. Fog flowed through the grove, and ragged clouds covered the face of the moon. The priests, their white beards and robes blowing around them, looked up into the sky as though searching for an answer. Uncertain, they went ahead with the sacrifice of the remaining ram; with a grim face and a firm blow one priest brought the hammer down on the head of the ram, then quickly cut its throat, the fresh blood squirting out into a cup. At the altar the priest scattered the blood, and it made dark spots on the white marble, blowing around in the fiendish wind.

There was a loud commotion behind me, and a shout. "The tomb! Look at the tomb!" A spectral shape had formed on the steps of the tomb, a vague misty shape, it seemed wrapped in a long cloak. Its formless head seemed to speak. "Thaagggennes, Thaagggennesss...." The voice may have come from the gaping mouth of the figure or from the moaning trees, but the words were blown away. The shape seemed to raise its arm, pointing at us. We drew back in fear.

"It's the daemon of Iolaos!"

"It's only the mist from the stream and the blowing wind."

"It's a keres, a dog from hell, who eats our guts and drinks our blood."

"Thanatos, thhhaannattooos," the misty figure seemed to say as it faded from sight.

"I thought it said thanatos. It carries the message of death!"

"It was only a mist and the blowing wind, and means nothing." Theagenes looked around, his face set in a grimace as though to challenge any who would doubt his word. "Go back to your positions, the ritual will continue." He spoke sharply, then he bowed to the priests. They opened the leg of the dead ram and cut off several slices, rolled them up and placed them on the altar as our gift to the gods. After the rite the ram would be carved up and shared. The twigs had blown away and new ones were gathered and placed on the altar. Protecting the twigs and the rolled meat with their hands the priests tried to light them with a blowing torch. The wind defeated them, though, and they stood for a moment hoping the gusts might go down.

From far away came a noise, the sound of many rustling wings and the harsh, raucous cries of ravens. "Caw, caw, caw." From out of the night sky the noisy birds swept down onto the priests and the altar. The priests flailed their arms but it was no use. The birds grabbed up the meat and made off with our offerings. Fearfully we watched as the evil-looking ravens disappeared into the dark heavens.

"Ravens are sacred to Apollo. The god himself has taken the sacrifice," Theagenes shouted, as if to quiet our fears.

"There is something more." The elder priest of Herakles brushed himself off, smoothing his ruffled hair and looked grimly at Theagenes. "The gods have spoken. The sacrifice is wrong. The ram escaped, the vision warning of death, the ravens. . . . I say that these are signs of danger and of coming death."

"What danger? Whose death?"

"The signs will be studied. Only the gods know and they will reveal their plan in time. Now let us go from this holy site. No! Leave the sacrificed ram. It is unholy and should be left. The shrine must be purified of any evil." The priest spoke, his voice resolute and firm. We turned silently from the tomb of Iolaos, uncertain whether the signs were of good or of evil. The affair was never mentioned again, though the sudden fear it caused would remain in our thoughts for the rest of our days.

Thebes sparkled beneath a cloudless warm May sky. Theagenes and I stood high on the massive walls of the Cadmea looking down at the city. The houses were freshly whitewashed, their roofs covered with new red tiles. Statues, standing beside the doorways for protection, were wreathed with flowers. In fact the entire city seemed festooned with garlands of flowers, the air sweet with their fragrance. Thebes was in a festive mood. It was time for the panegyreis, the gathering of all, and for the festival of Thargelia, the gathering of the first fruit. All of Boeotia came to the city to celebrate, some drawn in ox-carts, some on horseback, others on foot. Even the streets were filled with farmers, their calloused hands raising wineskins to their mouths, their faces bright and proud of the crops they had brought with them.

For five days the city would be alive with celebration, dance and song, revelry and drunkenness, games and sport, and with prayer and thanksgiving to the Immortals by whose blessings we all live. The fields would be purified of any evil that might prevent the precious crops from ripening — a frost, a drought, or the coming summer heat. The Thebans remembered the harshness of the winter last: the empty grain bins, the anguish of slow death, the starvation of many. Now they called on their agricultural skill, passed down from generation to generation, to bring the earth to blossom. But without the help of the Great Gods their efforts would come to nothing. The gods are all things, as the saying goes.

Full with the excitement of the day, Theagenes and I left our high parapet to join the people below, following them to the agora, where stalls had been set up by peddlers of all kinds selling food, religious charms, slaves, pots and everything else. Magicians, tumblers, acrobats and beggars filled the square. Perfumed and painted pornae plied their trade with provocative gestures. Since I'm always hungry, Theagenes bought some cakes to eat as we watched the excitement swirl around us in mad array. Tomorrow, when the festival began, there would be parades of boys carrying the eiresione, the May bough, a fresh-cut branch of greenery weighed down with the fruits of the earth. They would sing a little song:

> Eiresione brings
> All good things,
> Figs and fat cakes to eat,
> Soft oil and honey sweet
> And brimming wine-cup deep
> That she may drink and sleep.

The new eiresione would be hung over the doorway replacing the old dried one as a charm against pestilence and famine. Other celebrants would carry maypoles, baskets of phalli, and the first fruits of the season, all in an exuberant explosion of joy. On the fourth and fifth days there would be games at the stadium, the victors crowned with pine wreaths in memory of Herakles' funeral pyre.

I had just stripped and left the loutron, prepared for the day's matches when I ran into Phobos, a boy aptly named "Fright" after one of the squires of Ares, the god of war.

"Why don't you look where you're going, you dumb shit?" Phobos snarled. "Ah, it's Pantarkes, the darling of Theagenes. Rosy of cheek and sweet of mouth, and I hear your asshole is pretty good too, hey, sweet thing."

I hated Phobos with a grim passion and if my sword had been handy I would have run him through on the spot. "Ah, it's Phobos, the darling of farm girls and farm animals, from what I hear. Fuck any pigs lately, Phobos?" Phobos turned red, his ugly face twisted with rage. "You're so cute when you're angry, Phobos. One of these days you'll get your big cock stuck in a cow and how will we ever pry you out?" I sneered as I walked away. Phobos shook his fist at me.

"You just wait until the day of our match, I'll get you, you son of a she-bitch! I'll smash you flat. There won't be enough of you left to stuff a sausage skin."

"I didn't know little mice could bellow so loudly. Pshaw, fellow, you'll wake up all your beloved cows and pigs! You're red in the face, dear Phobos, did I say something wrong? Smash me flat, did you say? I doubt that... go wrestle your pigs and wallow in their slop, that's about all you're good for. Oil yourself up with pig slop and go to it, dear Phobos. I think you've already done that, I noticed a bad smell when I came into the palaestra and it comes from your direction."

"Oh, go lift one of Kratos' rocks. You'll be pushing those boulders around until you're a gray-beard and you'll never has as many muscles as I have." Phobos flexed his arm so that his biceps bobbed up and down, his heavy pectoral muscles thick with firm fiber, his belly flat.

"Mercy, great Phobos, you are a fright. Shivers of fear cause me to quake all over. Why should you lift rocks in the field when you have so many in your head, eh, Phobos?" One of the reasons I hated Phobos so much is that I had to nearly work myself to death to gain an ounce of muscle, while I'd never seen him exercise at all. "All of your muscle popping will do you no good when you face me, all you can do is strut and pose, making a pompous ass of yourself. I've better things to do, go pop your muscles for the pigs." I walked away, but I knew Phobos would be a problem. He was my only competition for the victor's crown of pine, and I had to throw him since it wouldn't look good for a member of the Sacred Band and eromenos of the strategos of Thebes to loose a wrestling match. Followed by my slaves, I walked to the sand-pit for the day's matches.

The next day the palaestra was filled with onlookers cheering for their favorites, hooting those who lost. My matches had gone well and I'd won them all without much trouble, but in the afternoon I had my

60

bout with Phobos. I entered the loutron to scrape down and eat a light lunch — it's not good to fight with too much food in your belly, as it can all come up if you are hit or get scared. My slaves fussed over me, massaging my sore muscles, telling me how good I was and that I was certain to win the crown.

The paidotribes, Melesias, walked in with a smile on his face. "Ah, Pantarkes, my boy, you've done well today, but watch Phobos, he's out for blood. He's out there getting everybody to bet for him; if he wins he should rake in a pile of drachmas. Theagenes just came in to watch and shifted the betting to your side."

"There's always been bad feelings between Phobos and I."

"Probably my fault. He's jealous of you and Theagenes. To tell the truth he's so ugly that no one wants him, his big ears and bulbous nose make him an object of ridicule, which enrages him. When you showed your abilities in the pit my attention turned to your training. I rather neglected Phobos, and now he hates me as much as you, I'm afraid. Be careful. I've never actually caught him cheating, but there has been talk behind my back. No one would think of squealing, of course. Watch yourself." Melesias grasped my forearm in friendship, then greeted Theagenes and left the loutron.

"Pantarkes, dear friend. Melesias said that you're winning. I'm glad."

"One more match to go." I smiled.

"Things have been busy at the stadium. Lots of competitions this year. The runners and jumpers are in their final heats. I am to judge the discus and the boxers this afternoon. Then the chariot races are in the morning and the crowning of victors tomorrow afternoon."

"There was no one who could even come close to your javelin throw yesterday."

"I always win that. Next year I'm stepping down, I'll let some other man win for a while. I'm losing my coordination, thanks to age and sore muscles. I've got to get back for the afternoon judging. Phobos is a mean fellow, but I know you can win."

"He's no problem. I'll win all three of the falls." Theagenes left. I could hear the shouts of the Thebans calling his name as he was much loved by the city. I relaxed under the soothing hands of my masseur.

The noon sun had passed its zenith. Phobos wiped the sweat from his brow, grinning. He was proving to be a difficult opponent as the afternoon match went on; neither of us had achieved a fall, and the match seemed to be reaching an impasse because of our equal strength. But I had no wish to fight the ugly Phobos all day long, as sometimes happens. I had to get a fall.

Again we took the systasis, our legs open and bent at the knees, our arms held out, looking for a hold. A flicker in Phobos' eyes betrayed a break in his concentration. Quickly I moved in to grab at his waist and lift him up, trying to throw him backwards. On the side away from Melesias, who judged the contest, Phobos gave my ear a vicious twist and dug his knee into my groin. The dirty moves made me mad; I dug my fist into the small of his back, rubbing the knuckle of my thumb into his backbone. He arched back in pain, in an instant I knew I had him. With a heave I tossed Phobos over my head and he crashed into the sand. I had my first fall.

The second came as Phobos gripped my hands, bending the fingers backwards in an effort to break or sprain them, but I knew the trick. Straining to move in, pretending that I was about to trip him, I suddenly moved away. With a downward yank, I slammed Phobos into the sand, face first.

I rubbed my sore fingers as I watched the downed Phobos get up, brushing the sand from his face. The afternoon sun was low, the wrestling pit was almost in shadow as I went in for the final throw. Both of us were tired, our bodies aching from the constant pounding we had given each other in the long match. As I shifted around the pit I looked for an opening, hoping I still had enough stamina to take him for the final fall. Phobos' nose was bleeding and he looked exhausted. I grabbed his hands, trying to twist him around, looking for any hold I could get. His resistance was fading, but not by much. Grappling hand to hand, our knuckles white from the pressure we stood nose to nose. "Fall, you bastard," I said gritting my teeth. With a vicious twisting yank I spun Phobos around, pining his arm against his back, and I brought it sharply upwards. The sweating, greasy Phobos, the final rays of the sun glinting off his broad back, moaned with pain as I kept the pressure on his arm. "Fall! Take the fall!" I commanded in desperation. Still he resisted but slowly his bent-over torso gave way beneath my steady pressure and he sank to his knees. I had my three falls.

Dazed and bone-tired, I let my slaves almost carry me back to the loutron. Phobos had passed out from the pain of the bout and we left him in a silent heap in the pit. I had broken his arm and it would be a long time before Phobos would wrestle again. I was sorry about that.

All of Thebes gathered the next morning at the hippodrome to watch the chariot races. The cleared space was marked with two pillars, one showing the start and finish line and the other the turning post. The entire length of the hippodrome was lined by spectators. Theagenes had entered four chariots in the race; each would be driven by professional charioteers. These chariots, called tethrippons, were pulled by a four-horse team, and were especially exciting to watch. They demanded great skill of the charioteer, who tried to take the shortest possible path as he maneuvered the speeding car around the treacherous turning post. The tethrippon was required to make twelve circuits of the race-course to win; the completion of each circuit was marked by the turning over of a bronze dolphin.

A trumpet sounded and the teams were off; there was trouble right away as an axle broke on one chariot, sending the driver to the ground. The thundering, sharp hooves of the stallions shattered his body and after the horses had passed the unfortunate man's limp body was carried away. Theagenes cheered his teams from the viewing stands as the furious race went on. Six dolphins fell, as the dust kicked up by the stallions covered the hippodrome. There was a scream from the turning post and we watched as a chariot unable to make the turn careened into the crowd, the spectators fleeing for their lives. An eighth dolphin fell. Ten. Then there was a loud crash, the yelling of men and the snorting of horses as three chariots piled up at the turning point. Other chariots, trying to avoid the crash, ran off the track. At the twelfth dolphin only two chariots crossed the finish line of the twenty teams that had entered. Theagenes' charioteer was the first of them.

The end of the festival came that afternoon, with the army of Thebes on parade and the crowning of the victors at the stadium. I was excited as this was the first time that I'd won any competition, and while a crown of pine may not seem very much it did mean recognition for my deeds. The day also marked my seventeenth birthday, and I felt I had much to celebrate, thanks largely to Theagenes. I now had slaves to tend my needs, a home and the camaraderie of the men of the Sacred Band, and above all I had the love and devotion of Theagenes.

I stood that afternoon with the other winners while the priests of Herakles crowned us with wreaths of pine. As a member of the Sacred Band I was dressed in military finery. The stadium was filled with joyous crowds, yelling and screaming their approval. Theagenes, as winner of the javelin toss, stood beside me. The white-robed priests moved down the line of winners, placing the wreaths, and they finally reached us. As we bowed our heads, our helmets tucked under our arms, the priests crowned us with the wonderfully pungent-smelling woven boughs, gave us their blessings, then moved on down the line of men. Theagenes embraced me. It was the happiest day of my life as we stood there in the stadium surrounded by Thebans, all well on their way to getting drunk.

There was a commotion at the other end of the stadium. Several mounted cavalrymen thundered through the gates shouting, and the crowd scattered before the oncoming horsemen who careened to a stop before Theagenes. The lathered horses snorted and pawed the ground before us. The leader jumped from his horse, shouting, "The Macedonians are at Elatia, two days march from here! They have taken the pass at Thermopylae!"

The crowd grew silent, listening to the shouting horseman. Theagenes turned to me. "Phillip advances his armies. Two days march from Thebes, three to Athens. This could mean war."

"I thought Thebes was Phillip's friend."

"I thought so too. We must send word to Athens. A parley must be arranged with Phillip. We'll see what his intentions are."

A few days later Phillip's envoys arrived with the envoys from Athens, led by the painted orator Demosthenes. The bouleuterion of Thebes was filled with army men, silently waiting to hear what the envoys of Phillip had to say.

A splendidly dressed Macedonian strategos stood up. He looked around the great room, smiling. "What is all the fuss? Phillip wants no war. He looks back with great fondness at his days of exile here in Thebes. He reminds Thebes of the treaty he has with great Thebes. And he only asks that they respect that treaty. He asks only the right of passage through Boeotia into Attica. The enemy is Athens, which has been against Phillip. Demosthenes, there, has raised his voice against my King, saying that he will destroy Hellenic culture and enslave her. This is not true. Were he and his son, Alexander, honored at Delphi? Have not Phillip's race-horses won at Olympia? Has not Phillip welcomed Hellenes at his court in Pella? The enemy is Athens and Phillip offers Thebes an equal share in the victory spoils for right of passage through Boeotia. If Thebes goes against Phillip in his desire to avenge himself against Athens...." The strategos sat down, his words unfinished but his meaning plain.

The unsmiling Demosthenes stood up. He looked haggard, his face unpainted, his gray hair unwashed with its usual henna. He gripped his black robe with one hand and raised the other in the air, waiting for silence. "Warriors of Thebes, young and old, listen to me. For years I have raised my voice against Phillip and with just cause. He is a barbarian, a tyrant and an enemy of democracy. Are we not free men? Raised in freedom and dying in freedom. We have known the rule of the tyrant who takes our freedom away. Phillip is such a man, and if he gains supremacy over Hellas and the city-states there will be no more freedom. This aggressive barbarian who is now at Elatia, two days marching time away from Thebes. . . I put it to you, will he stop there? No! With or without Thebes' permission he means to march on Attica and take Hellas for himself.

"What has Athens to offer Thebes for their alliance? We offer those Boeotians under our control and the Plataeans, long granted Athenian citizenship. These people and their lands will be given to Thebes. These are solid gains, not 'the spoils of victory' promised by the Macedonians, which they don't even have. I say rebuke Phillip. Send him back to the mountains of Macedonia where he belongs. Send him back to the witch-woman he calls his wife."

Theagenes stood up. "Your offer is not accepted. What are we to do with left-over Athenians? I say to you, Demosthenes, go back to Athens and prepare its armies. Phillip is against Athens, he is not against Thebes. A city as rich as Athens will bring much booty."

"Ah, Theagenes, still with your beautiful wrestler, I see. How are things with the fabled Sacred Band? Still noble? Still valorous? It comes to my mind that it's been quite some time since you've fought any battles. How are your armies, dear Theagenes? Are they prepared?"

"What do you mean?"

"I mean that an army can rest only so long on past glories. After a while the battle-standards, the shields and spears will get rusty. The soldiers think they're the bravest, but it's only a lie, repeated and repeated until they believe it."

"Are you accusing our armies of not being the finest?"

"It seems that I am. Another thought has crossed my mind. You're hiding behind your treaty with Phillip only to cover up your cowardice. In truth you are afraid of Phillip!" All the military men in the great room stood up to boo the orator. "It would seem I've struck a raw nerve and uncovered the plain truth. Theban men are cowards and afraid of Phillip. It is you, not me, who are the women in this room. You're soft, out of shape, your weapons of war rusty, your phalanxes confused, useless. Perhaps you've spent too much time with your legs raised and not enough time on the training fields."

"That's the kind of lie I would expect from a coward!" Theagenes, his face red with anger, shouted back at the orator.

"You once asked if I would march into battle. Against Phillip I would march and alone face his armies. Can you say the same? I'm more noble, more valiant, than any Theban in the room."

There was a long moment of silence. "Who is this Phillip? Why do we owe him anything? A barbarian who will make us slaves, I say we break our treaty and go with the Athenians," someone shouted.

"Let's have an end to Phillip. We're not afraid of Phillip or anybody."

"Aye. Are we to bear the taunts of the orator from Athens? Our army is better than that of the Macedonian barbarian."

"Death to the invaders!" All around the great room there was common approval of breaking the treaty with Phillip, the Theban men shaking their fists and jeering at the Macedonian envoys. Demosthenes stood smiling.

"It seems that the men of Thebes have come to their senses. Have I misjudged you all? I see now that you are brave men. The armies of Thebes and Athens will march together and crush Phillip. Envoys of the barbarian, go back and tell your master that he'll go no further than Elatia. If he tries he'll find the brave men of Thebes and Athens waiting for him." Demosthenes' voice was clear and loud, filled with bravery. The ruffled Macedonians rose and walked from the room.

"A clever ruse, dear Demosthenes, accusing Thebes of cowardice. Well, you've got what you wanted, war with Phillip. Perhaps you're correct about Phillip's intentions and perhaps he intends to make us slaves. Perhaps not. But it's just as well we put an end to Phillip, before Hellas becomes part of Macedonia. We'll put past differences behind us for the common good. Bring your men and stay with us at my villa; wars take much planning." Arm in arm, Theagenes and Demosthenes, walked out of the council hall, laughing. I and Aristarkhos, the orator's eromenos, followed.

As he was strategos of the Theban armies, Theagenes' villa became a military garrison. High-ranking officers, Theban and Athenian, met daily to lay plans for the coming war. The air was charged with excitement and energy. Phillip sent more offers of peace, but they were rejected. The pace of training increased as the citizen-soldiers of Thebes, men who had once known battle, were pressed again into service. The days began early with a hot meal and then we were off to the training fields for army drills. I returned to the villa exhausted each day, quickly falling asleep, much too tired for the drinking parties.

One evening, after a hot sweaty day of drills in the heat of the early summer, my chariot-driver pulled into the courtyard. My armor gritty with dust, I jumped down to head for my room and a hot bath. Standing near the fountain-house at the far end of the courtyard were several Macedonian hoplites, messengers sent by Phillip. They were talking to Aristarkhos, Demosthenes' eromenos. I had never liked Aristarkhos; he was handsome and had a good figure, but he was lazy and spent his days flirting with Timokleia's orphan girls. Besides, I thought it dishonorable that one should receive pay for his services in bed. I passed the hoplites and Aristarkhos without a word. They were laughing and smiling and seemed very friendly towards Aristarkhos, slapping him on the back. I thought nothing about it at the time.

I was weary, and glad to be relieved of the weight of my body armor as my servants unbuckled the stays of my bronze cuirass, then unlaced my leather boots. I smelled like a dead horse and was glad to see the servants bring my bath water through the curtained doorway. I removed my dirty tunic and was about to step into the bathtub. "Nice, very nice." I looked around. Aristarkhos stood in the doorway.

" I'm about to take a bath. What do you want?" I was in no mood to put up with the indolent young man who stared at me.

"Oh, nothing. I saw you come in. I was talking to Phillip's men. Such beautiful enemies." Aristarkhos came into the room and plunked himself on my bed. "Go ahead, take your bath, you certainly need one."

"It's better to smell of honest sweat than of a perfumed hetaira," I said with some anger.

"My perfume is the best, imported from Egypt, made of crushed lotus leaves, and very expensive. Demosthenes gives me the best. He's such a dear man and I was lucky to find him."

"It's shameful for a man to be paid for... what you get paid for doing."

"You're so old-fashioned, Pantarkes. I do it for love or money, but doing it for money is better. Besides, you have little to complain about. Theagenes keeps you in the best of style, and he's handsome while Demosthenes is old. I work hard at what I do; if I don't the old man will find someone else and then where would I be?"

"You could get an honest job."

"I hate work, that kind of work, anyway. To be reduced to common labor, like your slave who must bathe you and cart your bath water around. Ugh, I'd rather be dead. Demosthenes has been so busy with his war that he barely notices me. I really hate the old man, you know. If I could just get some money I would leave and maybe go to Corinth. They pay high prices for good-looking men, I hear. Everybody hates the old man for stirring up so much trouble, he's an old reprobate. But with him so busy now I can play around without him knowing. That Macedonian wants to see me tonight, he's got a big purse of money."

I got up from the tub, and my servant entered to dry me off. "I feel sorry for you, Aristarkhos, having to sell your love."

"I don't sell it all of the time. I make exceptions. . . for good-looking wrestlers, like yourself. Why don't you send the servant away, I'll finish drying you off." Aristarkhos took the towel from the slave, who left the room.

"No, I don't play around. I can dry myself." But Aristarkhos briskly wiped the water from my body. I should have sent him away but Theagenes had been busy with his war and seemed to have forgotten me. Aristarkhos' hands felt good. He kissed my ear as he rubbed my back, drawing nearer. It seemed silly to protest as I felt his hardness against me.

"The omens and the stars are against this war. We were unwise to side with the Athenians. There's nothing we can do now — Ah, Pantarkes, come in, I want to talk with you." Theagenes sat at a table with another army officer as I passed by, entering the villa from a day on the training fields. It was the first time he had noticed me in many days. I stopped. The officer saluted his leader and left. "Pantarkes, I'm sorry that I've been so busy. I haven't been able to be with you. I'm so tired after a day of conferences. You understand, I hope." Theagenes got up from his chair to come to me, taking my hand into his.

"I've a full day training with the Thebans. Is it true about the omens?"

"Yes. If it weren't that we had broken our treaty with Phillip and were now in this so deeply, I would say we get out. But the die is cast, so they say. I know about you and Aristarkhos; the slave told me. Why were you untrue? I love you, Pantarkes. Don't desert me now, like the others. This is a difficult time. Be with me." Theagenes looked deep into my eyes as if to see the hidden corners of my soul. Unable to meet his piercing gaze, I turned away.

"I'm sorry. I didn't mean to get involved with Demosthenes' lover. It happened, but it won't happen again."

"I know it won't. I need your love and support at this trying time. We're to march against King Phillip in a week, and we must all be strong. I fear this war," Theagenes said, turning away. "Demosthenes was right, you know. We're not prepared. Even with the combined forces of the Athenians, an army of thirty thousand men altogether, I don't see things going well with us. Phillip's armies have been on the field and are ready for war. We're not."

"Phillip will win?" Surprised by Theagenes' black mood, I took his arm, turning him around. "Thebes will be defeated?"

"No, of course not. I don't know what I was thinking about. You, perhaps. I don't know how I would face the morning without you. Be with me." Theagenes took my head in his hands, kissing me with great tenderness. "Your head is damp from perspiration. You smell like a man."

"I haven't had a bath yet. I'll go. . . . ."

"No. I like the man-smell, sweet, pungent, sweaty. Let's go to my room. Who knows when we'll have another moment for love-making."

I lay on my side, my head propped up with my hand, and gazed down at the sleeping figure of Theagenes. The room was hot from the afternoon's summer heat. Sweat glistened off Theagenes' muscular body, dampening the linen sheets. I was disturbed by his words. He seemed doubtful about victory over Phillip, in a war that could start in a week. I had never thought about really going to war; marching and training was routine, a thing a man did. But war? What would it be like? Theagenes' eyes opened, he looked up at me. "Deep thoughts. What were you thinking about?"

"Nothing, just looking at you. Watching you sleep."

"Lay back," Theagenes whispered. "I can't get enough of you." He kissed me with great passion, licking away my sweat. I forgot about the war.

The days passed quickly. Theagenes kept me at his side as the pace of war preparations accelerated. Conferences with military officials were held daily. Demosthenes looked on with the Athenians as plans for the coming war were plotted. Aristarkhos was not with Demosthenes, which made me curious. In the past they had rarely been apart except when the old man went to Athens. I asked Demosthenes about his friend. His lover was despondent about the war, he said, and stayed in his rooms, fearful that if Demosthenes went with the armies he might be killed. The old man praised his friend's loyalty and faithfulness endlessly. I was surprised by his words for Aristarkhos had made it plain to me that he hated the old man.

After each day of conferences we would gather for the evening meal. The usual joy had gone out of the symposia, the mood was now somber and restrained. Theagenes and I lay on our couches; other men, army officers, lay together around the big room. Demosthenes munched on his supper alone, looking dejected. Then wine was brought in and soon the mood became more joyful as the fruits of Dionysus took effect.

One evening as several men were dancing to the pipes, the large wooden double-doors of the room were suddenly thrown open and a drunken Aristarkhos stood there, the soft light of the oil lamps catching his staggering figure. He was stark naked, the light glinting off the bronze dagger that he held in his hand. "Where is my lover? The great Demosthenes. I've got some things for him. Both are hard." His other hand held his erect cock.

"Aristarkhos! What are you doing?" Demosthenes cried as he swung his bony legs over the edge of the couch. The party stopped at the amazing sight of the naked youth who stood obscenely in the doorway. "What are you doing?" Demosthenes was about to gain the floor and go to his eromenos, when the youth threw down his dagger, and ran from the doorway into the darkness. Demosthenes gathered up his ornate himation, then began running after the drunken youth.

"What was that all about?" someone asked.

"Just a lovers' quarrel. Poor old Demosthenes always finds these bitchy young things who give him a bad time. It's the gossip of Athens and has been for many years. Ha! They'll make peace and all will be well until the next time. Where is the wine-server? I'm dry. Let me tell you...." The Athenian officer went on, telling us about the orator's stormy but amusing relationships in great detail for the rest of the evening.

The party broke at a late hour. The crowing of a faraway rooster greeted us as we went to our rooms. Groggy from the wine, I fell into bed. There seemed to be shouting. I was in the Spartan palaestra, a dream that seemed to haunt my sleeping thoughts, a vision my mind would not release. Milo lay dead beneath me. I got up as from a deep pit. Milo's body faded from my vision and I was surrounded by angry, shouting men who wanted to kill me, their swords ready. I heard my name called in the distance. Aristion's face appeared, gold-bronzed and shining, radiant with beauty. "Pantarkes, I'm looking for you. Where have you gone?" I wanted to reply but no words came and the vision faded away. The shouts came back, loud and real.

"Help! He's killing me!" The voice was near, the screams frantic. Crash! Someone was being hit. "Help! Aggggggh!" It was Demosthenes' voice. Breaking the spell of my dream, I sprang up, ran from my room down the hallway, and shoved the curtain aside to enter the old man's room. Aristarkhos stood over the slumped figure of the orator. The youth turned, his grinning face catching the light of the dawn. He was fully dressed in armor, a dagger red with blood held in his hand.

"Out of my way, Pantarkes. See this? I got my money. The shitty old man will cause no more trouble for anyone."

"What have you done? You've murdered Demosthenes!" Aristarkhos looked down at the motionless body of his lover.

"If I hadn't got him someone else would have. Some Thebans don't want his little war with Phillip. It's all over now. Without Demosthenes stirring up hatred, Phillip will march unopposed. The Macedonians paid good money for his death. So did the Athenians. Now out of my way!" The youth came at me, his dagger held high, still dripping blood. "My horse is in the courtyard."

"You'll not leave this room. The screaming woke up the entire house. You'll never escape." I stood firmly in the doorway. Aristarkhos lunged at me. I jerked away. He slammed his fist into my bare chest and bolted away, running down the hallway toward the stairs and the courtyard. I followed. As I came into the courtyard he was grabbing the reins of his horse and was about to throw himself on the back of the animal. With a burst of speed I reached him, grabbed his cloak and pulled him backwards while he struggled to hold on to the saddle-blanket. I seized the front of his bronze helmet and again pulled backwards; the leather chin-strap caught his throat. With my other hand I reached out to take his dagger. The strangle-hold on the throat made the youth gasp for air. The horse snorted, then suddenly lifted us off the ground. Aristarkhos lost his grip on the blanket and as we fell in a jumbled heap the dagger was jarred from his grasp, landing a short ways away. We scrambled for it. With a long reach, my fingers wound around the hilt and it was in my hand. Seeing that I had the dagger, the youth stood up, backing away toward the horse who had settled down.

"Don't kill him! I love him!" Demosthenes staggered into the courtyard. His hand held his blood-spattered bed linen against his thin body. "Surrender. I'll forgive you." His voice was barely audible. Aristarkhos' mouth flew open, his eyes wide, his handsome face contorted with shock. I moved in, the blade of my dagger pointed at his belly, just below the edge of his bronze cuirass. "No! Don't!" The old man cried out, his hand extended as if to stop me. I looked at the youth's finely chiseled features, the straight nose, the beautiful mouth that I had kissed, and the square jaw, lightly covered with the first beard of manhood. I could not deliver the fatal stab. It was the old man's problem.

"This youth who you loved was evil, treacherous. You are lucky to be alive." I cut the leather purses from Aristarkhos' belt, spilling the gold and silver coins on the ground in a bright clatter. "One from the Athenians... one from the Thebans... one from the Macedonians... the price paid by your enemies for your death. Your lover has betrayed you, Orator. Watch yourself, there may be others who seek your death." Aristarkhos sank to the ground, softly whimpering, his eyes pleading. "As for this dog, I'll leave his fate to you." I walked away. I never saw Aristarkhos again.

It was going to be another hot day. I could feel the cold ribbons of sweat trickle down my back beneath my cuirass. But they were caused less by the heat than by raw fear as I stood with Theagenes on the massive walls of the Cadmea, watching the armies of Thebes gather for their march to meet the Macedonians on the plains of Chaeronea. As far as my eye could see on that bright day the Thebans, with their allies from Athens, Megara, Achaia, and Corinth, stood ready for war. The phalanxes made a forest with their long pikes aimed into the sky. The cavalry with heavy spears, the archers and slingers with wicker shields, the infantry with sword and shield: all awaited the command to march. Demosthenes, though still weak from the attack, ran around like a small boy, so great was his excitement about going to war. As for myself, I felt the excitement but deep in my thoughts were the memories of the omens — all bad — made by the priests and the star-readers, and that grim scene before the tomb of Iolaos.

Theagenes' mood continued black. His face was hidden now by his crested helmet, only his dark eyes showed, his movement slow, methodical as the various military officers reported to him. When all seemed ready, he motioned for his officers to follow. We moved quickly down the stone steps leading from the ramparts of the Cadmea. As syntagmatarch of the Sacred Band, Theagenes took his place in the front line and I fell in behind him. The older of the Band were placed in front of their eromenos to protect the younger in battle. The pipers, heralds and provision-bearers stood ready. With a blast of the trumpet and a loud cheer, the thirty thousand men marched out of Thebes into the Boeotian countryside.

It was dark before we reached the flat plains of Chaeronea. The armies would move against King Phillip at first light. The plains sparkled with campfires as the warriors settled down for the coming night. The crescent moon and the myraid stars shone bright in the blue-black night sky, the home of the gods. Many eyes watched the sky, feeling life intensely as the Fates spun their fragile web, now deciding which thread to cut, which life to end in the coming battle. Many would never see the moon or stars again.

"Don't look so glum," Theagenes said as we sat by the flickering campfire. "Tomorrow we'll send King Phillip and his Macedonians back to where they came from: Hades." Theagenes seemed to have cast off his depression; I heard a note of cheer in his voice.

"The bad omens and everything — you're the one who has been glum. The men in the Sacred Band are frightened. I've been talking to them."

"I should have kept quiet about the omens. We can't have a bunch of scared men marching into battle. I'd best talk to them." Theagenes stood, signaling the pipers to call attention. The Sacred Band lay around us munching on bread and dried meat, drinking from their wineskins.

Standing beneath the standard of Herakles, Theagenes addressed them. "Men of Thebes, listen now. Tomorrow at first light we face the legions of Phillip. Our reports show that our armies will be of equal size. Some have said that the gods are against this battle. But how can they be? The Immortal Gods are on our side and will not leave us. The soil of Hellas is sacred and the Gods will not permit barbarians to enter. We have only one choice: to defeat the Macedonians who would enslave us. Our war song will be: Freedom and Liberty for Hellas. By this sacred standard we, the Sacred Band, with love and courage, stand together or die together. Herakles, our patron, protect us all in battle."

The erastes and their eromenos stood as a body, cheering their leader. The mood of the camp changed from gloom to joy. They took up the chant: Freedom and liberty for Hellas. Theagenes drank deeply from his wineskin and joining hands, we began dancing with the others. The pace became more rapid and then frenzied, wild. At last we all fell to our bed-rolls and to love-making — not the soft love of intimate caresses, lingering kisses and light touching, but a lusty love of driving passion, hard, savage, painful. For many, it would be their last carefree moment on this earth.

It was to be another hot day. The sun rose as the armies put on their battle gear and took up their weapons. The phalanxes, the cavalry, the bowmen and slingers took up their positions in a battleline two miles long, ready to march. The Sacred Band formed the center, with the Thebans taking the left flank, the Athenians on the right. Ahead, nearly a mile away, stretching away into the dawning horizon, the armies of Phillip stood beneath a field of long pikes, blotting out the skyline. To the high pipings of the flute, to the sound of the trumpet, the signal came to attack. A great battle cheer rumbled like thunder around the plain and we began our march.

The sun brought beads of sweat to my brow which trickled into my eyes, and the dust of the dry plains rose up around me. I kept my eyes on Theagenes' back as the pounding of thousands of feet blotted out every other sound. We lowered our pikes and the two armies collided. New sounds reached my ears: men screaming in pain, the crash and the clank of metal hitting metal. We stopped; I nearly ran into Theagenes, so abrupt was our halt. The hoplite behind me did hit me, knocking me forward. My pike ran into something, it jerked in my arm, but I kept on pushing. Like the tongues of many giant serpents the bronze heads of the enemy pikes probed into our ranks, seeking their target. The whistling, whizzing of arrows and the lead pellets of the slingers filled the air with a deadly drone.

Hoping that my pike had done its business and unable to push the long pole any further I dropped it and drew my sword. My shield before me, I started to run into the confused fray of entangled fighting. "No! Pantarkes, get back! Fall back!" Theagenes' face loomed before me through the heavy dust. I started back at his angry face, surprised by his orders. "All is lost! Get back!" A sharp pain flashed through my upper arm. I strained to see what it was. The last thing I remember was the sight of Theagenes' hard fist slamming into my jaw. A feeling of shock and betrayal filled me. Darkness came.

I opened my eyes. I was face down in the hot earth. I seemed to be at the bottom of a pit, with dim streaks of light poking through. A heavy weight pressed on top of me. Struggling to throw it off, my hand sought a grip of the earth, but slipped. Through the hazy light I could see that my hand was covered with blood and mire. With all my strength I pushed upward, throwing off the heaviness. Remembering the sounds of battle I strained my ears; there was now only silence. Again I heaved upward, not realizing the weight that fell away from me as I stood was dead bodies. An arrow stuck from my upper arm, and without feeling I pulled out the offending shaft.

Rubbing my sore jaw, I suddenly remembered Theagenes' fist. As far as I could see the plains were covered with dead warriors. Great black buzzing flies feasted on their clotting blood. I called out Theagenes' name, then I spotted him just a few feet away. His handsome features stared into the afternoon sun. I ran to him, pulling

74

his turned head, but there was no other side: only cartilage, brain and bared teeth remained. There were no lips, no eye, no ear, only jagged bone and severed flesh. I choked. I now understood that Theagenes had hit me to save me. In desperation he must have hoped the battle would go over me and all would think me dead. He had been right. Turning away from Theagenes' broken face I looked to see if any of my friends had been spared. None. The noble elite of the Sacred Band had perished; I was the only survivor. What right did I have to be alive? I should have been dead with all the rest. I returned to Theagenes' body and took the sword from his tightly clenched fist. Holding the hilt with both hands I stood, the point of the sword pressed against my belly. I would join my fallen companions in the afterlife. But the contemplation of more blood, after all the pain and horror of the day was too much, and I collapsed into a semi-conscious helplessness. Through a haze I saw the god Apollo himself come to help me into the afterworld. Then darkness closed in once again.

"He's waking up, Hephaestion. Someone get water to cool his brow." I heard voices and felt a damp cloth on my forehead as I struggled to open my eyes. Slowly a face swam into my vision. It was Apollo, the Far-Shooter and I was on Mount Olympus, the home of the gods. I had always thought the underworld was a dark and gloomy place filled with ghostly shades, a place of cursed torment. Perhaps the teaching had been wrong. The golden Apollo looked into my eyes. He was as beautiful as the statues I had seen of him.

"Lord Apollo. Am I on Mount Olympus?"

"The lad is delirious. He thinks he's on Mount Olympus and that I'm Apollo."

"You had better tell him differently."

"No, brave youth. I'm Prince Alexander of Macedonia and this is my friend, Hephaestion. We found you on the battlefield. You were crazed, it looked as if you had been about to put a sword to yourself. We brought you here to my tent and we've bandaged your arm. I think you'll be all right."

The ghastly events of the day came to me in a rush. "Why didn't you leave me to die? I've no reason to live. All my companions are dead. Theagenes saved my life, I owe it to him."

"Theagenes? The leader of the Sacred Band? You were his eromenos?"

"Yes. I loved him with all my heart and I should have died with him. Only you stopped me."

"It is right and just that you should feel that way. Honorable. But don't you see Theagenes meant for you to live? It is his gift to you. Live and don't think of death. The altar of Ares, god of war, is glutted with blood and the broken bodies of strong warriors this day. What is your name?"

"Pantarkes... from Sparta. The battle was lost?"

"Yes. The armies of Thebes and Athens were shattered and broken and exist no more. The harvest of this summer is death. The funeral pyres will roar hot. King Phillip, my father, will move into Thebes tomorrow. The city will suffer his anger. He will seek vengeance on those who betrayed him. All Hellas is now at his feet. No army stands in his way. Victory belongs to the Macedonians."

The words of the battle paean came to me. "Liberty and freedom for Hellas." The words had seared into my brain as we sang them going into battle. "King Phillip will make Hellas a nation of slaves for Macedonia."

"No, I don't think so. My father is not stupid. He seeks only the unification of Hellas. He will try to bring the city-states into a league for the mutual benefit of all. Already emissaries are being sent down into Hellas to seek such a league. I think with our armies breathing down their necks, they'll comply. When news of our victory reaches Hellas they'll bend to our will. There are greater prizes to be won: great Persia, our old enemy, must be destroyed. King Phillip will seek their support for the invasion. Now sleep, Pantarkes. Regain your strength."

When I woke it must have been night for an oil lamp stood near my bed and I was alone. The tent-flap opened; Alexander and his handsome friend walked in. They were both dressed in fine clothing woven with gold thread. A slave followed with a gold plate holding roast meat, bread and cheese. "Ah, Pantarkes, you're awake. How do you feel? I've brought you some food." I answered that I felt better and since I was ravenous I bolted down the food. "Do you think you could get up? I want you to meet my father. You're something of a hero and he wants to meet you."

"Yes, I think I can get up. I feel much stronger." After I finished the meal, the two young men helped me to my feet.

"How old are you, Pantarkes?"

"Seventeen, last spring."

"I'm only a year older," the Prince said. "Come, my father is in a festive mood, a bit too festive — too much wine. You must realize that it is the crowning day of his life. A day of great victory."

Leaning on the Prince's arm I walked to Phillip's brightly lit tent. From inside came the sound of loud talking and merriment. Alexander opened the flap and we walked in. Some thirty men lay around on couches. Near the far edge of the tent was a middle-aged man, his dark-bearded face lined, rugged, his grizzled hair set with a golden diadem. His rich clothing looked odd on his massive body. His face broke with laughter.

"... And you should have seen old Demosthenes run from the battle, his skirts lifted high. That silly demagog probably still hasn't stopped running, even though he must have reached Athens by now. Did you see how Alexander took the Athenian flanks, driving them back? Certainly no man can claim to have a better son." The drunken Phillip sat up from his couch. "Who is this? The boy you told me about? The last of the Sacred Band?"

"Yes, father. Pantarkes of Sparta. We found him alive."

"Join me, boy. Sit here beside me." Phillip's breath was sour with wine as he shoved his face near to mine. He appeared to be blind in one eye.

"He was Theagenes' eromenos."

"Theagenes... it seems so long ago. He was my friend, so long ago. He was once my lover." Phillip looked away. "We've both lost a friend. I was young and wild in those days. Virile, with enough love for anyone. I grew away from a warrior's love, much preferring the hot passions of women. I've got wives scattered all over the place, but I remember how it was." Phillip stopped talking, his eye glazed over. "... except for Pausanias. Pausanias seeks my death. Olympias, my wife, seeks my death. You.... Alexander?"

Drunkenness had soured Phillip's mood. He looked ugly, his face twisted in a grimace. Pausing, he looked down into his lap, but suddenly stood up, nearly falling. "Damn you, Alexander. I've sired a daemon who'll bring my end! I'm better than you are. You'll amount to nothing. History will remember Phillip and forget he ever had a son. Am I not the conquerer of Hellas? And now my armies will march on Persia." Phillip was in a rage, shaking his fists at his son, spilling his wine as he lurched over the couches, falling.

"He wants to cross the seas to Persia and he can't even get from couch to couch." Alexander's face was grim. "Is this my father? This drunken old man? The conquerer of Hellas? By my mother's dark gods I deny his paternity. You are not my father. Olympias was right. I was sired by a god." Alexander's voice was low. It was as if his words were coming from a long distance away. A strange inner light came to his face as he ran his fingers through the tawny, leonine mane of hair that framed his clean-cut features.

"The world will forget Phillip and remember only Alexander. I am part man, but also a god with a god's mission. I shall reach out my hand and the world will be mine. It is my destiny. The god, my father, has told me so. Nothing can stop me." The young man stood for a moment. Everyone stared at him in awed silence. The strangeness passed.

"Now get my father off the floor and put him to bed. Tomorrow we march into Thebes and on to Athens. Hellas is ours. Issue orders for the wood to be gathered. The funeral pyres will be lit."

The next day the black smoke of the funeral pyres blotted out the hot sun. With rags tied around their faces, hoplites gathered the dead warriors and piled them up like firewood. The stench of death hung heavy in the still air, as noisy black flies feasted on the rotting corpses. While many had died as brave men facing the enemy, it was clear from the marks on the bodies that others had died in full retreat.

The members of the Sacred Band were burnt as they had stood: together. Phillip commissioned a great marble lion to be carved and placed over their pyre in memory of their bravery. My eyes were damp with tears. I had cried myself out as I saw Theagenes and my comrades vanish in the sea of flame, consumed in the purifying fires. I turned away at last, unable to stand the sight any longer.

I stayed with the Macedonians for several days while I recovered. I was treated with kindness and was served by Alexander's slaves. Nearly two thousand prisoners had been taken by Phillip. To demonstrate his goodwill he let them go, rather than holding them for ransom as is the usual practice. I felt no hatred toward the Macedonians. It was the will of the gods that they had won, but I missed Theagenes and the friendship I had known with him.

As the days passed my grief lessened and I knew I had reached a time of change in my life. The Theban army was no more; whatever obligation I had to them I had certainly fulfilled. Perhaps it was time now to return to Sparta and seek my family. Soon I would be eighteen and would be a citizen. I would have to think about taking a wife and raising children, as bachelors are heavily fined. But in Thebes I had become used to the comforts of life with the riches of Theagenes and I had a certain position in Thebes as a champion wrestler. Perhaps I would stay there with Timokleia.

I faced a crossroads in my life. I had some savings from my dole as a soldier, but I was uncertain with the destruction of the Theban armies that my claims would be honored. Perhaps I could buy a small farm, though I knew little about agriculture. Thus did my thoughts tumble over and over in confusion as I considered my future. The days passed and I regained my health and strength. A week passed.

The tent-flap opened and the Macedonian Prince stood before me. He smiled. "Pantarkes. How are you feeling? Father and I have just returned from Thebes. The two-faced city — they'll regret the day they tossed away the treaty we had with them! Those who went against my father have been put to death. Our garrison has been stationed at the Cadmea. We'll march to Athens in a few days." Alexander sat on the edge of the bed as he removed his helmet, tossing his hair back and looking at me. "Is your arm better? Healed?"

"Yes. It's a clean wound with no infection. Thank you for your kindness. Now that I'm better I should return to Thebes. As an enemy hoplite what will be my position? Will my claim for wages be honored by the Macedonian strategos? Perhaps I'll return to Sparta to find my family."

"Your claims will be honored. We seek no vengeance against the army but only with Theban traitors. I've grown fond of you, Pantarkes, in our days together. After this business of placating Hellas we go to Persia. There'll be great adventure, much riches, enough booty to make you a very rich man. The streets of the Persian cities are said to be paved with gold, their temples lined with it. Their kings have unimaginable wealth and it's ours for the taking. Come with us. A boy of your courage and bravery would find high rank in our army."

Alexander flashed a wide smile and placed his hand on my leg. "Join us and you will have adventure and riches beyond your wildest dreams."

I was surprised by the proposal and flustered. Adventure and wealth — it was certainly appealing and perhaps I was a fool to turn the offer down. "I cannot. To tell you the truth I hate the life of a soldier. It's not for me, though I cannot say what I really want. I know that someday I must return to Sparta and find my father and brother, and an old slave. Persia seems far away, the other side of the world. Who knows if I would return from such a journey? It's your destiny, I can feel that, but I have to find my destiny whatever it might be."

"Well spoken, Pantarkes. Who knows, perhaps the Persians will defeat our armies and my dream of untold wealth and great conquest will end in the desert sands of Persia. It's the will of the gods. I don't think we'll meet again, but think of me now and then." The Prince cupped my face in his hands, lightly kissing my lips. Early the next day I rode away from the camp towards Thebes.

Thebes was a stricken city. The hand of Phillip had come down hard on his unfortunate former ally. Bodies of his opponents hung by their legs from the massive walls of the Cadmea as a warning against any uprising. Many fine buildings had been looted and burned. The smell of grim death lay over the city. Wheeling my horse around I headed out into the countryside, glad of fresh air, taking the familiar road that led to Theagenes' beautiful villa. From a distance everything looked as it always had but as I rode into the courtyard the destruction became clear. Part of the house had been burned and lay in ruins. Inside, the statuary and furniture had been smashed and lay in pieces around me. The gardens were destroyed by the heavy hooves of many horses. The painted walls and carved fluted columns were blackened by torches. The villa looked deserted. I called out and my words echoed around the silent house. In despair I was about to leave and return to Thebes.

"Who is it? What do you want?" I recognized Timokleia's sharp voice as she came out of the back. She was heavily veiled and limped; I could not see her face. "Pantarkes? Is it you? I thought you were dead like the rest. By the gods it is good to see you! A man just came from Sparta to see you. We thought you were dead. He was about to leave." In the early morning light a lean man emerged from the shadows, the sunlight falling on his bronze-gold hair. It was Aristion.

❦ 4 ❧

"Pantarkes, good friend. How good it is to see you again. I had an idea that you might have escaped to Thebes, like other Spartans. I asked the men at Cadmea if they knew you and they said you might be here but then the news of the battle came. We had given you up for dead." Aristion and I embraced warmly.

"I almost was. It was your brother, dear Timokleia, who saved my life. It was terrible. A great defeat for Thebes. It's so good to see you again, Aristion. What brings you so far from Sparta?" We sat down.

"I'm on my way to Delphi and the Pythian Games. They're held in the late summer after harvest. And to look for you."

"You were to be married, as I remember. You were there that awful day — it seems like a bad dream of long ago — when Milo died beneath me. My family! Father, brother, and that old helot . . . you must have news of them. I shouldn't have left. I was a coward, a shameful coward."

"No, Pantarkes, no. It was the only thing you could do to save your life. Your father and slave were killed that day in the palaestra. There was a riot between the Dorian nobles and the landowners; many were killed. The Persian and his henchmen waded into the perioikoi putting them to the sword. I saw your father and slave fall before the slashing sword of the Persian. There was nothing that I could do."

"My brother, Damon?"

"I saw him running out of the palaestra, urged on by your father. He escaped. I don't know where he went. I searched for him but he had disappeared. Your father's house was confiscated by the Ephor and a decree was posted for your death if you ever enter Sparta again."

"I somehow knew it. I left my family to die while I ran away."

"No one could have stood up before the swords of Krypteia. It was the will of the gods and of Fate."

"At least Damon escaped. I wonder where he went, probably into the hills to hide. He can take care of himself. I didn't mean to kill the Ephor's son. It was a fair fight and my victory."

"The Ephor was horrified by the death of his beloved son, so he lashed out at anything he could get his hands on. With your escape he turned his vengeance on your family."

"It's my turn for vengeance now. If it's the last thing I ever do on this earth I'll destroy the Ephor of Sparta and the Persian."

"A formidable task, Pantarkes."

"I know, but I'll do it."

"Yes, Pantarkes, I think you will." Our eyes met. There was an invisible bond between us, a linkage, unspoken as yet. The Fates entwine our lives together on this earth, sometimes for good and sometimes for evil. I felt our bond was for the good.

"You were married? As I remember you hated giving up the life of a runner."

"Ha! It would have been better if I'd paid the fines for bachelorhood and remained single. A husband's life is not for me. Because of my prestige as an Olympian, great care was taken to find me a strong wife so Sparta would have strong children. The girl was an Amazon and dedicated to Spartan ideals. We had a child, a boy, born with a lame foot. She felt disgraced. I was delighted by the child, I wanted to keep the boy and escape. I pleaded before the Council of Elders to save him. I pleaded with my wife. It was no use. She took my boy to the throwing-place and tossed him off into the abyss. That was only the beginning of our troubles. Since I'd failed to produce a healthy child my wife was loaned out to other men. I saw little of her and when she came home she belittled me. I told her she was nothing but a whore for Sparta. We came to blows and she beat the hell out of me. I left the next day. So here I am, a rejected husband on my way to Delphi to look for the good old days of freedom."

"Your wife beat you up?" Timokleia spoke. "Amazing. In Thebes things are the other way around, I'm afraid."

"Sparta has different values from other cities. And you, Timokleia, veiled in sorrow for your brother, the brave Theagenes? They've destroyed your beautiful villa. I'm sorry."

"I mourn my brother, but these veils are not for him. See what your proud war has done!" The woman tore off her black veils. Her face was bruised, cut, her eyes blackened. She lifted her gown to show the ragged scars of a knife wound. I was shocked by her condition.

"The soldiers came in the night, pounding on the door. There were about ten heavily armed men on horseback. They charged in, just as I sent the girls into the woods to hide. We were terrified. I asked what they wanted, but they brushed me aside and began looking for anything of value, smashing and burning in a brutal rampage. They demanded to know where I kept my money. I wouldn't tell them. They beat and raped me until I thought I would die. I had no protection against them. They found wine and got drunk. I lay broken and bleeding, but must have passed out from the pain.

"In the morning their captain found me, cut and near death. He yanked me to my feet and demanded to know where my gold was kept. I told him I kept it in the garden-well behind a loose stone. We went there, and he looked in. Every bit of anger I could muster surged through my blood. I hit him over the head with a bucket and pushed him in. The guards, Thracians, accused me of murder, and took me into the city to face their King.

"Half dead from the beatings and rape, I faced that daemon from darkest Hades, Phillip of Macedon. I stood before him and told him that I was Theagenes' sister. I demanded that he honor the memory of my brother. I had suffered the greatest wrong from his plundering hoplites, and I demanded justice. I didn't know what he'd do; having seen the results of Macedonian justice around me, the hanging corpses and burning city, I expected death for killing that Thracian bastard. He must have been impressed with my bravery. To my surprise he let me go, arrested the Thracian hoplites, and expressed his private grief over the destruction of the Sacred Band. When I returned I found your friend."

"Oh, Timokleia, I'm sorry," I said, shocked and grievous for the woman. "The war was not of our making. I want nothing to do with war. There is no glory for the side that is defeated. All of us have suffered deep wounds, not only of the body, but of the spirit. Yet life goes on, doesn't it?"

"Yes. In time the wounds heal and the bitter memories fade."

"So what of you, Pantarkes? How has life treated you?" Aristion asked. I told him of the soldier's life in Thebes, "but the thing that has the most meaning for me is that I won the victor's crown for wrestling. Where is it, Timokleia?"

"That part of the house burned."

"Oh, well, it was only a bunch of pine branches, the needles were falling out. My poems are gone, well, they were not very good anyway. But I won the crown. I was very proud. It was the first time I'd won such an honor."

"I know the feeling of pride. As a youth I won my first crown at Delphi, the laurel wreath, in honor of Apollo. You were always good at wrestling. Why don't you come to Delphi with me and enter the Pythian Games? A winner has national prestige."

Before I could reply, Timokleia spoke. "You can't do that! My brother left his inheritance to you. In his will he has given you everything, his lands, his stables, his wealth and his name. He would want you to carry on in his footsteps. There is much gold. Happily I put it in a very safe place."

"But I wanted to return to Sparta to search for my brother. He still may be alive if he escaped to the hills. He knows the land and no one could find him. He's a survivor."

"To go back there is a sentence of death. Stay with me. We'll restore the villa. I'll find my orphans and everything will be just as it was. Perpetuate the memory of my brother, your lover. I need a man's strength here. Stay, Pantarkes."

"I don't know." I looked at my two friends. Again I faced a crossroads in my life. Should I return to Sparta? Remain in Thebes with Timokleia? Or go to Delphi with Aristion? One path could mean my death, which I no longer feared. Another was safe, secure. My third choice — Delphi — meant a future of uncertainty. My athletic victory was a small thing, fought in a provincial town with real little competition. But the Pythian Games drew the best athletes from around the Hellenic world. My two friends understood my quandary. Timokleia excused herself. I removed my helmet and cuirass. Aristion watched me.

"You look so different from that frightened boy of long ago. You've grown up. You're all muscle. I am impressed. And your beard makes you look older."

"Yes. I've worked hard to make myself stronger. My beard finally came out better. You should have seen it a year ago, it looked like a dead rat's fur. You look thinner than I remember. You were my idol, you know. I was adolescent, I guess."

"There's nothing adolescent about love."

"I didn't mean it that way."

"You loved Theagenes very much?"

86

"Yes. He was always kind and considerate, even when I'd b
unfaithful. He gave me everything, even his life. I gave him very li
in return."

"Even if for a fleeting moment, the greatest gift we can give anoth
is ourselves, if the love is true and genuine."

"It will take me a long time to get over it."

Timokleia returned. She held up the front of her gown with botl
hands, the linen apparently carrying a heavy weight. She gracefully
knelt, dumping the leather bags on the ground. "They are filthy, but
safe. Nobody would think of looking down the latrine," she said as
she opened the smallest bag, spilling the contents. The bright glitter of
gold caught the sunlight. "My brother's gold. It's yours, Pantarkes.
Stay with me. There's more in the other bags."

"A king's ransom!" Aristion stared in wonderment at the wealth.
"The Games offer only a laurel crown, not gold."

"I don't know much about farming or taking care of horses," I said.

"The slaves do that. My girls are very beautiful, educated and
trained in household duties. I'm certain you would find one to your
liking. Why risk going to the Games?"

"I'm a good wrestler."

"Ha! I thought I was a good runner until I got to Olympia," Aristion
said. "To be honest, I nearly lost. It took every last bit I had to win. If
I were you, I'd settle in Thebes."

"Perhaps . . ." My voice trailed off, my mind was a muddle of
confusion. What if I won at Delphi, and again at Olympia? A
champion wrestler! It would be a chance to prove myself. *Be the best
and excel over others.* These words cut into marble on the Theban
palaestra, words spoken by demi-gods of long ago, still they rang out
over the centuries. I would be the very best wrestler in all Hellas. I
would go to Delphi and win the Games. But doubts entered my mind.
Perhaps I would be a fool twice over. Having rejected Alexander's
offer of adventure and riches in Persia, should I now also reject the
chance to settle down to a life of respectability? But there were other
things in life besides wealth and respect: a chance to prove myself.

"I'm sorry, Timokleia. I must go to Delphi and enter the Pythian
Games. It's my dream."

"The dream of a fool, a misbegotten dream. Men are so stupid.
You're just like my brother, out chasing his dream of battlefield glory
and you see what it got him. Go on then, if that's what you want. I'll
miss you, boy. I've several suitors, perhaps I'll accept one of them. A
woman is defenseless in this world without a man. Take the gold, I

87

can't see you going to Apollo's holy city dressed in rags. As for me, my dream is just getting from day to day in the best way possible. I've baked some fresh bread, and there's some cheese. Let's go out of the hot sun."

Timokleia was upset with my decision. I had no wish to hurt her and we stayed at the villa as long as possible. When we left, the villa had been restored and she'd taken a husband. Her adoptive wards had returned and everything was much as it had been when I first met her. It was a sad day when Aristion and I waved a last farewell to her. She was an admirable woman, almost Spartan in her bravery and courage.

A slow, hot wind blew the blistering late summer heat of the Boeotian plains around us, causing whirlpools of dust to rise beneath the hooves of our stallions as, with our slaves and pack-asses, we set out to cover the fifty miles to Apollo's sacred city. It was a welcome relief from the heat to arrive in the cool, green refuge of the Trophonian gorge which would mark the beginning of our ascent into the rugged and wild regions between Mount Helikon and Mount Parnassus. We would follow the winding, stony roadway alongside the Pleistos river. Pilgrims and athletes on horseback or in ox-drawn carts rambled along with us in a slow pilgrimage. One day, Aristion and I rested on a grassy slope, drinking the cool waters from a nearby spring. "It's an old tale of how Apollo killed the monstrous Python," Aristion was saying, "thus making Delphi his holy place on earth. The dying gasps of the huge snake are said to inspire the oracle, its death throes are said to cause earthquakes which plague the region. The Pythia, a very old woman, is a priestess and has the power to foretell the future. No one can understand her babbling except the priests who interpret her strange words. It is said that the priests are not above taking gold and having the words come out any way the buyer wants them to."

"The priests are crooks?" I asked.

"No, not really, just cunning. They have enormous power to sway those who wish to take the woman's prophecies in earnest, though few do anymore. Hellas has been consulting the Pythia for so long now that it's become a necessity, especially if one is faced with a difficult decision. After all, Delphi is not called earth's belly-button for nothing."

We rode on. The walls of the gorge rose above us, in jagged and rugged cliffs. There was a wildness about the place, a strange feeling of unknown forces at work. Except for the trotting horses and the

creaking wagon wheels the gorge was silent, as silent as the eagle that circled in the bright sky overhead. If the strange satyrs, centaurs and wood spirits who are said to live in such places had appeared, I would not have been surprised.

A full week passed and we sensed that our journey was coming to an end. One evening we rounded a great cliff that hovered above us, and as we came out the narrow gorge widened into a broad valley. The sun had almost set, turning the mauve of the valley into a soft blend of red and purple. Far away, sea mists clung against the mountains. They cleared and the final rays of the sinking sun hit Apollo's city. It seemed to hang, to cling on its precarious perch above the river and below the great ragged cliffs. It floated like a dream city suspended between earth and sky. The last rays of light touched the shrine, highlighting the dazzling white of its marble temples and monuments, causing the gold and bronze to flash in a radiant brilliance. The city stood for a moment bathed in unearthly light, before Apollo's sun fell behind the great cliffs.

We took rooms in a hostel. The next day I would enter as a contestant in the Pythian Games. It took hours for me to get to sleep as my mind raced with anticipation.

In the morning Aristion and I waited with a large crowd before the eastern gate. The pilgrims who had come to consult the Pythia and to worship at the shrines stood silently. Towering over them by sheer brawn, the athletes talked and boasted in loud voices, oblivious to the sacred ground they stood on. Occasional attempts to quiet them were met with sneers and a clenched fist or an obscene finger. I stood silently, in respect.

At last a priest came to open the gates and the crowd flowed onto the Sacred Way, a winding path that led up to the Temple of Apollo, high above us. All of Hellas vied to raise monuments at Delphi and they surrounded us in gaudy, glittering splendor as we walked up the path. Commemorative monuments for wars fought or victories gained and painted stone and inset bronze statues of notables stood everywhere. Up the path were the little temple-like buildings: the treasures of the Siphnians, the Thebans, and the Athenians, holding vast accumulations of gold and silver vessels given to Delphi.

Going up the hill was like reading a history of Hellas, and our progress was slow as Aristion and I stopped often to read an inscription. Besides statues of politicians, authors and poets, there were many statues of athletes who had won the Pythian Games. One beautifully painted stone caught my attention. It was a full-scale athlete carefully painted with wax to give the image a life-like appearance. His brown arms stretched out, and one hand held a bronze strigil. His weight was shifted onto one foot, the figure poised and tense, and the handsome face had the feeling of weariness, as though the strain of the contests had tapped the man's utmost energy. I read the inscription: Agias of Elis, wrestler and pancratiast, winner once at Olympia, three times at Delphi, and five times each at Nemea and Isthmia. Impressed by the many victories, I thought that Agias must be a fine man, noble and excellent, the very best. Secretly I dreamed that my statue might be immortalized in this holy place, my name admired and remembered. "Agias must be one fine wrestler and a very fine man to have won so many Games."

"I won almost as many," Aristion said, looking up.

"Where's your statue?"

"They didn't vote me a statue, but my name is inscribed somewhere around in a list of victories. I've never seen it. Let's look for it." After a long search we found his name inscribed in marble at the bottom of a great wall.

"Here is it," Aristion shouted. "It's all covered with weeds, but there it is: Aristion of Sparta, winner of the diakulos."

"What's that?"

"Running twice the length of the stadium, twelve hundred feet, my best event in running. Not much, but they did vote me a statue in Sparta. The last time I saw it my statue had become a resting place for birds and was pretty dirty. So much for fame and glory," Aristion concluded with a smile.

The sun was high overhead when we reached the beautiful Temple of Apollo. From the high vantage point we could look back down at the monuments, across the sun-browned valley of Krisa, and there in the far distance sparkled the waters of the Corinthian Gulf. The port city of Itea served as anchorage, bringing pilgrims and athletes from the cities of the Peloponnesus and beyond.

We watched as those who had come to consult the Pythian oracle gathered before the portals of the Temple, waiting while Apollo's priest received their requests and gifts. Some waited on a marble bench for their turn to see the famed oracle. Above and beyond the Temple was a large theater and on a flattened slope a stadium had been built for the Games. I was so engrossed by the magnificence of Delphi that I'd almost forgot the Games, until Aristion mentioned the stadium.

Then we moved on, pausing to drink from the purifying waters of the Kastalian spring which gushed down from the great rugged cliffs, the Phaidriades. Taking a thin path we saw in the distance a complex of buildings, the gymnasia, the palaestra, the covered running tracks, all gracefully placed in the midst of a grove of shade trees, overlooking the rocky ravines, the valley and the splendid mountains beyond.

The noisy, brash and brawny athletes had gathered before the portico of the gymnasium to register their names for the contests. Many athletes were military men so they had worn armor, as I had, but I wished I hadn't since the heavy bronze grew uncomfortable on such a hot day. Some had removed their helmets and were wiping their sweating brows. Other men were dressed in colorful tunics, their professions unknown. Some spoke in strange dialects and wore non-Hellenic clothes. And there were the older veterans who knew their way around, paid professionals sponsored by rich patrons or by cities eager for victories. Their scars and battered faces showed they had competed in the Games for many years, and they stood in marked contrast to the younger men, whose clear faces and timid ways told that they were newcomers. Aristion went up to the running tracks while I stayed with the heavy-weights, the wrestlers, boxers and throwers. The bulky athletes jostled for a place in line and were not above shoving or pushing some other man out of line. Several fights broke out and the armed guards rushed in to stop the pounding fists.

Time passed and I neared the tables where the gymnastes, the trainers of professional athletes, sat to record each entrant's name, city, and a list of our victories on long papyrus scrolls. It was late afternoon and only two men stood ahead of me. Sweating beneath the heavy bronze cuirass and helmet I wanted to get back to the hostel to rest from the tiring day. I heard a loud cheering behind me. I looked around to see a dozen men coming down the path. It looked as though they'd been drinking the good red wine found in the taverns below as they staggered around, almost falling from the steep path into the valley. Their leader, a big man, a helmet tucked under his arm, seemed the drunkest and had his arm thrown around one of his friends.

As he came near the face seemed familiar. "It's Agias, the champion," someone shouted. It was the face from the statue that I'd admired coming up the Sacred Way, but it was an older face, lined, fatter, scarred and growing bald. I moved to first place and was about to step up to the table when Agias staggered down the line of men, his friends cheering his progress. In a loud, boasting voice the Olympian announced he was back at Delphi for his fourth win. As I stepped up to the table he grabbed me.

"Out of my way, boy!" he said, shoving me back.

"You son of a bitch!" I said through clenched teeth. "I've been waiting here all day. You can't shove me out of line."

"You runt, I'm the champion, the best and the first. Go back in line." Agias laughed, angering me more. I charged him in a blind rage. The drunken athlete fell over even before I got to him. There was a gasp.

"Young man! If you don't stop fighting I'll disqualify you from the Games."

"Disqualify *him!*" I said pointing to the sprawled figure who was dusting off his fine armor and trying to get up.

"Agias is an Olympian champion and should be treated as such."

"He may be an Olympian to you but to me he's nothing but a rude drunk who stole my place in line." Agias' friends stood around me shaking their fists and trying to push me away. The gymnastes, his face next to mine, shouted to me to get to the back of the line or he would disqualify me. There was nothing I could do, so galled and humiliated I moved to the back of the line while the arrogant athlete took first place. The line soon closed but I placed my name on the rolls the next day. My one win at Thebes looked small against the long lists of victories of other athletes.

Over a supper of baked fish, black olives and deep red wine, Aristion and I watched the athletes, our competition, gulp down their food. A few tables away a boisterous gang of men surrounded the drunken Agias. He got up to make a speech, fell over, and was carried to his rooms.

We watched the night sky as the silvered moon gained its fullness. Soon, at its zenith, the Pythian Games would begin. After a light morning meal the athletes would trudge up the sacred hillside to train and prepare. Aristion and I, followed by our slaves with lunch and athletic equipment, would join them. I had retained my faithful Charmis from Thebes. His expert hands, his soothing massage before and after exercise, were important now. We wished Aristion the best, then Charmis and I entered the cool splendor of the colonnaded gymnasium where we stopped for a moment to watch the big boxers bind their hands for the day's contests.

Walking down a short flight of steps we entered the bright sunlight of the palaestra where the wrestlers and pankratiasts were oiling up, their hard muscles tense as they nervously watched the gymnastes, trainers, judges, and the douchoi — the rod bearers whose duty it was to flog any of the short-tempered atheltes who violated the rules. Charmis helped me to strip, removing the buckled cuirass and the

92

valuable armor. As always, Charmis was afraid of thieves in the dressing-room but he knew that the death penalty would be imposed for the theft of any item valued over ten drachmas. As I stood naked, Charmis ran his hands over the back of my legs and kneaded the muscles of my back. I always have trouble there, all of the tension and nervousness that athletes feel before a day of matches centers there in my legs and back, and Charmis is always able to get the kinks out and to relax the knots. He oiled me and dusted me with fine peach-colored powder, then I was ready for the day.

Back in the palaestra the athletes drew lots to determine the matches. The lots are small rocks marked with letters of the alphabet: two have Alpha, two Beta, two Gamma, and so on. The Alpha men are matched, the Beta men, the Gamma men; if the matches are uneven someone has the luck of drawing an unmarked lot, but all of the lots were numbered this time and I was paired off.

My first match was with a big man from Athens. We took our stances and moved in, looking for a hold. It was to be a long sweaty day of throws, holds, grappling, grunting and agony, and for some who lost, a day of heartbreak. There is no pity for losers. Jeered and hooted, the defeated athletes, the young and inexperienced, the old and broken, quietly fade away. The young would go back to intense training and on to the next games, but for the old it could be their last. They would have to content themselves with memories of past victories, days of glory. They would return home to bore their friends with often-repeated tales of years gone by.

I faced three men that day, taking two matches, losing one. The winners would face the other winners the next day. Charmis scraped me down, the cool bronze strigil removing the sweat, then with oil and powder he massaged my aching muscles and torn tendons. Around me the sweating, grim-faced, and bleeding athletes, many too exhausted to move, sank to their knees, shivering and groaning, a heap of tired muscles and battered nerves.

After a day of matches, my belly still in knots, I would go outside to the cool splashing fountains, where fresh mountain water flowed through lions' heads of stone into marble basins, or I would take a refreshing dip in the large circular plunge bath, to enjoy the view and talk with my fellow athletes. As Hellenic culture had spread throughout the world, so had the ideals of athleticism and every city supported a palaestra and held games. I met men from the many isles of the Aegean sea: sailors and fishermen; urbane men from the great cities of Asia Minor; dark, sullen men from Italy; great black men from Egypt, their muscles carved of ebony; and a Jew from Syria, Ben Isaac, whom I got to know quite well. While not powerfully built, he was quick and agile in the ring and had won his matches. He said his people were shocked by naked athletes and were disturbed by the many young Jews who became Hellenized and had entered the games. He'd had a fight with his religious family and had left home. His religion scorned a man who'd had sex with another man and his family was appalled and disgusted when young Ben Isaac had brought home his first lover. Even so, I felt that his religion, family, and country had a strong pull on Ben Isaac, and that someday he'd give up his adopted life as an athlete and go home to become a rabbi, as their religious leaders are called. We dove into the stone-lined pool, tossed a leather ball around, and dunked each other under the water.

At the end of each day Charmis and I went off to the taverns and to have supper, passing the Temple of Apollo on the way. I'd forgotten about the religious side of Delphi, except for a brief prayer to Apollo that we all said before taking lots, and one day I grew curious about the Pythia, who could read the future deep in the bowels of the majestic temple. I told Charmis to go on and arrange for supper at the hostel while I stopped to look at the suppliants who waited outside. I looked up at a larger-than-life statue of Apollo, an offering bowl and a bow held in his great hands. How could one worship one god, I wondered, remembering what the Jew had told me about his faith, when there are so many? Gods of the sea, gods of the fields, goddesses of love and devotion. Lost in my thoughts, my belly rumbling with hunger, I bumped into a middle-aged man, his hair and beard silver with the passage of time. He, too, seemed lost in his thoughts.
    "Sorry," I said.
    "Watch where you're going," the man snapped back, disturbed away from his thoughts.
    "I said I was sorry."
    The man breathed deeply, and looked back at the temple. "When will that damn priestess see me? I've been waiting for days. Just too many people with too many troubles." He turned to me. "Are you waiting to see the Pythia?"
    "No. I'm an athlete and have entered the Games."
    "Those damn Games. Those big, stupid grunters had taken all the rooms when I got in from Sparta. My staff and I were lucky, some athlete hung himself and we got his rooms. He lost, I guess. Damn those prophetes, they must realize the importance of my question. The fate of Sparta hangs on her answer. Damn."

The silver hair, the powerful build, Sparta. I looked deeply at the agitated man. Somewhere, long ago, I'd seen that lined, hard face. I faced the Ephor of Sparta! "I. . . I've never been to Sparta." Fear and anger and countless other emotions filled my heart as I faced the man I'd vowed to kill. He chatted on, unaware of my identity.

"That damn Phillip and his Sacred Hellenic League. Sparta is accustomed to leading, not being led. We'll never join his League. It's an insidious plot to get soldiers for his wars in Persia, he can't fool me. No Spartan will go to that hellhole, with a foreigner at the head of the army."

"Phillip? The Macedonian king?" I was trying to sort out my feelings in this chance encounter with my enemy, but blood rushed to my head and I felt dizzy. "The League?"

"The Pythia will tell Sparta what to do. And she'd better have the right answer, too. Certainly she and her priest are against this invasion by barbarians, unless Phillip got to the prophetes with gold. No, that could never be. He did restore their treasuries, maybe he'll collect the debt. I see you wear a soldier's garb. Have you fought?"

"Yes, for Thebes."

"Chaeronea?"

"Yes."

"The blackest of all black days for Hellas. Sparta thought Phillip would be stopped, now the country bows to his will. Sparta will never concede."

My hand was on my sword, my mind buzzing. I knew the Ephor must die. But how? He must know the reason for his death, and who I was. I would drink full from my cup of revenge, but not here in the presence of Apollo and on sacred ground. I could slit his throat while he slept, but then he would never know. I needed time to think. "Perhaps we'll meet again. You can tell me about Sparta." I turned, walking away. My heart was full of hatred.

That evening my mind was not on the delicious food set before me. "You seem far away," Aristion said, looking at me from across the table. I told him of my chance encounter with the Ephor. "It appears that Apollo has delivered your enemy into your hands. You'll kill him?"

"Yes, I've vowed my revenge. He'll die."

"How?"

"I don't know."

"Be careful, the Ephor is a physically strong man. You're lucky he didn't recognize you. There's a warrant for your arrest and he'd only have to report you to the Delphi police. I've nothing against the man, he was always kind to me. This is your battle, Pantarkes, your revenge, but take care the revenge doesn't turn against you. Now eat, the Games begin tomorrow and you'll need your strength." Aristion smiled.

The moon hung full and suspended amidst clusters of bright stars. The air was soft and warm, and the sweet smell of pine and the last flowers of summer caressed Delphi as the athletes stood at the bottom of the Sacred Way, the red-yellow light of many torches flickering off the high walls, waiting for the processional to begin. Far away, from up the hill, we heard the sound of trumpet, drum and flutes, and the five hundred naked, oiled and jubilant men and boys marched up the hill to the great stadium.

The Pythian stadium was filled with shouting men as we came through a large ornamental gateway at the eastern end, out onto the flat space flanked by the marble banks where the audience sat or sprawled eating grapes, drinking from wineskins, and cheering their favorites. On the northern side, in the center of the stadium, the Amphictyonic Council sat in marble stands, stately, distinguished and richly robed, the sponsors of the Games. Priests of Apollo stood beside a small altar at the western, curved end, their sacrificial animals beside them. They waited for the arrival of the lampadedromia, a boys' relay torch race, bringing the sacred flame from the temple to light the sacrificial fires.

The athletes stood in two long lines along the banks of seats, making a pathway for the torchbearing boy who entered at a fast run and, reaching the altar, placed his torch to the wood. The ceremonies had begun. Tomorrow runners, jumpers, discus-throwers and warriors in armor would run here in final competition.

The priests said their prayers, made wine oblations, and sacrificed the animals to the god. The athletes recited vows not to cheat and to fight cleanly — vows which would be forgotten in the coming days of competition.

"Young man, young man. Soldier," I heard someone calling. I was going up to the theatre to watch the new plays, poetry reading and flute playing, a welcome alternative to the awkward, noisy boys' wrestling scheduled at the palaestra. I turned, recognizing the Ephor's voice. "Good news, the Pythia will see me this morning and my staff and I will be able to return to Sparta at last."

"Oh." My heart froze. Was I to miss my chance at revenge?

96

"The sea voyage is long and Spartans have never been good sailors."

"I remember a sea voyage I made long ago. No, Spartans don't make good sailors."

"Well, the Pythia's words will clear up everything. Sparta will know what to do about Phillip." Clearly the Ephor was nervous. He picked at the edge of his rich himation, pulling out the threads. What would the prophecy be? Would the warriors of Sparta fight Phillip? Inflexible Sparta and their ingrained traditions! An island of tyranny, in the midst of freedom and democracy. Autocratic suppression and narrow-minded thinking would someday destroy their iron rule. I wondered what the drunken Phillip, whom I'd met so briefly, was thinking about that nest of vipers. "Apollo knows I've given his priests enough gold. I'm certain that her words will be in our favor."

"I'm curious to see the Pythia and her mighty powers. Though I've no questions for the noble lady I would like to see her. May I come along? I'll stay out of the way," I asked. I wanted to keep the Ephor in sight. There might be a chance to send my sword through his ribs.

"All right. But there is a fee for visitors."

Several white-robed men waited before the bronze gates to lead the suppliants down into the underground chamber where the Pythia spoke her prophesies of the future. The interior of the temple was cool and silent, the smell of stale incense hung in the air. We were lead to a small door and down a flight of steps into the marble-lined, torchlit room. A small golden statue of Apollo stood at the side, helmets and other votive offerings hung about on the walls. In the center of the room, marking the center of the world, stood a great tripod, a stone bowl suspended in its center. A thin line of smelly vapor rose from the bowl, the dying breath of the great serpent slain by Apollo in legendary times. The air was heavy with incense, the view fogged by mists and vapors, and it took my eyes a moment to adjust to the darkness after coming out of the bright daylight. I blinked several times before all of the details of the ancient room swam into view. I stayed to the back and watched as the Ephor sank to his knees, waiting for the Pythia.

I heard a shuffling sound and the tiny, wizened, very old form of the priestess came out of the darkness at the other end of the room, almost carried by two priests at her side. Her toothless mouth chewed laurel leaves, the drool dripping onto her formless gown. Her priests held tablets, poised to write into the soft wax her every word. She said nothing.

My eyes watered as the foul-smelling incense swirled around in the hot closed room. The Pythia moaned from deep in her throat. Suddenly, with wide eyes, she looked down at the Ephor kneeling at her feet. Violently she shook the tripod, adding to the mystery of the room a note of terror as the god took hold of his priestess in an outburst of holy frenzy. She was shaking, rolling her head, drooling and moaning, and several worshippers fell to their knees in dread before the terrible Pythia and her wild ravings. She stopped, her mouth opened like a tragedy mask used by actors. "Ohhhhhhhh, ahhhhhhhh, eyeeeeeee," the Pythia spoke in a gutteral, masculine voice as her priests marked on the wax. Her thin legs twitched and she shook as though having a fit, while she spoke her strange and unintelligible words.

Much awed by the holy woman, I watched her through the smoke and darkness. Suddenly her withered arm shot out, straight at me, and she said one word in plain language: "Lykous." Was she pointing at me? I was scared. Had she read my mind and seen my thoughts of dark revenge? *Lykous,* a wolf, one who kills his prey. "Lykous." She repeated the word and lapsed into her gibberish. Her head fell backwards as though dead, her tongue grotesquely sticking from her dribbling mouth. The priests lifted her and carried her off into the darkness. The high priest spoke in rolling, echoing, sepulchral tones: "Rise noble Ephor, the divine Pythia's words for Sparta: 'Without walls, Sparta falls. Sparta falls, without walls.'"

The Ephor rose to his feet. "But holy father, what do the words mean? Sparta has no walls. Its warriors are its walls. Should we build stone walls? What do the words mean?"

"I can only repeat what the Pythia said. The meaning is for you to understand. I cannot say more."

"The Macedonians got to you. Phillip paid you to make up a confused, unclear and stupid prophecy. I know it."

"The words of the Pythia are correct. The charge is unjust. It was the god who spoke through her, not Phillip."

Red-faced, stuttering and angered, the Ephor looked for a moment as if he would strike the priest, but he turned on his heel, tramping up the staircase. I turned to go after him, not wanting him out of sight, but the priest called to me. "Young man! Stop. There are words for you." Surprised, I swung around. The priest read from his tablet: "Lykous. Fangs of blood, vanquished prey. Victory and a curse for you this day."

Astonished by the prophecy, I gaped at the bald priest. The Pythia had read my mind. "What do the words mean? What curse?"

"I think you know." The priest walked off into the darkness. Confused, I stumbled up the steps, out of the temple, and into the brightness of day, wiping the pungent sharpness of the vapors from my eyes. I saw the Ephor standing with a group of his officers, talking and gesturing wildly.

". . . her words are false. I do not understand this at all. Sparta falls, no walls, no walls Sparta falls. Stupid."

"The words of the Pythia are not always clearly understood. They must be submitted to the councils at Sparta for their ruling. It is all we can do. I had expected a clear answer, however," one of the armored soldiers was saying.

"We have no clearer answer to Phillip's aggression than we had before we came. I must think about this — and pray to the god, perhaps he'll reveal his thoughts to me." The Ephor slapped the shoulders of his officers. "I must think and meditate." He breathed deeply as he walked away from his men. He must have forgotten about me, for he brushed by me and started up the pathway toward the theater and stadium. I waited for a moment, then followed.

He passed by the theater and the stadium, then took a pathway north. High above the great ragged cliffs of the Phaidriades dwarfed his form, hovering like talons of an unknown bird of prey. The path narrowed as we came up against the barrier of the rocks. I thought he might stop, but he kept going along the pebble-strewn path, his figure hidden at times by trees that dappled the ground with shade and sunlight. Delphi looked toy-like from the heights.

So intent was I on watching the Ephor that I accidentally kicked some stones from the path. With a clatter they rolled into the deep ravine. I stopped, my hand shot to my sword hilt, afraid that the Ephor might hear, but the faint sound of his footsteps ahead didn't pause. Was he going all the way to Mount Parnassus? The air grew cold. I saw a bright flash of sunlight ahead and what seemed to be a clearing. I advanced slowly, looking through the trees. I could hear heavy breathing as the Ephor came out into the terraced clearing. At the far end stood a small temple; beyond that was only blue sky, and I assumed the temple overlooked a chasm. I paused, watching the silver-haired man walk to the marble temple, his hand upraised as if in prayer. "Divine Apollo, hear my prayers," his loud voice echoed around the surrounding cliffs. I stepped quietly from the trees into the cleared area as the Ephor sank to his knees, his hands held out, imploring the god. He kissed the air in salutation. I now had my moment with my enemy, the slayer of my beloved father and slave, the one who had caused my downfall and sent me into exile.

"Ephor of Sparta!" I shouted. He looked around.

"What! Ah, the young soldier. You've come to this lovely spot to meditate. I come here while I'm in Delphi, it's quiet and away from the crowds. It's the shrine of Apollo Hekatebalos, the Apollo of sudden death. But the temple is misnamed, I think, it's so tranquil and placid."

"The Pythia spoke with me after you left. I, too, know how to interpret the will of the gods, and she has told me where to seek the truth about your destiny."

The Ephor smiled. "The Pythia spoke in riddles to me. I would be happy to hear more. But if you have this ability, why have I not heard of your skill?"

"Perhaps you have. Let me read your future, and you can judge for yourself how accurate I am."

The Ephor nodded his agreement.

"I will find your future reflected in your sword. Lay it here on this altar." The Ephor did as I asked, and I polished the blade briefly, then gazed into it.

"I see a wrestling match, a grudge fight, a death—"

"Milo!" gasped the Ephor. "You see my dead son!"

"Quiet! I see confusion, more fighting, innocent people forced to flee — What's this!" I cried, picking up the sword by the handle as if to gaze more intently into the blade. "I see the murder of innocent people by a mad tyrant—"

"Stop!" cried the Ephor, "You cannot see—"

"And I see revenge!" I cried, twisting the sword away as the Ephor desperately grabbed for it.

"I see revenge by Pantarkes, who was forced to flee his home, his father killed, all at the hands of a wretched man who will now pay for what he did."

The Ephor, petrified for a moment, now began to try his escape. I was faster, though, and I slashed his leg with my sword. A moment later I was on him, and without the slightest remorse I plunged the blade into his chest. Leaving the sword in his body, I turned and started back down the pathway.

"Well, the gods have helped you take care of one enemy," Aristion said. "I doubt if the Persian will be as easily killed and don't forget there's a warrant for your arrest."

"And the curse. It was just like the Pythia said: vanquished prey and a curse for you this day. I don't think she's a fake."

100

"What curse?"

"The curse of Apollo and Achilles, called down upon my head by a frightened man who saw his death in my eyes."

"How can Apollo curse you when he may have helped you kill the Ephor? The curse of Achilles, the hero of the Trojan war? He was fated either to gain glory and die in his youth or to have a long inglorious life at home. He chose a short life, but gained immortality. Is that what the Ephor had in mind? Is that the meaning of the curse, dear Pantarkes? To have a short life, but filled with glory?"

"Who knows? But if that is my fate I'll accept it. Death holds no terrors for me."

"Brave words. I wonder what you'll say when death looks you in the face. I think you'll change your mind. Better to serve on earth than to reign in Hades, some said. Guess what? I won my heats and have placed as a finalist. And I thought age had caught up with me!"

"Aristion, I'm so proud! Once an Olympian, always an Olympian." The lean runner smiled. I could tell he was happy and I was pleased with his success. The Games had slipped out of my thoughts and tomorrow was the final day of competition. The palaestra would be crowded.

My belly was in knots. "What in the shit have you done with my aryballos? Theagenes gave it to me and if you've lost it—" I screamed at Charmis, who frantically searched through a cloth sack for my oil jar. "It's my good luck piece, without it I'll lose. You know that." I had stripped and now the missing oil jar would mean my defeat on the final day of competition. "You had it tied to your arm. Did you put it in the sack when you took off my armor? Did you leave it down below?"

"Here it is. I put it in the locker when I put your armor away."

"Thank the gods. Don't do that again." Charmis held up the small painted jar. "Now let's go." The athletes, the trainers and attendants ran everywhere, fussing, nervous and edgy. The morning matches would be decisive. I had managed to get enough falls to qualify for the finals. Some of those had been difficult, some easy, but today's matches would all be difficult.

I knew this would be a sweaty, grinding and bloody day of hard falls. I must keep my mind clear, must not let petty things like lost jars upset my sense of balance, my mental preparation, and my physical coordination as I faced the finalists. There would be only one winner and that had to be me.

The great palaestra was filled with men as Charmis and I walked out. The naked athletes jumped around, rubbing themselves to keep warm, but the morning chill would soon burn off as the sun rose. Accustomed to the high-strung, arrogant and aggressive athletes, the gymnastes and the police stood ready with whips and sticks. The colonnades were filled with spectators, some in rich dresses, some in rags. It seemed as if the entire world were represented. Old philosophers who had come to argue and not to watch the games, eager boyhounds, exotically dressed wizards, magicians and astrologers selling charms and horoscopes, artists and sculptors who wanted to observe the body in action for their art, hawkers shouting out the virtues of their sausage and honeycakes, wealthy foreigners borne on elaborate chairs by sad-looking slaves, army men in crested helmets and brazen swords. Seated in throne-like chairs were the Hellanodikai, high officials from Elis, scouting the athletes for the Olympics that would be held next summer. I put them all out of my mind. A single distraction could mean defeat.

We were to draw lots from a silver bowl placed before a golden image of Apollo Pythia at the far end of the palaestra. The wrestlers and pankratiasts gathered around the image. After reading a prayer to ask for divine help, each would reach into the bowl and draw a marked lot. Then we stood in a circle while each lot was examined and we were paired. I looked for the mark on my lot. There was none; I had drawn the bye. It was a great stroke of luck for me, as I could stand around and watch and stay fresh while my opponents would be worn and tired. Charmis brought a stool and I sat down to watch.

Just before the drawing, the pompous, strutting, naked pankratiast Agias had entered the palaestra with his friends and slaves. A loud cheer rose for the golden-crowned athlete, who waved and smiled at his many admirers. He'd drawn his lot and was paired with my friend, Ben Isaac. Time had taken a heavy toll on the proud Olympian, his belly sagged and his muscles looked flabby. Athletes have nicknames for the various types and shapes of men: Agias was a lion, with a great chest and arms, but narrow hips and feeble rump and legs. Some men are bears, thick-set, heavy and difficult to throw. Some are badgers, small, short men who have developed special skill at throwing bigger men and who, like their namesake, are mean and aggressive.

Agias clearly meant to take his fourth win and the crowd was with him, their shouts of approval must have sounded all the way down the hill. There was still a lot of fire left in his sagging gut as he strutted around boasting loudly, ignoring Ben Isaac who stood quietly composed, his arms folded across his broad chest, waiting for Agias' performance to end.

I think the Olympian would have been there all day milking the cheers, but finally the gymnasiarch grew tired and called for the match to begin. I sat on my stool and waited as the competitors were oiled and dusted. Agias removed his crown of golden leaves, holding it up for all to see. The police waved their menacing whips and Agias took his stance. With an agility that would have put younger men to shame he moved in with style and precision, drawing more cheers. I had to admire his skill. Each hold was cleanly executed and long years of training made his moves almost ritualized. I could see right off that the younger Ben Isaac was in trouble, as Agias took his first and second fall. But going in for the third, the Olympian showed signs of his age. There was a slowing, a sagging of his bravado, while except for a bloody nose the Jew stood firm. I hoped Ben Isaac would take the next fall. Rivulets of sweat, mixed with oil and dusting powder caked his hairy body as he took his stance for the third time.

Instantly Agias moved in taking a hold around Ben Isaac's waist and lifting him off the ground. Ben Isaac clamped his legs around Agias' waist, locking his arms around the other in a strangle-hold. Agias dug his fists into the Jew's back. They stood there, locked together, and the crowd hushed. Pressure, strength, and sheer grit would decide the winner of the final fall. The thin legs of Agias wobbled from the weight of the Jew, who had made good his strangle-hold. Agias' face turned red, his tongue purple and the veins of his neck and bald head seemed as they might explode. Ben Isaac arched back, the tendons of his chest taut, the muscles of his arm knotted with powerful strength. Surely they looked like they would burst apart from the pressure. There was no sound, except for an occasional grunt. The two men seemed carved of stone, their movements slight as the pressure grew. And then it was all over. Ben Isaac, his body red from welts caused by the tight holds, screamed and threw his arms around wildly, reaching down his back to break Agias' fierce grip. Freed from the strangle-hold, Agias arched back, and in a tremendous heave he threw the Jew over his head. Ben Isaac landed in a crumple, his arms and legs askew, his mouth full of sand. He raised his arm in surrender. An exhausted Agias sank to his knees. The hush broke and the crowd went wild; not even the police could keep them back as they surged into the palaestra, lifting the soggy Agias to their shoulders, carrying him around and shouting his name. They'd forgotten that I was still to fight Agias. Several gymnastes rushed over to ask me to declare an akoniti, to concede victory to Agias "without dust," as it's said. After such a display of skill I would be foolish, and would certainly be defeated, if I went against Agias. "There would be no dishonor, the Amphictyonic Council would understand your decision to give the laurel crown to Agias," one gymnastes said.

"There's no way I'll concede to that old man," I said, drawing myself up. "I came here to win, not to take an akoniti."

"Silly, stupid boy. Take it!"

"No!"

"So be it. You'll meet Agias in the skamma, now that the jumpers and runners have finished at the stadium, before the Council." The gymnastes turned with a huff. I think he really expected me to be so fearful of the match I'd accept defeat without a blow being struck. It was clear, too, that Agias was everyone's favorite. While Agias was borne into the stadium on the shoulders of his admirers, I walked behind.

The stadium was packed with spectators as we entered. Near the high ornamental gateway leading into the flat area, the winners of the running and jumping events were walking away from the marbled stands, having received the victors' crowns. I saw Aristion and waved. Aristion, all smiles, waved back. Sacred red bands had been tied around his arm and thigh and fluttered back in the cold air. Clouds covered the sun, but even the grayness of the day couldn't quell Aristion's joy. He ran to me, his hands held branches and a wreath of laurel leaves covered his golden hair. I was falling in love with the runner all over again, now that the memories of Thebes slipped away. He would sometimes catch me with his clear blue eyes, and sometimes we'd kiss, but nothing more than that. Most athletes decline love-making while at contests, fearing that to spill their seed would sap their strength.

Aristion came running, the leaves flopping up and down against his ears. "Pantarkes, Pantarkes, I've won the diakulos! I can't believe it!" We embraced with exuberance. "Haven't you wrestled? There's not a mark on you," he asked. I told him about the bye and the victory and my decision to reject an akoniti. "It was the right thing to do, Pantarkes. The Olympian will be tired and you'll be fresh. It will give you a great advantage."

"Yes, his match with Ben Isaac drained him, but he's strong and has years of experience over me. Stay and watch, if you like. I want the laurel crown."

"You can have mine. I feel silly wearing this thing."

"You can keep yours, I'll get one for myself." Before us a layer of sand was being spread before the marble stands where the Council sat. My contest with Agias would be the highlight of the day. Agias' admirers put him down and he stood near the skamma, his hands on his hips, his face grim as he saw me walking his way.

"It's that shitty runt that took my place in line. Throw him out! I'll not debase myself. I order the Council to declare an akoniti. Give me the laurel. This little shit doesn't stand a chance against the great Agias!"

"I think, great Agias, you're full of crap. You're old and tired. Why don't you go home? Your championship is finished. I'm Pantarkes, the best and greatest. When I get finished with you... I'll teach you to knock me out of line, you old, beaten shit." I shouted out my challenge with bravery. I had no intention of letting the bastard take my crown and if I were to win against an Olympian— the thought dazzled my mind.

"Silence, you two empty-headed braggarts." A portly, well-dressed man stood up. "My name is Artemidorus. As the agonothete, I am the sponsor of the Games. My gifts have been abundant, there has been enough food and oil for the athletes, though brought here at great cost to me. Victory is sweet as Agias knows, there is the prestige of the laurel and there are gifts from one's home city. A very sweet pie for the winner. I'll fill the pie even more: a gift of five hundred drachmas to the winner." A hush fell over the audience and then a loud cheer. The prize was a small fortune.

"The agonothete is indeed generous," Agias said. "This boy has an advantage. I'm slightly tired and he stands unmarked. I'll have no mercy on him. No sissy wrestling, I challenge the stupid boy to a pankration."

"That's unfair. I'm a wrestler, not a grubby pankratiast. I'll not get down in the dirt with him." The advantage was shifting to Agias, who had specialized in the pankration. Things had evened up, I was unmarked, but not mentally prepared for the brutal pankration.

The members of the council conferred. "Agias is favored here, we approve his request. You will fight until one of you surrenders," a member of the council announced.

A gymnastes held up his stick. "You know the rules: no gouging, no biting, no grabbing the balls." A drop of rain fell from the dark sky, landing with a splat on his nose.

I leaned forward and looked at Agias across the sand-covered skamma. "Kill him, Agias," the crowd shouted. Agias raised his arms but I was wasting no time. I moved in and grabbed his upraised arm, giving it a sharp twist downward. He yowled with pain. His hard fist caught me on the ear, then he swung his knee into my groin, but I backed away. His arm flew up against my jaw. I grabbed his wrist, and with my other hand sent a hammer of blows into his soft, flabby belly. He pulled my arm to his mouth and gave it a deep bite.

"You're biting, you bastard. Just like a woman."

"No, just like a lion."

"I call a foul. You saw that. Agias bit me."

"The noble Olympian would never do a thing like that. Get on with it." Several of Agias' friends left the grassy slope and rushed to the pit to shout obscenities at me, but they were whipped back to their places.

I ran at him, my fists ready, sparring, dodging blows. I landed my fist to his jaw and something cracked as Agias backed off, his hand at his mouth. The drop of rain had turned into a light shower and the sand stuck to my feet, droplets fell into my eyes, fogging my vision. If I could get the man by his feeble legs, I'd have the match. Agias gagged and spat out several broken teeth. I made a grab for his waist, but his knee caught me in the balls, then he grabbed my nipples and gave them a nasty twist. His finger went for my eye, but I moved away in time. I looked at the gymnastes. Clearly no foul would be called, whatever the violation. Furiously I landed a hard vicious fist into Agias' belly, and another to his nose. Blood spouted out, the rain washing it down his mouth, onto his chin, to drip to the muddy ground. There was fear in his eyes as he came at me. I grabbed his arm to spin his soggy body around. With a thud Agias fell face down into the mud. As I fell on his back, my foot twisted beneath him, I grabbed his slimy leg, trying to get his foot. Propped up on one knee, caked with sandy mud, oil, and powder, I knelt exposed over the struggling man. I felt his hand going up my inner thigh, his fingers touched my genitals. I jerked away. There was no dirty trick the man wouldn't try. "You bastard," I cried. Somewhere, out of the rainy mists, I heard my name being chanted, almost as loudly as that of Agias. Slowly the crowd was shifting sides.

My hands found his foot and I gave it a nasty twist, plunking myself down on Agias' rump, trying to get my balls out of reach, I twisted again. He thrashed around, howling with pain. But now my foot was lost beneath his chest, shot through with pain. I settled into my grip, I had the Olympian where I wanted him, and I had only to await his surrender.

The fresh coolness of the rain washed the mud from my face as I looked up, asking the gods to grant me victory. Feeling Agias' backbone beneath me, I leaned backward to get a better grip on his foot. Agias screamed in agony as a bone cracked and his heavy body dug into the wet sand, writhing with pain. "My foot!" I cried, but he dug in and I felt a snap. The gymnastes moved in, watching for a sign of surrender since both of us seemed defeated, our bodies weary and covered with bloody mire. Finally the Olympian raised his arm in defeat. I had won the match.

Men rushed in to untangle our bodies. There was no sound except for the soft pat-pat of the rain. Both Agias and I had gone to the limits of our strength. Exhausted in victory, I could barely stand. My ankle was twisted, perhaps broken. Agias, his face bloody, his nose broken, his teeth shattered, his leg dangling under him, looked at me one last time as he was carried away through the rain while I was dragged to the victory stand. In a single voice the seven thousand spectators shouted my name as the wet laurel crown was placed on my head. My head spun from joy and pain and I fainted.

Voices came at me from a dark emptiness. Faces appeared and swam away. "He'll be all right, the opium in the wine should deaden the pain... the ankle is broken, but it set nicely... there should be no problems... watch for blood poisoning..." The voices disappeared into the void. I opened my eyes and looked into a soft, plump and rosy face.

"He's awake. Good boy. Aristion, everyone." Soon a flock of faces were looking at me. "Remember me? I'm Artemidorus, the agonothete. Here..." he placed the wreath of laurel in my hands and held up several bags of heavy coins. "Delphi has a new victor." The plump man beamed a bright smile.

"... where am I?"

"I had you brought here to my room. Now that the Games are over there's plenty of space. My physicians mended your foot and there should be no problem, but you need lots of rest. We were all anxious for you. We'll look after you. Are you hungry? I'll send for some bread and meat." The plump man went away, and I greeted Aristion and my slaves.

"Who is this Artemidorus fellow?" I asked, as Aristion sat down beside my bed.

"He's a wealthy olive grower from the town of Amphissa, fifteen miles west of Delphi. He's been like an old mother hen to you, fussing and worrying. When you've rested he wants us to come with him to his estate at Amphissa, where you can recover your strength. Your defeat of the Olympian has made you a hero and the Amphictyonic Council has voted you a statue to be set up on the Sacred Way. They've hired a sculptor and you must pose for him. It's a time of glory for you, Pantarkes." Aristion clasped my hand warmly.

"I can't believe it."

"It's very true. Since you've missed the victor's banquet after the Games, all Delphi will turn out when you've rested a bit. Agias had enormous prestige in Hellas, and now, all of that is yours. The world loves a hero, Pantarkes. Take it all while you can." Aristion looked at me strangely. Perhaps he really believed in the curse of Achilles and that an early death awaited me.

"It looks like I'd better start training for that. I'll take some boxing lessons. I've got to defend my title, until some upstart takes it away from me." I gripped Aristion's hand tightly, as he bent over to kiss me with warm lips.

I rested for several days and tried hobbling around on a walking stick. Occasionally people from Delphi came to chant my name and to throw flowers and branches beneath my window. The wealthy sent me rich gifts and bags of money. Athletes came for advice about training, and love-sick boys and girls mooned outside my door. The high officials of the Amphictyonic Council and the Olympian officials, the Hellanodikai, came to see me. A lavish banquet was given for me and I rode around in a golden, flower-covered chariot receiving the cheers of Hellas.

The air was cold as we left Delphi, heading west to Amphissa. The plump olive grower had become a friend and benefactor, and I now dressed in such rich robes that I looked like a high-born aristocrat. The plain between the towns was planted with groves of huge gnarled olive trees, some of which looked very old. The "Amphissa olive" is famous throughout Hellas — large, black and fleshy, these olives are among the world's best.

We arrived at Artemidorus' country villa early the next day. Since it was nearly winter the olives were being picked. Men and boys beat branches to shake down the fruit, which was collected in baskets and taken to a stone press block, where oil ran out of a spout and into an oil jar. Several large jars stood around the courtyard waiting to go to town or to be shipped to the ports of Hellas. The villa was alive with dogs and with the children of the slaves, who helped in the harvest. The train of pack-asses, horses, armed guards and the sculptor and his assistants gradually unloaded and we went into the rambling house.

Artemidorus, his plump, pink and shining face constantly wreathed in smiles, his fat fingers encased with rings of gold and inset stones, patted his hands joyfully as he showed Aristion and me our rooms. His wife and three young sons were nearly as plump as he and they followed along after us. My livery had increased greatly in the last month, and my ten slaves carried my baggage up the stairs, escorted by an armed guard who watched my gold. So many letters had come to Delphi congratulating me that I had also hired a letter-writer to answer them. It was getting complicated to be famous.

Settled into the room, I dismissed my slaves. Thankfully, Artemidorus and his entourage left — his constant fawning annoyed me. I stretched out on a bed, gently lifting my gimpy foot up onto the covers, and there was a knock at the door. I turned to Aristion, who was unpacking, asking him to see who it was. A handsome young man stood waiting. "My master, Polykleitos, wishes to know when he may view the athlete."

"Polykleitos?"

"The most famous sculptor in Hellas. He's been retained by the noble Artemidorus to sculpt the athlete in stone, and he wishes to begin his work on the marble as soon as possible. He has other commissions and must return to Athens before the winter sets in."

"Are you tired? Do you want to see this sculptor?" Aristion asked.

"Might as well get it over with. Show him in." Without a word the sculptor swept into the room. I sat up with a mild case of shock. The handsome young sculptor was extravagantly dressed, his himation shot through with gold thread, his scarves trailing behind him with a strong scent of rose petals. His elaborately curled hair was dusted with gold powder, and he carried an ivory baton in his hand. He came, almost dancing, into the room and pointed his baton.

"Which, may I ask, is the athlete?" His voice was high and lisping.

"We're both athletes," I said.

"No, no, silly, the one I'm going to sculpt."

"Me."

"Oh, well, you'll do, I suppose. Take off your clothes."

"What?"

"I can't do a nude statue if you pose with them on, now can I? Athletes are always nude, philosophers and statesmen have their clothes on and that's the way it is." I stood up and stripped.

"Hum," the sculptor walked around me, lightly tapped me with his baton. "You're a trifle too muscular for today's fashions, lean and supple is the word, but I'll rearrange your parts when I start on the marble and I'll take out those nasty scars. They're quite unbecoming when done in marble, I think. Some of the sculptors are putting them in. I just can't stand that. Ugly, ugly, ugly. Athletes should be beautiful, graceful, and a little sad. Poetic, if you know what I mean. The athletes I've done have been such clods, insensitive to the higher things, art and beauty. I'll start the sketches tomorrow. A studio has been set up in a room on the first floor, the marble has arrived, and all you have to do is pose. That's not asking too much, is it? Artemidorus must have money to throw away, he could have ordered a stock athlete statue and then all I'd have to do is sculpt your head and glue it in. Of course that would look rather shabby since there's always a dirty ring around the neck. Be in my studio early, this provincial town looks like a bore and I don't want to be stuck here all winter. Ah, for the parties of fabulous Athens, they know how to live there! As for this place, ugh." With that the sculptor swept from the room, leaving a strong scent of rose petals.

"Great heavens, what was that?"

"I'm not quite sure," Aristion laughed.

The next morning the house was awakened by the noise of hammer and chisel. I opened my sleepy eyes as the steady pounding on cold marble bounced around in my head. After a quick bowl of porridge I went to the sculptor's studio. The small plain room was thick with marble dust as several men, hammers and chisels in hand, worked a seven-foot block of marble. Through the dust I saw Polykleitos reclining on a couch while one of his handsome assistants fanned him with a scented handkerchief. "The master will be ready in a moment. He's waiting for his muse to inspire him."

"Ahhhhh," the sculptor moaned, his hand held to his forehead. "I just can't make contact with divinity today. My mind is dulled by this commission, but..." his eyes popped open "... one must think of the money. Athens is expensive. Good, I see you're here. You, prepare the clay." His assistant scurried to a table and began to knead the brown clay. "I'll do a clay study of you today, just to get the kinks out. Strip and stand over there where the light is good."

"How should I pose?" I asked, standing naked against a wall and feeling silly as Polykleitos looked me over.

"Well, there're only so many poses possible when you carve in stone, bronze is different, of course. Damn marble dust, gets into everything. I hate white marble, until the statue is painted, it looks so dead. For you, the athlete at ease pose. Lean on that stand and relax.

110

Good, good." The sculptor returned to the table and watched while his assistant began to dab clay onto the wire frame.

"I thought you made the model," I asked.

"Heavens no, I never touch the slimy stuff. A great artist like myself would never get his fingers dirty. I let my students do the work and I supervise. Now be quiet, perhaps my muse will find me, but I don't see how she can in this rat hole."

For the next several weeks I watched as the students carved the marble away and a human form began to emerge. "You must be in there some place," Polykleitos quipped one day. Even with a brazier the studio was cold and I would stand there, shivering, goose-fleshed and covered with marble dust. "Just think of the art, you'll be immortal when I've finished with you," the sculptor said. "Beauty is everything."

A month later the hammering stopped and the house was blissfully quiet. "It's finished. My masterpiece. I'll unveil it tomorrow." And so the next morning, the entire household gathered in the dusty room and at the far end stood a sheet-covered statue. With great ceremony and a wine oblation and flair, Polykleitos ripped the sheet away and there I stood in marble.

"It doesn't look like me," I said.

"Of course it doesn't, silly. I've smoothed out the rough edges, and there were a lot of those. People want to see the noble, the idealized, the perfect and the beautiful. When it's taken to Delphi and set up on the Sacred Way the people will stand in awe of this, long after you're dead and forgotten." And so there I stood, noble and idealized, the perfect athlete, relaxed, leaning on a plinth, my face pensive and soft. No one would imagine the pain, the agony and the hard blows that I'd suffered to get that statue.

"Well, I must be off. I've had my students sign my name on the base. You can get some local stone-cutting hack to carve the base and inscription. Be careful when you move it to Delphi, I don't want my masterpiece damaged by a bunch of clods." With a dramatic flourish the rose-scented sculptor, his purse fat with money, his handsome students in tow, rode off down the road back to the bright life of Athens.

"Your ankle looks almost healed. The swelling has gone down. Can you stand on it?" Aristion asked as he removed my bandages.

"Yes, I think so." I stood with my weight on my lame foot. "It still hurts, but I can stand on it."

111

"Good." Aristion smiled as he rose to his feet.

"You know, I've been thinking of going. Artemidorus is kind and all that, but. . ."

"Going where?"

"To Sparta, to look for my brother. He may still be alive."

"The snow is two feet thick out there. It's best to stay until spring."

"No. I've had dreams, I hear him calling to me out of the night."

"It's foolish."

"I must go. You can stay if you like. It's my own mission."

"We're friends, aren't we?"

"Yes."

"We'll go together. I'll ask Artemidorus about pack-animals. But I think you should wait."

But Artemidorus' chubby face fell and turned ashen. "It's foolish, the port of Itea is closed. I can't even get my olive oil out, the seas are too rough. It's a hard winter. Stay here until spring. I thought you wanted to see your statue placed at Delphi. If your brother is alive, he'll be alive next spring."

"I must go," I said, my face set with grim determination. When he saw that my mind was set, Artemidorus gave us horses and mules, and soon we set out for the port of Itea. Wrapped in heavy cloaks, our breath white in the cold air, we plodded slowly through the drifts of snow. A bitter wind blew off the gulf of Corinth as we arrived in the little town of Itea. Its wharfs and quays were empty of ships. Small fishing boats lined the shore, broken and battered by the high frothy waves that beat in from a dark sea. We spotted a small house, with a faint light escaping through the boarded windows. We knocked and a withered old man opened a creaky door.

"A ship going to the Peloponnese? You must be crazy. There hasn't been a ship in here for nearly a month and won't be until spring. Can't even fish. I may starve before the seas go down. Worst winter in years. Better go back where you came from. Now get out of the doorway or all the heat will escape." He slammed the door and we were left in the bitter, freezing wind.

"What now?" Aristion asked, his voice shivering with cold.

"We'd better go back." My voice was bitter as the wind, and I looked for a moment across the stormy water. Somewhere I knew my brother was alive and I hoped he was warm and protected from the cold. With a prayer I mounted my horse, and we returned to Amphissa to wait out the winter. And I came down with the worst cold I had ever had, spending my time coughing and sneezing and wishing that the miserable winter would end.

In early spring we took my statue to Delphi to be set up on the Sacred Way. The heavy statue, carefully wrapped and bedded in straw, was lifted into an ox-drawn cart for the trip. It took almost a week, as the wheels kept getting bogged down in the still-muddy road.

Pushed, pulled and hoisted, the statue was taken up the Sacred Way and placed on its pedestal next to the statue of Agias. A strange irony; the vanquished stood next to the victor, but it was the only place available in the crowded forest of statues. The carved inscription read: "Pantarkes, winner once at Thebes, winner once at Delphi. Defeated Agias, the Olympian, in the pankration. Voted and sponsored by Artemidorus of Amphissa." I looked up at myself, immortalized in painted marble, wishing that the sculptor had carved in my scars. But what did I know about art? After a brief ceremony of dedication and fond farewells to my chubby benefactor, Aristion and I, with our slaves and pack-mules, set out for the port of Itea and home to Sparta.

❧ 5 ❧

"Aye, can't see why you fine looking men want to go to Sparta. It's no place for the likes of you now that the Krypteia have taken over. Runs the place like a prison now they've started building those stone walls." Aristion and I sat looking up at a beefy tavern-keeper, sipping his bad wine. Stale cooking odors hung around the rough timbered room. I had taken one last look at the small, lumbering merchant vessel before it pulled away from the wharf and was glad to get my land legs back after the long voyage. Like most ports Gytheion, laying twenty-eight miles south of Sparta, was dirty. Its wharfs were draped with torn nets and its choppy bay waters were full of small fishing boats. The air was pungent with the odor of dead fish.

"What walls? Sparta never had walls."

"The way I heard it was, some oracle told them if they didn't have walls the city would fall. Besides they're shit scared of Phillip, who's marching around the Peloponnese with the Macedonian army. He's trying to round up recruits for his invasion of the old enemy, Persia. That's the way I get it."

"The oracle at Delphi," I spoke quietly to Aristion. "I told you about it."

"Nope, I wouldn't go to Sparta or they'll put you to working slave labor on those walls. The whole town been turned out with whips and swords of the Persian behind them."

"The Persian?"

"Yes. He's some sort of strange foreign bastard. The Ephors and the councils of Sparta have given him absolute control over the building of the walls and he drives the poor bastards like oxen at the plow. I've

115

seen him — he came down once to supervise a shipment of stone. He's got a ready hand with the whip, all dressed in black armor, looked like a black hound from Hades. Wouldn't want to get on his bad side. Nope, better stay away. Sparta's in the iron grip of terror." The tavern-keeper walked on to the next table.

"With the Persian and Krypteia in control we are at the mercy of the gods. I had no idea they would believe the Pythia and really build the walls."

"Sparta goes by the books and keeps the traditions of old. So what are we going to do? With Sparta in control of the police, if they catch you—"

"Yes. I know. But I must keep my vow. The Persian must die and I must find Damon."

"Oh, Pantarkes, let's get out of here. Damon is dead. He couldn't have survived the winter, and a year and a half of being alone, that's asking the gods for too much. And the Persian, shit, Pantarkes, be reasonable."

"I made a vow of vengeance and I mean to keep it, if it's the last thing I do."

"If I've read the curse of Achilles correctly, it just may be."

"The old man was scared. He was babbling."

"A curse made at the time of death is powerful."

"I accept the challenge of Achilles: to be brave and strong."

"Childish thinking, my friend. It's best to leave this viper's pit. There's only death and terror here."

"I must."

"All right, we'll go into Sparta. I can see from your face nothing can stop you. You must enter the city without being caught, find Damon and leave. We can go to my house. I left my slaves in charge, if they haven't deserted me. I have some prestige. We can disguise you."

"They will have forgotten me by now."

"Sparta never forgets. We have slaves and the guard. He's in armor, go along with him. They'd never notice a second guard."

"It might work. At least I'll have a sword in my hand if they spot me. We'll buy some horses and donkeys at first light." By the time we finished haggling over the price of the animals it was midmorning before we set out on the muddy road to Sparta. The spring rains fogged the surrounding countryside as we slogged along. I rode beside our guard who smelled of stale wine and complained of a hangover. Late the next day we saw the misty mountains of the Taygetus which cradled at its base my home, a home I thought I'd never see again.

There seemed to be some sort of roadblock up ahead as a long line of horses and ox-drawn carts stretched along the road. As we drew near we saw heavily armed hoplites searching the wagons and questioning all who would enter Sparta. Aristion pulled up before a guard and, leaning down from his horse, spoke to the man.

"What's the trouble here?" His voice was loud and commanding. "I'm Aristion, the Olympian. I'm returning from a glorious victory at Delphi. I'll not put up with this shit. I demand an escort to my house at once!"

The guard seemed unconcerned by Aristion's demands. "The city is under martial law." He looked down at a scroll. "Aristion? You're not on the wanted list. What's your business in Sparta?"

"Business? You stupid fool! I live here! Need I report you to my friend, the Persian? He'll have no mercy when he learns I've been detained by a stupid guard." Aristion threw his cloak up around his shoulders. The guard, flustered, raised his face visor.

"Aristion? The Olympian? I remember you. I've seen you run many times. There was a report you'd left Sparta for good — the word about your wife got around." A wisp of a smile crossed the hoplite's lips.

"My wife? Oh, her. I'd forgotten about that poor creature. Who thinks about women when there are contests to be won?"

"Sparta is much changed now and very suspicious of anyone, with the Macedonians marching around and our walls not yet built. You'll understand, we can't be too careful. Can you vouch for your slaves? We don't want trouble."

"My slaves are loyal to me." Aristion looked down at the hoplite, his voice disdainful. The guard looked at our caravan, and seemed to have second thoughts about letting us pass without a search. I watched, my hand on my sword. Then abruptly he turned and called for a few mounted men to escort the Olympian into the city.

Sparta, beneath gray skies, looked drab and grim. There was no gleaming marble, no golden monuments, no glint of polished bronze except the points of spears. The hoplite armor and even the red cloaks of the soldiers looked muddy. Passing into the center of the central village I saw the walls, Sparta's defense against Phillip. One watch tower stood completed, its height carried crenellated battlements where in time of war the archers would stand. The thirty-foot walls stood proud and defiant, but only for a short distance. Nearby I could see that only the lower courses of stone had been laid. A group of

Spartans labored on crumbling ramps, pushing and pulling a heavy stone. For a moment the squared stone moved up the ramps but the weight was too much and it slid back to the bottom with a soft thud. Doggedly the workers tried to pull it up again. Certainly the tortured Sisyphus, who in the underworld rolled his rock up a steep hill only to have it eternally roll back down, was shown more mercy than the Spartans who labored here under the crack of the leather whip. I saw all of this only for a moment when we passed the grim walls of the Spartan garrison and the Spartan assembly hall, called the Skias. As we passed the road leading to my father's house I glanced up the muddy path. I knew I would take that path soon to find my brother.

We came to Aristion's house, which was better built than most. The rain had soaked its white walls to a putty color and rain dripped from the red tile roof as we came to a halt. He jumped down from his horse and shoved the gate open. "Shit, there's no one here," he said after calling out some names. The gardened courtyard had grown over and the locked door buckled as we came against it with our shoulders.

"The servants have left," he said when we had entered, the mosiac floors and painted walls covered with dust and dirt. "The servant quarters are in the rear. Stash your stuff and get back in here to start cleaning. Go to the market and get something for supper. Shake your butts." The servants rushed around as Aristion sat down on the edge of the stone hearth. "Well, Pantarkes, we're back home again. Not a very good homecoming, but things will be better in a while."

"Where are your wife and slaves?"

"I've no idea. The slaves were provided for and as for my wife, she's probably been married off to another man by now. I don't care, that's the last marriage. I suppose you'll go out tomorrow and search for Damon?"

"Yes. I just know he's still alive. I'll go to my father's house and ask around. Our old neighbors knew Damon well; he was not above making raids on their fruit trees and gardens. They might know where he is. I'll go at first light. Where do we sleep?"

"Upstairs. We can sleep in our bed-rolls. Damn, I'm hungry, where are those servants?" After a long wait the servants came with food and wine. Aristion and I went upstairs and climbed into our bed-rolls. I blew out the oil lamp and darkness settled. But we were barely asleep when a cry sounded at the door.

"Master, master, wake up. There's a woman downstairs claiming to be your wife, demanding to see you." Aroused from my sleep I saw a servant shaking Aristion, who was rubbing his eyes.

"Who?"

"Your wife Aspasia is downstairs."

"Shit. How did she know we had arrived?" Aristion got up, pulling his blanket around his waist. "Come on, Pantarkes. Let's see what the bitch wants." Clutching our blankets we went downstairs. A tall, statuesque woman stood in the middle of the room, wrapped in a heavy cloak. A servant beside her carried an umbrella. She looked the personification of the warrior-goddess Athena: square-jawed, narrow-eyed, thin-lipped, her face framed by a bountiful mass of blond hair that hung in braids about her shoulders. Her walking stick seemed like a spear. Aristion drew himself up to full height, but she towered over him by at least a head. There was a scowl about her lips as she looked down at him.

"Sooooooo, my errant husband has returned. News of your arrival is all over Sparta. The return of such an important citizen is not an easily kept secret. Welcome home, Olympian." The woman's booming voice echoed around the room as she swept up Aristion in a bone-crushing hug. His lean, frame seemed lost in the folds of her robes. I hid a smile behind my hand, pretending to scratch my nose. She must have noticed the movement as she put her husband down. She looked at me with cool eyes. "Who's this? Your lover?" She pointed her stick at me.

"No, no, that's... my assistant guard. He watches the gold box."

"Ha. Sleeping with your slaves. How curious of you. He looks like an athlete, a wrestler; broad shoulders, firm arms, strong neck. Boy, what's your name?"

"Ah, Damon, of Thebes," I said, taken off guard by her unexpected question.

"Thebes? What were you doing in Thebes, Aristion? Looking up your old friends? Traitors, those who've escaped, like that boy last year who killed the Ephor's son. Your eromenos looks Spartan. Those arms have seen spear-throwing. I'm not wrong."

"Damon is a brave lad. He fought with Thebes against Macedonia, a war that Sparta chose to ignore. Where were the brave Spartans as Phillip took the field? Phillip is war-chief in Hellas, not the Spartans, not Thebes, not Athens. Sparta is nothing, a flea on Phillip's rump which he can slap anytime he wishes. That silly wall won't keep him out."

Aristion's sudden vehemence drained Aspasia's face white as she clenched her stick. "Sparta is strong and prepares for Phillip's invasion of this sacred land. Artemis will guide us. Oh, beloved, let's not fight.

Things have not gone well for us, I know. There was nothing I could do about the child. It's the law which all true Spartans must obey."

Aspasia turned away, wiping her nose with her gown and brushing tears away.

"My dear, I know it wasn't your fault," Aristion said. He placed his hand on hers, and she clutched it tightly.

"I'm still your wife and my place is here with you, beloved. We'll make a new start. Things will be better, you'll see. I'm afraid your slaves were sent to work on the wall and I moved the furniture to my father's house. I'll stay with my family tonight and move back tomorrow. Oh, yes, I have two strong children, healthy boys. You'll love them. You'll have to dismiss your eromenos, he's no longer needed. I'm home to stay." She threw a kiss to Aristion as she walked out.

"I should have stayed at Delphi and taken holy orders," Aristion muttered, looking at his departing wife.

"She's huge," I said as soon as she was out of earshot.

"And formidable. A product of Spartan training. She seems to have mellowed, it's the first time I've ever seen her cry. She's not a bad sort, really. I wonder who her boys belong to? Not to me, that's certain. Be careful of her, she remembers Milo and might put two and two together in that iron mind of hers."

"Damon's name was on my mind and I just blurted it out. She saw that I was a wrestler. It looks like I'm your ex-lover, tossed out into the cold, and a slave too. I came down fast in the world," I said with some amusement.

"It's your protection. Stay out of her way and let her think anything she wants, except the truth. She'd turn you in at the blink of an eye if she knew who you really were. Be careful."

At dawn I rode out of Sparta, taking the familiar road toward my father's house. I tried to recall his face and that of my mother as the mare trotted along, but time had erased the hard edges of my memory and the images that came back were hazy. After riding a while I realized I had taken a wrong road and forgotten the way home. Had it been that long ago? Where was that great olive tree that marked the turn? Had it been cut down? I took this path and that, searching. Finally I saw the tree just where it had always been, and with a sigh of relief I heeled the mare onto the correct road. A half mile on, I saw my father's house standing in ruins. Only the lower part of stone stood, the upper parts of brick had crumbled and the wood beams were gone.

With a sad heart I tied the horse and went inside, calling my brother's name. There was only silence as I stepped over the rubble. I looked up into the low hills; they had been a favorite retreat for Damon and I found a footpath leading up into them. Untended, our fields and vineyards had dried up. A short distance away the trellises of a neighbor's vineyard sprouted green, a promise of rich harvest. I saw an old man trimming branches from the grape arbor and he watched me closely as I went over to him. "Pardon me, sir, I'm looking for a boy who once lived in that abandoned house."

"The old house, Panyasis' place. He got killed. Who are you?"

I paused, afraid the old man might give me away. "I'm a friend of his family. I knew the boy when he was younger and we were friends."

"There was a boy around here for a while, but he went away. The police were looking for him a while back. They still are, from what I can tell."

"No, I'm not from the police. I've been away, in the north."

"There was an older boy, about your age, I guess. What did you say your name was? You look like him. He ran away, never heard where he went. His name sounded a lot like his father's name... Pan... Pantarkes. You're Pantarkes."

"Yes. I've come home to find my brother." My heart jumped a beat as I told my secret.

"The police were looking for you. They were here last year."

"There's a warrant for my arrest."

"Panyasis was a good man and my friend, but things can go wrong even with the best of families. I'm not saying that anything could be done, but if you are who you say you are, your brother might still be around. . . ."

"He's still alive?"

"Might be, might not be. The police send clever spies. I went to your mother's funeral, what were her grave-goods?"

"Er... an old iron pot and her weaving stuff."

"The name of Panyasis' helot?"

"Timon." I slowly began to remember the old man.

"Not saying anything, but if your brother could be found, where might you be staying?"

"At the house of Aristion, the Olympic runner." I saw that further questioning would accomplish nothing so I mounted the mare and with a final glance to the farmer on the hill, I rode away.

It was late morning when I returned to Aristion's house. The

121

Spartans hadn't forgotten their hero; a small crowd had gathered and shouted his name. Servants carried furniture back into the house, painters were giving the place a new coat of whitewash, and men on the roof repaired the tiles, all under the watchful eye of Aspasia who directed operations with her stick. I found my possessions had been moved into the slaves' quarters by her order. That rubbed my nerves, but to her I was only a guard and a slave. I heard a loud bang and looked around. It was Aspasia.

"There you are. Where have you been all morning? Get upstairs and help move the furniture. And stay away from my husband. He said you were a good man, sober and reliable. I'll allow you to stay. But you're in my service now, and you will do what I say. I'm the mistress of this household. Now get upstairs." I burned around the edges as I carried out her orders. After that I saw very little of Aristion or his wife. Several days passed and late one night Charmis woke me.

"Sir, an old man was at the front gate asking for you. The servants woke me up asking if there was anyone named Pantarkes with Aristion's slaves. He was about to be sent away when I caught up with him. He's at the back door."

I got up and went to the rear of the house. A man stood wrapped in a heavy cloak.

"Pantarkes?"

"Yes. You're the man from the vineyards!"

"I've come to take you to your brother."

"Gods of bountiful blessings, he's alive!"

"I saw him only yesterday. He couldn't believe you were alive either. We must move quickly, you're both wanted men and it would be certain death if we were discovered. You must not know where Damon is, if you were to be taken, tortured and revealed his hide-out. . . Men stronger than you have broken, the Persian has his ways. You'll be blindfolded until we reach Damon. Get dressed at once. It's a long ride, but I have horses waiting." Moonlight revealed several mounted men waiting in the shadowed street. Charmis helped me dress and I explained where I was going. He was overjoyed that Damon was alive.

The old man blindfolded me and I mounted the horse which was led through the streets of Sparta. My heart raced at the thought of seeing Damon. The gods had been merciful. After what seemed like hours of travel light began to come through the cloth around my eyes. Dawn was arriving. As I bounced along I mused that I knew nothing about the men who were leading me. Had the police been told? Had the old

122

man betrayed my secret? Were they, for some strange reason, taking me somewhere out of town to kill me? I thought of jumping down to run away, but the horse started uphill and I had to grab the wiry mane to keep from falling off backwards. The light disappeared and the clopping of the hooves echoed around me. We went downhill and the fresh air grew stale. I thought we must have entered a cave somewhere in the Taygetus Mountains. We stopped. "We're here. You can remove your blindfold."

"It's him!" My heart leapt as I heard Damon's voice. Yanking the cloth away I saw him standing, his face glowing, surrounded by our mastiff hounds. I jumped down to embrace Damon. The dogs sniffed me, and the old bitch, recognizing me, nearly knocked me to the ground with her great paws. Never have I known such joy.

"Blessed gods. I've thought of this moment since that day when I stood high in the mountains looking down at Sparta. I've cursed myself every day for running away."

"No, don't do that. It was all you could do at the time. Forget. We've survived and that's all that counts. I knew you'd return if you could. You look good, really great."

"You too. You're still a puppy-dog, eager and full of bounce."

"Yes, I haven't let things get me down. Here, now, let me introduce my friends, other Spartans who have had trouble with the police." Thirty men stood around us; some were young like Damon and others old like the farmers who brought me to the hidden cave.

"This is my long-lost brother. I've told you about him. These men, Pantarkes, are all escapees from the tyrannikos of Sparta. The Persian would give his balls to find us — if he has any. One by one we've come here waiting for a chance to bring the tyrants down. Enough of whipping, torture and oppression. Sparta must be free!"

"Death to the Persian and the Dorians!" the men raised their swords, chanting the words. Their voices seemed the voice of a thousand as their bold cheer echoed around the dark, torchlit cave.

"Come, brother, let's talk. We have much to catch up on." Damon and I sat down near the fire-pit of the great cave, telling how our lives had progressed since that horrible day at the Spartan palaestra.

I told Damon about Thebes, and the war, about my confrontation with the Ephor and my wrestling victories at Delphi. His mouth dropped when I said that my statue stood on the Sacred Way. "What honors, what glory, what adventures. I'm afraid my life has been dull compared with yours. Trying to stay one step ahead of the police has been my only concern. I stayed around the house waiting for you, but the Ephor's men watched the place and I finally took off for the hills. I stole and killed game to keep alive. One night I raided a farm, with a goose under my arm. I was caught and I thought it was my end, but the farmer knew me. The perioikoi stick together. I stayed with his family for a while, but the police came one night and I barely escaped. The farmer led me to this cave where other outlaws had come. The young, the old, helots and slaves, the dregs of Sparta. We were down and out, but you know me, I'm not going to lay down and die just for a bunch of shitty Dorians.

"Secretly we went to farmers and into town, organizing and seeking help against Dorian tyranny. We steal Dorian food and weapons, we raid shipments of gold. We're much hated. Ha! We've got those bastards where we want them, down in a hole in Hades. Someday when we've got enough men and weapons we'll march down into Sparta and take the place over. The Persian will be stuck on my sword, just like he stuck my father and Timon."

"Sparta will never rise in revolution."

"When they've had enough of being ground into the dirt, when they've grown weary of oppression, of tyranny, and of being scared of their own shadow, only then. . ."

"I'll stay here and help you fight."

"No, you'd be missed. I know of Aristion's wife. Her father is the current Ephor of the third district. He replaced the other one — I wish I could have seen you kill him. When his officers returned from Delphi they said he'd died of natural causes. Her father is now head of the Krypteia. Take care, beloved brother." With that I was again blindfolded and taken back to the city.

It was late afternoon before I returned to Aristion's home. Charmis greeted me and I told him about the meeting with Damon. He was joyful, but only for a moment. "Aspasia has been looking and asking for you all day. The place has been like a madhouse. She's giving a party for her husband to celebrate his victory at Delphi. She wanted you to shop and deliver the invitations. You'd better go see her and have a good excuse for being away for so long."

"Damn that woman. Help me dress. Where is my clean tunic?" Aristion and his wife were reclining on couches as I entered the ornate megaron. I bowed as she looked up from a cup of wine.

"There you are, you good-for-nothing. Where have you been? Always running off. Aristion, can't you do something? I'd have him whipped. You've such a soft heart."

"Ah, Damon was running errands for me. I sent him to the street of

124

craftsmen looking for a gift for you, beloved. A present for tonight's party. I didn't want to tell you. Now stay here, I want to see what he's brought. He has good taste. Come, slave, let's walk in the gardens." He got up and grabbed me by the arm, taking me into the garden. "Now, where have you been? Someone was here last night asking for you by your real name. He was sent away."

"I know. That man came to take me to my brother." I told Aristion the story.

"You and Damon must escape. It's too dangerous here. You and he are bound to be discovered. What can a few do against the trained army of Sparta? It's hopeless. Leave while there's still time."

"I can't leave yet. The Persian must die; both Damon and I have vowed revenge."

"He'll be here tonight to celebrate my Pythian victory."

"I'll kill him then."

"No, you fool. He'll be here with members of the Krypteia. You couldn't get near him. My wife suspects something. They told her about that man asking for Pantarkes. She asked me this morning if that wasn't the name of Milo's killer. She thinks we've been lovers. Now she's jealous, and wants you out of the way. It would be simple, I could just dismiss you and you and Damon could leave... she's coming. Here take this." Aristion reached inside his himation and shoved a small gold box into my hand.

"So what are you two talking about? Old times? Even if this boy, Damon — or Pantarkes — is your lover, he's not a very good slave, always going off somewhere just when you want him. Dismiss the worthless boy and I'll buy you another."

"Worthless? Does a worthless slave have such good taste? See what he's found for you." Aristion grabbed the box and held it out. Aspasia opened the little box and took out a pair of jewel-encrusted gold earrings. She held them up against her ears. "I was going to give them to you tonight, but now is a good time. Go try them on. You look beautiful, dear." Excitedly Aspasia left the gardens.

"Even a Spartan has some vanity. Look, stay out of sight tonight. Stay in the kitchens. I don't want any trouble. You can kill the Persian sometime, but not tonight. Because of my position I must get along with these people. Understand?" Aristion grabbed my arms, holding me tight. "Be careful, dear friend."

When I returned to the servants' quarters the chief steward sent me shopping and it was growing dark as I returned. The house was alive with the flickering of many oil lamps, wondrous odors of food scented the air, garlands of flowers decorated the doors and walls. It was a beautiful spring evening; clusters of bright stars covered the heavens while a sickle moon hung on the horizon as I entered the house. Servants scurried around making ready for the festivities. I helped around the kitchen. Aristion was right, it was best to stay out of sight. I'd have no chance tonight against the enemy, my vengeance would have to wait until the right moment.

The food was served and the clay seals of the wine amphorae were broken. Soon loud cheers toasting Aristion's victory at Delphi rang through the house. It was growing late as the servants carried more wine into the party. Charmis and I were breaking yet more seals when Aspasia suddenly appeared at the door pointing her finger at me.

"You there, boy," her words were garbled and she weaved a little. "The party is getting stale. The men are tired of the dancing and acrobatics. You look like a wrestler and one of the men has made a challenge, but everyone is too drunk. You'll do. Come with me. You, old man, bring some oil for the wrestlers and be quick about it." I was stunned by her imperious order and stood staring.

"Poor Aristion, he put away too many toasts and was carried up to bed. He'll not be in the best of moods in the morning. Come now, we can't keep the men of the Krypteia waiting."

Angered by her order, I wanted to throw the amphorae at her, but Charmis and I followed like obedient servants to the doors of the megaron, where Aspasia ordered me to strip. As I did so she cast a keen eye on every part of my body, licking her lips. I was embarrassed. Then she threw the doors of the room open. "Men, a challenger from my household, Damon of Thebes. Since the master of the house is indisposed, I'll sit in his place."

We entered the dark room. The low, flickering oil lamps cast dark shadows of the reclining men onto the walls, the air was heavy with the smell of wine. I saw the nude form of a muscular man, the light glancing off his heavy chest and massive thighs as a slave rubbed oil on his sleek body. He posed, drawing cheers from the men. "Acton of Sparta. Champion." The man stood, hands on his hips, watching as Charmis oiled my body.

"I'll make short work of this one. Bring more lamps and the swords, we'll have some fun with this slave." Fresh lamps were brought in and swords, sitting upright on their hilts, were placed in a square on the mosaic floor. I quickly looked around, searching for the face of my enemy, the Persian; his form loomed out of the darkness when the fresh lamps were placed around the room. He sat on a couch alone, sipping wine. The light caught his bald head, but the rest of his face was covered by a leather mask, with only slits for the eyes and mouth. The rest of his figure was clothed in dark robes. Around him lay paired men: the Krypteia. I had been cast into the very center of a vipers' nest.

The drunken Aspasia took her place next to the Persian and the light caught her bright eyes and wet lips. "Yes, yes, the swords, the sharp swords. I wonder if Aristion will miss his beautiful eromenos. One of those swords is for you, Damon, or Pantarkes, or what ever your name is." The Persian turned her way and then turned his strangely masked face towards me. "Do your work, Acton."

I turned to face the Spartan, who had taken the stance, and we each moved in, looking for a hold. He wasted no time coming at me. I grabbed his forearms, and dug in with my fingers. Yowling, he brought his knee up, forcing me back. I straddled my legs, trying to get a better grip on the smooth mosaic floor. It was a mistake. I lost my grip and slid backwards, falling flat on my belly. My feet hit several of the upright swords, which clattered and fell over. The Spartan dived on top of me, hoping to land on my back for a pin, but I dodged away. He stood, catching my arm and spun me around toward the swords.

"Pantarkes!" Charmis screamed as he saw me falling toward the sharp, gleaming bronze. A blade scraped my arm as I hit the floor. Angered by the blood and pain I grabbed the sword as I stood up. The Spartan backed away. I parried this way and that, watching him retreat. It gave me time to catch my breath and I threw the bronze down. I heard my name called out, the voices were angry. Reason left me and I was caught up in blind anger, as hatred for my enemies welled up within me. I went mad in that desperate moment. The young Spartan didn't stand a chance as I moved in with rapid fury. He took the normal stance, expecting to play with me a bit more. With all my force, every muscle, fiber and sinew filled with rushing blood, my mind crazed with anger, I moved against him, ignoring his stance, I grabbed him around the waist, lifted him above me, spun his frantic body like a sack of grain then slammed him to the hard floor.

My anger was not yet over. Grabbing a sword, I charged the Persian. Aspasia screamed as she ducked under the couch. My sword was not for her, but for the hated Persian. I wanted to see the expression on his face as the bronze sank into his belly, and my other hand was ready to rip his mask away. But before I reached him I was pulled to the floor. Firm hands held my legs.

127

"Pantarkes, you've come home." A boot drove into my ribs, turning me over. I looked up into the mask of dark evil as the massive form of the Persian stood over me. His black robe swirled around me like a fog from hell. "We've waited a long time for you." His voice, gutteral and broken, floated down from his hidden lips. "Arrest this man. Take him to the garrision for imprisonment and death."

A square of light floated high overhead. The feeble light fell across an empty room to a barred door a few feet away. I ached as I raised myself off the cold stone floor. I was naked. A dirty bandage had been wrapped around my arm, which was covered with dried blood. A clay jar sat near the door and on all fours I crawled over to it. It held water. I took a drink and with my cold fingers washed some of the blood away. Through the iron bars I saw an armed hoplite, his back towards me, and beyond him, at the far end of a corridor, a pinpoint of light.

I crawled back to sit against the wall, waiting. A guard came and slipped a bowl of wheat porridge through the bars and I ate the mush with great hunger. This was to be my end. At least Damon was alive and safe, and I had seen a moment of glory in my time. But the Ephor's curse had come true; mine would be a short life. I would never see my eighteenth birthday. My only wish was that the gods had given me a moment longer to sink my sword into the Persian.

My thoughts were disturbed by the sound of heavy steps in the corridor, and the light at the end was blocked as the guard snapped to attention. The Persian stood on the other side of the bars looking down at me.

"Pantarkes, the circle of life has come roundabout. This cell once held your father. He was here for many months, but you'll be here for only a short time, time enough to round up your brother. Rebellion cannot be tolerated. We know of his secret cave and it's only a matter of time before we take him and his little band of outlaws. We can always use more men on the walls. Soon their backs will feel the bite of my whip. Men are searching the hills, rounding up suspected perioikoi dogs. I have ways to make them talk. Your head will look very nice alongside that of your brother stuck on a pole in the center of town, a warning to would-be rebels."

Somewhere under that black helmet I knew a smile crossed those unknown lips. I wondered who the Persian was and why was he so unwilling to show his face? His cloaked figure turned and he went back down the corridor. His words were empty, I felt sure. No one would reveal the location of Damon's secret cave. He would be a sharp burr, forever tormenting Sparta's tyrannikos.

Two days passed, marked by the coming and going of light from the small cell. The guards gave me water and porridge. My arm seemed to heal and I searched the cell for a way to escape, but the stones were set into firm mortar. All I could do was sit on my naked ass and wait.

On the third night I heard screaming from far away. My eyes popped open. Flaming torches blinded my vision, but I was able to see a figure pushed along, dark shapes of armed hoplites at his back. The creaking iron bar holding the door was flung open and a tightly bound figure was thrown in, landing in a heap at my feet. I looked down into the frightened eyes of Damon.

"No! No! You bastards!" I cried, raising my fists in anger at the retreating guards.

"It's no use, Pantarkes, they've got all of us. They found the cave and were on us before we knew what happened. Some tried to escape, but they were split open before they got out. See if you can get these ropes off, they're tight and they hurt." Frantically I worked the ropes, unraveling the hard knots until Damon's arms and legs were free.

"Someone must have broken and told the Krypteia your location."

"Yes, I suppose. It was a risk. Oh, Pantarkes, you should have stayed away. This was my private war, you could have been safe, but now, all is lost." The thin light of dawn filtered through the window as Damon stood, rubbing his wrists and legs. His long brown hair, matted with sweat and blood, clung to his skull. His round face looked into the light as if for the last time; his boyish body stood firm and resolute as he wiped a tear from his brown cheek. He sat beside me, taking his hand into mine, and together we waited for death.

More days passed, marked only by day and night as we waited in the stinking cell. Damon's head rested on my chest. He was asleep, but his body twitched as though he were having bad dreams. Faint shouts came from the end of the corridor; by the end of the day our heads would hang in the city square.

The shouting grew, and the drowsy hoplites grabbed the swords and shields. I heard the sound of fighting, the loud clank of metal hitting metal, and screams of pain. Our guards rushed up the corridor. Still I couldn't tell what was happening. The guards stopped, their swords slashing at someone. Damon woke and we stood watching, our hands clutching the iron bars. One by one the guards fell before the aggression of the oncoming attack. As the guards dropped a young man ran down the corridor, a bloody sword in his hand.

"Samos, Samos!" Damon shouted, and his face broke into a broad grin. The youth threw the door open.

"Sparta rises in revolt. We've come, Damon. The perioikoi are taking the garrison. I don't know how long we can hold out, but we'll put up a good fight." Suddenly the youth staggered and fell. A sword jutted out of his back.

"Brave youth. Let's go, Pantarkes. Grab some weapons. Our time for vengeance has come." Taking swords and shields from the dead hoplites we ran, opening the cells of Damon's scruffy band, and our group ran out into the bright sunlight. The training field that had known the measured march of soldiers was now a confused melee of fighting men: Spartan against Spartan, aristocrat against helot, slave against master. Fires were started and the garrison was burning. Sparta was in revolt.

Damon looked at me. We knew what must be done. The Persian would be at the walls, supervising slaves, whip in hand. In a breathless run we took off in that direction. Work had stopped as the bloodletting swirled around the squared blocks of stone. We saw the black form of the Persian retreating up the steps of a completed watchtower. Damon pointed and we ran up the ramps and along the ramparts. The Persian stood ready, looking down from the high crenellated tower. Entering the doorway, we gained the steps, and in a moment we faced our enemy from across the stone platform. He stood against the stone battlements, sword in hand, waiting.

"Pantarkes. Damon. There's death in your eyes, my death. It ends. Spartan against Spartan. Kill me. There's not much to kill." The thick, gutteral, rasping voice of the Persian came across to us in the thin wind and bright sunlight. "You think I'm foreign. I'm Spartan, as good as any of you. I know Sparta well, see what she's done to me." He raised his gloved hands to remove his helmet and unbuckle his face mask. We stood back in horror.

Below the Persian's bald head was nothing but scarred flesh. His eyes were sunk into skull-holes. Two raw, gaping holes served in place of a nose, and for a mouth he had no lips, only yellow teeth hanging from bony cheekbones. He opened his teeth to speak. "Yes, I'm Spartan, but my words come out garbled, foreign-sounding. Look." As he removed his cloak and armor we saw his body. His arms and chest were withered and skinny, and a strange bronze frame surrounded the twisted flesh.

"So I was born, deformed and ugly, fit only for the throwing-place. My mother pleaded for my life, but finally took and threw me out, but she was grieved beyond words and at night she came back, before the wolves got me, and took me home. I was broken and nearly dead, but she nursed me back to health, hiding me from the world to grow up stunted and deformed. My father, a perioikoi blacksmith, made a frame to support my poor body. I set my heart against Sparta and took a whip into my hand. Why should I have felt mercy for Sparta? With my bronze body I was as good as any man. I was taken in by the Ephor; he was kind and I did his work. But now my body is in constant pain and I can barely lift the bronze any more. I am ready to die."

Damon and I stood stunned, looking back at the man who stared at us from that death-head. There seemed to be a smile on the toothy face. He leaned back, his spindly arms grasping the stone. Raising himself up, he sat for a moment looking around at the world, then he toppled backwards from the high tower. There was a loud clank as his bronze body hit the pavement below.

The sounds of trumpets came through the air from afar. We looked to the north. The sun glinted off a forest of bronze pikes and the armor of many men. The marching boots created the sound of muffled thunder as the immense army moved toward Sparta. The sunlight caught the golden standards and I recognized the sunburst design of the royal house of Macedonia. Cavalry stretched from horizon to horizon filling the Lacedaemonian plains.

"Look, look to the north, an army marches on Sparta," someone shouted from the ramparts. Slowly, as the word spread the fighting stopped, the field littered with the dead and dying. From our high position we could see a chariot, with an armed guard, break away from the battlelines. Phillip had come to Sparta. His name was chanted across the field, and in a mad frenzy the Spartans grabbed any weapon at hand, rushing north to form ragged battlelines against the oncoming Macedonians. Side by side, the low stood with the high, weapons ready to fight the Macedonian King.

Phillip, his chariot pulled by two milk-white stallions, their trapping heavy with gold, came at a slow trot toward the massed Spartans. Without walls, Sparta falls, and so it would be. I hated all that Sparta stood for, but at that moment my eyes blurred as I saw my fellows, battered and bloody, muster to the defense of their city. I knew they would fall like wheat before the blade of Phillip's immense army. And I knew that it must not happen.

"Come on, Damon. Grab a horse, we must act quickly. I think Phillip will hear my words. I pray the gods he will." We ran from the tower and mounted two mares who were wandering around in search of their masters. At a swift gallop we passed the wide-eyed Spartans, who must have thought we were Macedonian spies eager to rejoin our friends. Soon we were out on the road leading north. Phillip's chariot driver halted the stallions, the guard closed in and the King stood in his ornate golden carriage watching us approach. We reined up the mares and I shouted to the King.

"Majesty. I beg a moment, in the name of all the blessed gods and in the name of all you hold sacred."

"There's not much I hold sacred. Let the boys come forward. One, I think, forgot his clothes." At a slow trot we soon sat facing the King. He was smiling and rubbing his grizzled beard, and no doubt thought us mad.

"Majesty. My name is Pantarkes and this is my brother, Damon. We're Spartans. We met long ago, after the battle of Chaeronea. You were kind and gave me shelter."

"Er, I remember. Pantarkes, the last man of the Sacred Band. You're a long way from Thebes."

"Sir, Sparta is my home. I returned after winning a great victory at the Pythian Games."

"Good, my boy. Exactly what do you want? I tire of Sparta's arrogance. Their refusal to honor the Sacred Hellenic League and their refusal to recognize me as supreme war chief has greatly angered me. They need to be taught a lesson, a lesson the warriors of Sparta can understand." He looked back to his vast army.

"Majesty. Sparta has known days of glory and greatness. She's arrogant and stubborn, yes, clinging to the old days, days which have gone away. You face a shabby reflection of that glory. Barely three thousand hoplites stand in the battlelines, the rest are slaves, women and children armed with little more than their bodies — which they will gladly give to stop you and to protect their sacred land. I speak plainly. Someone once told me you were not given to the airs of falseness that many in high position have. Has there not been enough glory for you? Phillip is known for his mercy and benevolence. What will history say when his armies smash Sparta? And you can easily do that, there is nothing but easy slaughter. I ask mercy for my city." Phillip stood, rubbing his beard and looking to the south.

"Yes, I am known as a good man and that means something to me. I seek peace in Hellas, not vengeance. I want an end to the futile wars of the city-states. Victory in Sparta would be a small thing and as you say, they would die to the last man. History has a way of remembering only the black spots in one's career. Very well, Pantarkes, I'll not enter Sparta. It's an old dog, worn and mangy. History remembers those who do not kick old dogs. Warn their leaders, the Ephors and the councils, that I'll have no mercy if they raise their swords against anyone in the future. A good life to you and your brother; now you'd better go back and put on some clothes. Remember me." Phillip smiled as he gave orders to his driver, and the chariot wheeled around. With a blast of trumpets and a roll of drums, the army turned and marched away from Sparta.

"Thank the gods! Sparta is saved!" Damon shouted.

"Phillip is a great man, considering that he's a Macedonian barbarian. Let's go back." We returned to the battlelines of scarred, smoking Sparta. The lines of hoplites watched silently but seeing the army march away, one by one, they began to cheer. Someone must have known who I was for they began shouting my name.

"Pantarkes! Pantarkes! Pantarkes, soter!" I was being called savior by my fellow Spartans. My heart beat rapidly as we rode triumphant into the grim city.

Several days later Damon and his rebels and I were called to the Skias, the assembly-building in the center of town. The five Ephors, the Gerousia, and the Apella all sat in wooden tiers looking down at us. The powerful Ephors sat on stone seats a short distance from where we stood. After the opening ceremonies a list of our crimes against Sparta was read, charging us all with treason and rebellion. These were major crimes and the day would probably end with our death. The Dorian aristocrats sat facing us sullen and grim.

Speaking first, I told them of Phillip's warning against any aggression on their part, implying that the King was my dearest friend and would come to my aid if needed. I told them of my dark vows of vengeance against the Persian, but reminded them that as things had turned out, he had not died by my hand. I told them that I was a Pythian winner and about my statue at Delphi. Was I to be treated like a criminal when I had brought glory to Hellas? I demanded that the aristocrats free us all, restore my father's land, and dismiss the charges. I did my best to speak in the grand style of Demosthenes' stirring oratory.

Damon then made a speech calling for liberty and freedom from oppression. He reminded everyone of the recent uprising and told them that his friends, the perioikoi, would certainly rise up again if he and his band were put to death. Sparta had already seen too much of death and destruction. Many of the rebels bore wounds from the rebellion, a caustic reminder of that terrible day. Was there no end to it?

133

We finished our pleas and stood in the big room while our judgment was debated. Some called for death, especially for Damon who had stolen Dorian gold. It was unnerving to listen to the old men as they argued our fate. Some demanded banishment. The aggressive aristocrats came to blows and our case was almost forgotten as ancient rivalries were rekindled. Swords were drawn, but the five Ephors rose from their honored place to call for peace. Their word was law and the warring Dorians put their weapons away and sat down. And then when the Skias was quiet they turned to us. In a low voice an Ephor spoke. He agreed that I had been unjustly accused of murder and that I had fairly won my victory on that day so long ago in the palaestra. The charges against me were dropped. However, Damon's crimes and that of his band were too great to forgive. They were to be executed.

Many of the Dorians, especially those who bore wounds, then came to their feet. Sparta had suffered enough, they said, and if the rebels were put to death then others would rise up. There was fear in their eyes, for while they controlled the government, they were few in number compared with the helots and perioikoi. Their voices were small at first, but one by one the assembled men conceded to reason and the Ephors gave in to the demands. Some of the rebels were sent into banishment and a heavy fine was levied against Damon. I was able to pay the fine from my winnings at Delphi.

So the events that had started almost two years ago, when in pain I had yanked Milo's balls, had come to an end. Thanks largely to his high position, Aristion was elected Ephor, and has spoken of reforms that will perhaps bring peace to the warring factions. I know his wife was glad to see the last of me as Damon and I rode out to our farm which, with the help of our friends, was restored. We worked throughout the spring to rebuild the house and the lands once more became productive.

Fever struck Sparta: Olympic fever. Indeed, the hot contagious fever swept all of Hellas in late spring. It was the year of the Olympiad, the greatest and most important of the panhellenic games. One festive day the Spondophoroi arrived. These citizens of Elis sponsor the Olympiad. They go throughout the Hellenic world announcing the Games and proclaiming the ekecheiria, a truce made in the name of Father Zeus in which all hostilities are to cease, allowing free passage to all who wish to attend the great games.

Floral festoons of bright design hung from the buildings, the dour palaestra had been whitewashed and the citizens of Sparta put on their best to welcome the Eleans. The Heralds of Zeus rode into the city with appropriate flourish, the trappings of their stallions rich with gold. Dressed in gold and purple himations, bearing heralds' wands, and wearing slightly wilted olive-leaf crowns, the five Eleans announced the coming Olympiad. The athletes gathered in around them, excited and pushing. There were certain rules: all athletes must go to Olympia one month before the Games for intensive training under the watchful eyes of the Hellanodikai; the Games were only open to Hellenes; and all participants must observe the laws of Zeus. Our blood ran hot through our veins in anticipation of the event. It was the fulfillment of the dreams of many, including myself. I wished at that moment nothing more than an olive crown at Olympia.

A sacred mission, the theoroi of Sparta, started out for Olympia. They bore to Zeus sacrificial animals and gold, and tents to house the high officials of the mission. The athletes — runners, jumpers, boxers and wrestlers, discus throwers and charioteers, as well as the trainers and servants, the priests and aristocrats — all formed a magnificent procession. Damon and I sat astride our mares, our farm safely in the hands of our friends, waiting to get underway for the seventy-five mile ride up through the towns and farmlands of the Peloponnesus to Olympia, the sacred city of Father Zeus.

❧ 6 ❧

"Gather round, everyone. Telemachus, architheoros of the theoroi and Olympian, wishes to speak to you in the glen." Damon and I, grazing our horses, watched as Telemachus' messenger rode from group to group among the thirty Spartan men. Some of us were resting after the long journey, others were exercising, or nibbling on newly-roasted sweetmeats cooked over campfires by adoring mothers. Telemachus sat on his dappled mare while we assembled.

"Brave Spartans, athletes, mothers, wives, daughters and lovers, tomorrow we will leave this camp and go down into the river valley of the Alpheios and into the holy city of Olympia. This place marks the boundary and no women may pass beyond. This is the law of the Elean Hellanodikai who rule at Olympia. Do you see the high mountain yonder, Mount Typaeum? If any woman is caught in the holy city she'll be taken there and thrown down to her death. Only the honored priestess of Demeter Chamyne may attend and watch the games. Some of you may have been told of the only woman who was ever an exception to this rule, the noble lady Kallipateira, daughter of Diagoras. Her father, her husband and her sons won many games and were much honored. Her youngest son and her darling, Peisirodos, whom she had trained herself, was to enter and she was grieved that she would not be able to see his victories. She disguised herself as a trainer, with a tight wrapping across the chest, and entered the city to watch the games. Her son won. The good woman became so excited that she ran out to her son and her wrappings fell away, exposing her sex. The Elean officials were very upset, but her family had brought so much honor and glory to Elis and to the games that she was set free. I don't think any of you women could be so lucky." Telemachus looked toward the high rocky cliffs of Mount Typaeum.

"Unfair and unjust," a Spartan woman shouted out. "Shouldn't I see my son win? Olympia is unfair."

"The contests are fought naked and even the trainers are now also naked, because of lady Kallipateira. It is a mark of Hellene men to exercise gymnos and their pride, but they think it unbecoming and shameful for a woman to show herself before men."

"Piss on what Hellas thinks! Do not Spartan women run naked and even wrestle with men? It's no big thing — but it can get that way," the woman smirked.

"Every year when we go to Olympia I get the same arguments. I don't make the rules. You have the Heraia, women's games in honor of Zeus' spouse, Hera."

"Silly little running contests, run in modest skirts that cover you up all over."

"We can only abide by the rules. Now listen to me, you women can stay here for the month and the five days of contest, or you can return to the city. Your men will come back, olive-crowned with victory, crushed by defeat, and for a few, as ashes gathered from the funeral pyre. Look now. I'll have no more complaints. Give your man a good-bye kiss and go away. I've got to talk with them." Telemachus gave the women a harsh look as mothers fondly embraced their sons, wives kissed their husbands, and swearing love eternal, with wet kisses and streaming tears, young girls embraced their sweethearts. The women wandered away, some to set up camp for the long wait, others to begin the long ride back to Sparta.

"We hate to see them go, but it's a man's world down there. Tomorrow we'll enter Olympia to begin training. The Elean Hellano-dikai will be your gymnastes and judges from then on. You're the best of Spartan athletes and you may think you've trained hard, but you've had it easy. Though I don't agree with all their methods, the Eleans are the best trainers in the world. You'll find them strict, but fair. Behave yourselves and make Sparta look good. Generations of men have brought home the spoils. We'll get started with the first light." Telemachus smiled and reining his mare, trotted off.

"Tomorrow we'll see fabled Olympia," Damon said as we walked back to our horses and bed-rolls. "From the way he looked at you I think Telemachus means for you to win. My brother, the pride of Sparta!"

"After my victory at Delphi, who would expect anything else? I'll win a crown for Sparta, you'll see, if it kills me."

"You will. I want to win too. I'll take the crown for horse-racing, the keles, it's only six circuits around the hippodrome. I've trained that mare to go like the wind, like the fleet-footed, winged Pegasus. You know, when we get back I want to breed horses. But breeding stallions are expensive as all hell; if I could get a bet on the race and win..."

"You were always good with animals, Damon. We'll think about it when we get back."

Sunlight had barely penetrated the trees when Telemachus and his men prodded us all out of our warm blankets with a hard boot. After a meal of dried meat and bread, we mounted up and were off at a slow trot down the hill. Somewhere to our rear the great theoroi of Sparta, with its slow-moving carts, sacrificial animals and high officials of the mission, crept along.

The legendary heat of Olympia hit us as we entered the valley and passed through several small farming towns. Our eyes strained for a first glimpse of the temple of Olympia as we came to the tree-strewn river valley. I thought of high Delphi, the home of a young god, perched on the mountain edge: nervous, dramatic, imposing, tied to the sky. Olympia, the home of an elder god, was different: low, placid, secret, its roots tied to the earth. There was a break in the tree-lined road, a long whitewashed wall was visible just over the high wall, and beyond we saw the red-tiled roofs of many buildings. In the center there was the gleaming white marble roof of a great columned temple. It was the home of majestic Zeus, the Lord of Olympia. We had arrived at our destination.

The air was sweet with incense, but there was also the sharp smell of burnt sacrificial flesh as we rode past the high enclosing wall. Soon we saw the large palaestra and gymnasium which would be our home for the next month of hard training. Following Telemachus down the dusty road we came to the groves of pine and oak trees. Sunlight glinted off the river nearby as we were told to dismount and to set up camp. Already the area was filling with athletes, trainers and officials from the cities of Hellas. Bright standards proclaimed the name of their cities and its symbol: the Athenian owl, the Delphic tripod, the sunburst of Macedonia. Throughout the month all of Hellas would gather around Olympia pitching their tents beneath the hot sun and starry nights.

"Come on now, shake your butts. Hurry and line up. We'll march

139

over to the gymnasium and give the Hellanodikai a chance to look you over." Warned of the ferocious heat of the valley, Damon and I pitched our tents beneath a big tree, and while Damon groomed his lathered mare I followed the athletes, trainers, oilers and masseurs, as we happily marched behind Telemachus to the training areas. To our right the brightly painted pediments of temples, the statued tops of monuments and praying voices caught our attention. Gaping like curious tourists we paused to look, but Telemachus urged us on. "Hurry up, you can see all of that later." Around the corner we entered the shady colonnades of the great palaestra of Olympia.

Telemachus stopped for a moment to talk with a porter, who walked out into the sunlight where athletes were already at exercise. The porter returned with several men dressed in gold and purple himations. They carried a baton of ivory and gold, topped with the golden eagle of Zeus, the Elean Hellanodikai. Some of them were young and some were gray-bearded, but each carried himself with dignity and purpose. I thought I recognized one young man, an Elean I had met after my win at Delphi.

The himation of light wool did little to cover his magnificently built body. His arms were thick, muscular and bronzed; the pinned himation fell down over massive pectorals, stretching over the heavy broad chest. A golden belt clinched the narrow waist, and the fibers of his muscled thighs and calves bunched as he walked. His lean face, sparkling eyes and white teeth became alive as he saw me. His handsomeness had made a lasting impression on me at Delphi, and I felt the sharp arrow of Eros plunge into my heart. The Elean gave my hand a firm grasp.

"Pantarkes, dear friend."

"Herakleitos. We meet again."

"I hoped you might come to Olympia. I've thought about you."

"You've been in my thoughts also, very much."

"Have you settled in?"

"We just arrived from Sparta. We're camped down by the river — in the shade." I noticed the beads of sweat that ran down Herakleitos' smooth brow onto his sunburnt chest.

"It's hot out there, but it's cooler near the river. The Eleans are camped down there."

"Maybe we can see each other."

"Yes, I'd like that. Our meeting at Delphi was much too brief."

"Pantarkes! Come on. We're to meet with the Eleans in the ephebeion. Hurry." Telemachus' voice irritated me as Herakleitos and

I gazed into each other's eyes. "There'll be time for that later," Telemachus said gruffly.

The ephebeion, a large room with wooden benches, was filled with recent arrivals and the men talked loudly as we stood along the white walls waiting for the Elean gymnastes. A moment later the big, impressive man walked in, followed by his secretaries carrying rolls of papyrus. Busily he talked with his officials, pointing here and there, nodding and shaking his head like all important men do, and finally he looked at us with a smile.

"It's a little cooler in here. Hot enough out there to fry a wheatcake. Well, my name is Attalos and I want to welcome you all to the one hundred and eleventh Olympiad. You men have come a long way and endured many hardships, I'm sure, but the rough times are just beginning. We Eleans have trained generations of athletes and in time will train generations more. You've come here with only one purpose, to win, and we'll do our best to make you winners. The next month won't be easy, some will drop out if they lack the endurance, toughness, and stamina to enter, but for the selected few, the brave, stouthearted and courageous, the olive crown will be yours.

"A word about our training methods. Some of you have been using the tetrad, a four day training cycle: preparation, concentration, relaxation, and moderation. We've found this to be a dangerous schedule. Several years ago a wrestler from the Egyptian city of Naucratis, a young lad by the name of Gerenus, came to train with us. As usual he was wined and dined by his city and came to his exercises well hung over the next day, a thing that I hope you are all wise enough to avoid. His trainer, ignoring the boy's complaints, insisted that he go through the entire set of exercises. That afternoon the boy collapsed and died. Not a very good system.

"Here, we set the training schedule for each man according to his type. Some do well when driven hard, some need to be prevented from training too quickly. Some are as a perfect block of marble: able to face hard work, seldom ill, with a healthy appetite, easy to train and accepting instruction easily. I hope you are all like this.

"Besides seeing to your training, we're here to see that you obey the laws of Zeus: fair play, clean fighting and no cheating. When you visit the shrines I want you to examine with great care the sixteen Zanes, statues of Zeus purchased with fines collected from those who have been caught cheating. In hundreds of years the Olympiad has had only sixteen men caught cheating in the games. So be warned. Our special police, the alytarches and the alytai, will watch you, and if you are found guilty of any evil deed the rod-bearers will apply the whip. We tolerate no nonsense from stupid athletes who break the rules.

"Olympia has her traditions and one of these is that the athletes will be responsible for cleaning up the rocks, underbrush and rubbish that has accumulated in the stadium and hippodrome since the last Olympiad. Your assignments will be listed. Make sure you're there to help." The Elean looked around with stern eyes, then went on with his speech. "Our training begins at dawn. Wrestlers, pankratiasts, and boxers will meet here in the palaestra, runners, jumpers, discus and javelin throwers will meet in the gymnasium just north of the palaestra.

"You men think you've had it hard, but we Eleans have trained for the last ten months to prepare. You will find us to be skillful trainers, the best. You all know the famous Mys, five times Olympic boxer, the grand old man. He gets better as he gets older. Stand up." A gnarled and bruised old man rose and shook his fists above his head, receiving cheers from the assembled athletes. "You boxers will have the honor to be trained by Mys, the very best. The wrestlers and pankratiasts will be trained by Herakleitos, who took the crown last year. He's young but don't let those good looks fool you, he's mean as a mountain lion." My Elean friend stood, then Attalos announced the trainers for the other events, some famous for their athletic prowess and others not so well known.

"Now, one last thing. Remember this is a sacred shrine and deport yourselves with decency and good taste. Don't piss in the Altis and when you take a shit be sure to cover it up so somebody won't step in it. Good luck to all of you. Meet with your trainers and be good boys." The athletes gathered around their trainers. I joined with the other wrestlers around Herakleitos, who told us to strip and to meet him in the palaestra to begin training.

"This place is really big," Charmis said, as he looked around, keeping to my heels. "I hear they've got hot baths and a big swimming pool. They certainly have gone out of their way to make the athletes comfortable. My goodness, Herakleitos is very beautiful. Everybody was looking him over, but I think he has eyes for you."

"Yes, he is beautiful. I hope he's a good trainer and knows a lot about boxing, my weak point. I should have stayed a simple wrestler, then there would not be so much to learn," I said idly, making conversation as the big athletes threaded their way between the crowds who'd gathered in the shaded colonnade.

The walls of the palaestra were imbedded with memorials to past

Olympic winners. Some, in fact, had placed their ashes in the walls to be forever near the place of their victories. Statues of bronze or painted stone stood along the walls, and men of all shapes, sizes and pursuits lined the way. Some eagerly reached out to touch the handsome young athletes and there were the usual astrologers, soothsayers and magicians. Poets read their works to small audiences. Philosophers of many schools preached their ideas to any audience they could get. I often wondered why this noisy, shouting and chaotic melee of men are permitted into the palaestra. Most of them care little about an athlete's need for concentration and their ass-like braying can disturb us, and many of them think nothing of coming to blows to make a point. I suppose it's part of Hellenic freedom and that Hellas would be very poor without their exchanges of ideas, but I wish they'd find somewhere else to air their thoughts.

Charmis and I finally reached the loutron, where I removed my tunic. It was the first day of training at Olympia and the nervous tension had already set in. Would I be eliminated? I could imagine similar thoughts running through the heads of the other athletes as they talked noisily, stretching their muscles, hitting their servants over some trivial mistake. It's difficult to put into words what we felt that day. You might train every day until you dropped and master every skill needed, but there was always fate to consider on the grueling road to victory. There's a saying: After victory at Olympia, you might as well die, for you've nothing else to live for.

"Pantarkes, master," Charmis spoke while kneading the tight muscles of my back. "Sir, I've been in your service for a year now and I was wondering if I might return to Thebes after the games. I'm getting old and it's time to go home and die."

"You're not that old."

"Nearing fifty. Not many years left."

"I had no idea you were fifty. Who else knows my aches and pains? Who can so soothingly smooth the oil and dust me? Have I not paid you well enough?"

"Yes and I've put the money away. There'll be lots of ships taking people home at the port of Cyllene. It's only a short journey home. Have I not served you well?"

"Yes, you've done that. I hate to depart with you, but I know what it's like to be far away from home. Stay with me during this difficult time." Charmis' request surprised me. I'd become so accustomed to his patience with my sometimes angry nature and his tenderness to my pains that I'd forgotten he was only a slave in my hire. I could have demanded that he stay, but I knew only too well what it was to be homesick. "I don't know what I'll do without you, dear Charmis. We'd better get outside, the day grows late and I've much work to do."

Herakleitos took my breath away as I caught sight of him talking to the wrestlers. Oiled and dusted with a fine peach-colored powder, his magnificent physique gracefully poised on the ball of one foot, his arms outstretched, he was the perfect athlete. Probably in his late twenties, he was the center of attention. I have been called handsome, but all eyes were on Herakleitos. His penis was becomingly small and finely formed, caught in a brush of light brown hair, his testicles round and smooth. He looked my way and smiled knowingly. I hoped he was not against having sex during training.

"I want to do a few light exercises today." Herakleitos' voice was firm and commanding. And so, to the high-pitched pipings of the auletes, we exercised: side-bends, jumping and some exercises with the weights to stretch our muscles. When our bodies were warmed up and limber, our gymnastes lined us up for our first light matches, giving him a chance to study our movements before he decided on our regular program of training. That afternoon we went to a nearby room to exercise with the punching bag, our hands wrapped with the soft leather himantes for protection.

"You move well, Pantarkes, though a bit jerky. Try to make your arm movement smoother. Left, right, get those fists up there. More movement on the toes, like dancing. Feel your feet, be natural. Let the rhythm of the flutes guide you. You're stiff, like a statue, be alive. Here, let me show you." Herakleitos came over from the bench and I sat down to watch.

At once he was pounding at the leather bag with hard fists and graceful action. I thought he might rip the bag away in his fury. "You've got to watch the face. Keep your fists up. See how I keep my feet moving. Anticipate your opponent. Watch him. Watch his eyes. Be angry, after all it's only a leather bag. Left, right, right, left. Parry and thrust. Thrust and parry. Be the aggressor at all times. Never give the other man a chance to get in." I watched with great care as he bounced around pounding the hapless bag. His was a natural grace, instinctive, his hands and feet moving with grace and beauty, as masses of muscle fibers moved together without effort. The chiseled cuts of his lean belly quivered, covered with oil, dust and sweat. It

144

was with the greatest effort that I kept my eyes above his navel. He stopped to look over to me. "See, it's very simple."

"Simple when you know how."

"You'll get on to it. What do you eat?"

"Almost anything I can get my hand on: bread, cheese, vegetables, fish, and meat, when I can get it."

"Diet is very important. Easy on the bread. Meat is very easy to get with all the sacrificial animals being butchered. They give it away free after services at dawn and dusk. Eat lots of meat and vegetables, you can't go wrong there. It's almost time to call it a day. In the humid evenings I go down to the river and look at the stars. I've found a place where it is sandy and cool. After supper we could go together, if you'd like, and watch the stars." Herakleitos touched my arm.

I should have modestly drawn away, but I returned his touch. "Yes, I would like that." After a scrapedown with the strigil and a warm bath, Charmis helped me dress and we returned to camp. I stopped at the temple wall and picked up fresh lamb from the priests, and later we feasted on roast meat. Damon had spent his time at the stables with his horses and he was in good spirits.

"Pantarkes." I looked up from the fire and Herakleitos stood there, the flickering campfire glancing off his bronzed muscles. He wore a light tunic and carried a blanket under his arm. "Ready? Put on some sandals, it's rocky along the river." He put his arm around my shoulder and we walked towards the river. The night sky was alive with sparkling stars, matched by the flickering campfires scattered around the shrines of Olympia. It was a warm night, a warmth matched only by the warmth of Herakleitos' body next to mine as we stumbled over the pebbled dry river bed. Soon we came to a clump of bushes, and hearing the water lapping the shore we found our way through the tall water plants to a small clearing overlooking the river. "Here," he said, spreading the blanket and taking off his tunic. "I like to lie naked. Isn't it nice here?"

"Yes, beautiful. The river sounds are soothing and the stars are so bright." I removed my tunic and lay down looking up at the stars. After a while Herakleitos raised up on his elbow and looked into my eyes.

"The first time I saw you at Delphi I felt a desire for you. I could feel your pain. I was glad you beat Agias, he was such a pompous ass."

"I thought the Eleans might hate me for taking one of their heros. But they were kind to me. I noticed you in their group and was struck by your beauty, and though we spoke few words you remained in my memory. I never thought we'd be here, now, watching the stars."

"The Eleans recognized your great skill and courage. They have their eye on you and wonder if you'll be able to repeat your victory."

"I will."

"I know you will, Pantarkes." He touched my cheek, which sent a lightning-like flash through my body.

"You are the most beautiful man I've ever seen." He bent over, his lips brushed against mine and our bodies pressed together in the joy of love-making. His hard masculinity thrilled me, stirring an intense animal passion that carried us to the stars of heaven and to the earth below. His fierce lips left my mouth, traveling down my chest, biting, nipping. Finally, our energy spent, we lay together. I knew at the end of the games he would return to Elis and I to Sparta, but it was a magical moment that each of us would remember for a long time.

"Aieeeeeeee! Look to the skies! The stars are falling!" A loud, scream traveled out over the river. "Run! Run! The stars are falling." Other shouts joined the first and we heard the sounds of running feet nearby. The riverbank hadn't been as empty as we'd thought. We broke our embrace and our eyes shot heavenward. It looked like the stars were indeed falling, as bright points of light shot here and there like agitated fireflys. I was filled with fear; it was an omen of evil, the sign of an end of greatness.

"They are falling. Let's run." I jumped up.

"No, don't be scared." Herakleitos caught my leg. "I've seen them before. They're only meteors, things in the air. The stars are fixed and cannot move. I cannot explain them, but they're not supernatural. They mean nothing, and they're quite pretty."

His logic calmed my nerves and we watched the heavenly display. "Look, that star has a tail." A sparkling, slender object swept across the sky. "That is certainly an evil omen, surely a sign of disaster. Everybody knows that. Someone of greatness will die. The world will fall apart," I cried, clutching my lover as the strange object crossed overhead.

"No use running to the trees. Stars are as big as houses. If this is our time I'd rather die in your arms. It's a comet, a long-haired star."

"A sign of death!"

"It could be, but I doubt it. Many beliefs held by the uneducated are false. Yet it is scary. It might mean something. I wonder who's death it signals?"

"It is probably a false omen," I said, not wanting to appear uneducated. Soon the heavenly fires went out and only the firmly fixed stars hung above us. Returning to camp, men huddled together for protection.

Early the next morning a group of athletes appeared at the gates of the temple to receive the rations of fresh meat. Some laughed and joked and others were still groggy from the last night's parties. An old man stood watching, his face contorted in a fierce scowl, his frail body supported by a walking stick. He looked like a wandering philosopher and from his unkempt appearance I assumed he was a cynic, who hates everything, especially athletes. He called out to us, his voice filled with loathing.

"Pigs. Gluttons. All you athletes do is eat and sleep. There are ten thousand evils in Hellas, but nothing is worse than the race of athletes. Of what use are all those muscles? Vain, empty men, lop-sided with heaviness. Pompous, arrogant, bloated hulks of nothingness. Where are your minds? Lost in a pile of fat and grease. Seek wisdom, not vainglory, which passes and benefits no one."

"I can't say wisdom has done you any good, you old bag of bones. Be off with you before I smash those dusty bones."

"Even dead I'm worth more than you. I teach the truth."

"What truth?"

"Eternal truth. I'm afraid your mind is too soggy with layers of fat to understand."

"Shit. You ask these wise men to explain themselves and all you get is the bit about 'eternal truth.' Avoiding the question?"

"Truth is beauty and beauty is truth."

"Speaking in riddles? Old man, your words make no sense. What has beauty to do with truth? Beauty is when I throw some bastard in the pit. Be off. We're hungry." The old cynic wandered off in search of truth and beauty and we got our ration of meat.

Our training days began before dawn. Sometimes, before exercise, we'd be given the task of cleaning up the grounds, and with shovels, pickaxes and rollers we'd go out to pick up rocks, trim bushes, and clean the debris and garbage. And then came the training through the heat, flies and sweat. The bugs seemed attracted to the olive oil and dusting powder on my skin.

Antiphon is supposed to have said: "Training makes athletes as golden-gleaming as the columns in the palaestra — and as solid as stone." It was an idealized view, I'm afraid. We were not solid stone, but bruised, battered and beaten humans, creatures of tension and

147

nerves, and as the days of training passed our lives together grew more difficult. The understanding between an athlete and his trainer must be a close one. The athlete must trust his trainer, a trainer who is always demanding the best, though the athlete may not always be giving his best.

One hot afternoon a heated quarrel broke out. A wrestler, proud of his fine body, entered the palaestra to train. As his gymnastes watched, the wrestler began to strut and pose before an adoring audience. The trainer flew into a rage and gave him a good blow to the ears. "Shitty, worthless athlete! Get to work." The wrestler stalked off the sand, followed by his gymnastes, each shouting at the other. The trainer grabbed a sharp strigil and plunged it into the back of the wrestler, who fell to the dust, dead. "Let the strigil be used as a sword on worthless athletes!" The trainer was never charged with any crime.

Olympia was the home of the mighty Zeus and his divine wife Hera. The infidelities of Zeus with mortal girls and boys are the subject of many jokes and stories, but here at Olympia, wrapped in age-old tradition, one forgets the common, homely things that are said about the gods. Early one morning Herakleitos and I took a walk through the Altis, the sacred grove between the temples of Zeus and Hera. It was a delightful morning, with cool air, chirping birds and a soft breeze caressing the many trees. Hundreds of statues of athletes, winners at Olympia, stood around. Some of them, their statues covered with flowers and gifts, had become heros and demigods. Others were praised as healers, and it is believed by many that the strength of a dead athlete can cure illness. In fact, strigil-scrapings are sometimes sold to cure wounds. To these healer-athletes go the prayers of many.

Circling around, following a row of Doric columns, we reached the eastern end and entrance to the great marble-roofed temple of Zeus. The massive bronze doors of the temple stood open, as the morning services to the god had begun. Inside was the famous forty-foot statue of Zeus, sitting in solemn grandeur, his august bearded head nearly against the ceiling. The black marble floor and the pool of oil at his feet, used to prevent the ivory from cracking, reflected the image. The artist Phidias, who made the image of Athena Parthenos at Athens, had carved the great statue, its flesh rendered in softly glowing ivory, its robes molded of shining gold. The countenance of the god, calm, benign, and eternal, looked down as his priests prepared their service. I felt a lump in my throat as my friend and I placed a pinch of incense on a side altar, then quietly left.

As we rounded a bend in the pathway to the smaller temple of Hera, a round, unfinished marble building caught my eye. Slabs and drums of fine white marble lay about and a high fence surrounded it. A bold sign informed us that trespassers would be punished by death. Surprised by so harsh a warning in such a holy place, I asked Herakleitos what it was.

"The Phillipion. When it's finished it will house the statues of King Phillip and the Macedonian royal family. Everybody hates it. They write obscenities on the marble and throw offal at it. The Macedonians finally put a fence around it. It's rumored that the statues will be worshipped in the Egyptian style, a thing so offensive to Hellas that the building has become an object of great hatred."

"He's a barbarian, a foreigner."

"He rules Hellas and can do damn well what he wants. They even let him into the games. His arrogance knows no bounds. We ignore the Phillipion and wish it, like the Macedonians, would go away. The temple of Hera is over there."

Later we passed the Zanes, those inglorious statues of Zeus paid for by fines placed on cheaters in the games, then we reached the krypteia, a vaulted arch leading into the open stadium. In a few weeks forty thousand men would sit there on the sloping embankments, bearing the blistering heat and many discomforts to watch the Olympiad.

To our right was an enclosed grandstand, with twelve stone chairs, where the honored Hellanodikai would sit during the games. Across from it were the seat and altar reserved for the honored priestess of Demeter Chamyne, the only woman allowed to view the games. At that early morning hour the great stadium was silent, but in a few weeks all of Hellas would be cheering, shouting, booing, drinking, eating, scratching insect bites, and complaining of heat prostration, as athletes strove to win a crown of wild olive. Herakleitos and I returned to the palaestra for another day of hard training.

Damon sat near the campfire watching me. "Writing on your scroll again? Papyrus is expensive."

"It's easier than having to lug around a marble block to write on," I replied, smiling. "Someday when I'm old and have children I can take my book out and read it to them. These are precious times for me and the mind forgets. So much is happening that I want to write it all down while the moment is fresh in my mind."

"Did you write about me?" Damon asked, looking pensive.

"Yes."

"Something nice, I hope."

The days of training had become routine: exercise, eating and sleeping. The Elean judges had gradually eliminated the worst athletes, so the competition was now more fierce. The culls left Olympia, their hopes of victory smashed and shattered like a pottery jar.

One morning I went to the palaestra as usual, but noticed the big square was strangely quiet and the athletes stood around in small groups talking in low voices. Herakleitos saw me and came running over.

"Have you heard the news? King Phillip has been assassinated by a member of his own bodyguard. Alexander has proclaimed himself king."

"Phillip dead? I can't believe it." My mind raced back to the days after the battle of Chaeronea and my brief meeting with the Macedonian king. He had seemed fearful for his life and now his fears had been realized. And the strange Alexander, belittling his father for falling over a couch, with high aspirations of world conquest. Had his son ordered and plotted Phillip's assassination? Probably.

"King Alexander III. It bodes evil for Hellas, I think. Already cities rise up against the Macedonians and are throwing out their hated garrisons. What will the new king do with Hellas in revolt?"

"I don't know. I met him once long ago and I don't think he'll take any shit from Hellas." I heard my name being called. Telemachus, in full armor ran towards me.

"Pantarkes, bad news. Sparta has broken the sacred truce and has been disbarred from the games!"

I stood in shock, my mouth open. "Disbarred! It can't be! We can't be out of the games, we've worked so hard for victory."

"Sparta, learning of Phillip's death, renewed its ancient quarrels with the town of Lepron, which had started the thing by stealing some Spartan horses. The insulted Ephors sent a small army to get them back and destroyed the place. The Hellanodikai has judged Sparta to be at fault and will not allow her to enter the games. Sparta's honor meant more than any Olympic victories."

Bitter disappointment clutched my heart. The news was too much to bear. "We've come so far for nothing. Shit. The Hellanodikai say they are fair. The Spartan truce-breaking was not of our making. We're athletes, not crafty politicians, all we want is to compete. We'll demand the Eleans hear our case. Is that asking too much, Elean?" I said, fairly shouting at Herakleitos.

150

"Yes, you may plead your case, but don't expect the Eleans to reconsider. Once they make a rule they stick to it, and this is serious. All you can do is ask them. I'll try to arrange a meeting." Herakleitos rushed off. Telemachus and I watched with grave apprehension.

Early the next morning the eleven remaining Spartan athletes stood in the round-ended bouleuterion to plead our case. We watched the Eleans, who sat in majestic splendor at the far end of the hall. Telemachus bowed low as he approached them.

"Lords of Olympia. I've come to ask that my boys, good Spartans, be allowed to play the games. They've done no harm and they're not at fault because the Spartan hoplites went to Lepron to get some horses back. It was too minor an affair to have such sad consequences for my boys, who've worked so hard to place in the finals. You're fair men and all we ask is that they be allowed to compete."

One of the purple-robed Eleans stood up. "We've considered your request. The minor affair wasn't so minor. According to our reports an armed force of five hundred hoplites marched to Lepron and wiped out the town, leaving it a smoking heap in direct violation of the sacred peace of Zeus. We must bar your city from the games and fine them. We are in sympathy with the athletes but most of them are young and they can wait the four years until the next Olympiad. Our decision is final."

"That cannot be!" I shouted out. "The destruction of Lepron had nothing to do with us. Are we to be blamed? I say the noble Hellanodikai are unjust and unfair." I went on madly, boldly, my eyes almost in tears.

"The accusation is false. The Hellanodikai strive to the utmost to abide by their own rules of fair-play and honesty. There is something to what you say, Pantarkes. We know of your Pythian win and the defeat of one of Elis' greatest athletes, the noble Agias. We Eleans think that you should have a chance to prove yourself. We say this to the Spartan athletes: if you wish to enter the finals you must find sponsorship from another city. This may be difficult for proud Spartans, but it's the only way you can enter."

"Deny Sparta! You ask too much of my boys. They will never shift loyalties."

"I wouldn't be too sure of that," I said. "Sparta has abandoned us for their silly war. What loyalties do we really owe them? None, I say."

"Thebes will sponsor Pantarkes. I'm Melesias, architheoros of the theoroi of Thebes. I trained the boy not so many years ago. He was a

151

good student. Come fight for Thebes, Pantarkes. We're not rich, but you'll not find us poor either."

"Melesias, old friend, it's good to see you. Thank you for your offer. Yes, I'll fight for Thebes."

"You can't do that! To deny your birthplace, your city. You're a hero there. Forget this Olympiad, there's always the next."

"I put it to you, dear Telemachus, who knows what will come for me in the next four years? My chance is now. At twenty-two I'll be an old man, all weak and withered up by age and who wants to see a senile pankratiast?"

"If your win means that much to you, so be it. Go with Thebes, if you will. There's no disgrace. It is the fault of foolish Sparta to have lost a winner." Telemachus smiled. The Spartan athletes were split; some went home, some gained sponsorship from other cities. I was glad to have a friend in Thebes.

And I was glad to see old Melesias. Age had caught up with him, his bones were stiff with rheumatism, his eyes rummy, but filled with fire. Remembering my first days in his fine palaestra and the sharp blow he'd laid across my back for my hubristic arrogance, I was sorry to hear that he had retired. Many athletes would be denied his wisdom and his excellent training.

We talked of times past. Phillip's murder was much on his mind: he had hated Phillip and now hated Alexander even more. "He murdered his own father to gain a throne. He's a boy, a stripling. He's effete and though of age, refuses to grow a beard, just to keep his boyish looks. He's a common pornae, a girl-boy, who sticks his legs up for his husband, Hephaistion. After having his father murdered by the witless Pausanias, he struck out again and had his two brothers put to death. The throne of Macedonia went for a high price. The gods help us, for a monster, a true tyrannos, is king over Hellas."

"He was kind to me after the battle, offering me a high post in his army. I wonder where I'd be now if I'd accepted. Poor Phillip, brought down by his own son. He'll never be as great as his father, just a murderous barbarian. Don't worry, he'll go back to Pella and no one will ever hear about him again."

"Look back."

"Oh yes, beautiful." Herakleitos and I had climbed the wooded hill of Kronos, and a cool breeze whispered through the pine as I turned from my climbing to look back down at Olympia where thousands of campfires flickered. "It looks like all of Hellas has come to Olympia,"

152

I said listening to the sounds of laughter, song and merriment that filled the clear air of night, "to get drunk."

"Wine merchants get rich from this festival, along with food servers, potters, pickpockets, magicians, musicians, hawkers, and even a few athletes who know the right people."

"What do you mean?"

"There's only one winner, some must lose and he might as well get paid for it. It's never been proven, but we know it goes on. The big, wealthy cities will pay anything to get one winner, anything. The games have become too big, too famous for the Hellanodikai to handle. My father told me how wonderful it used to be, now he doesn't even come anymore. He said something was missing, the religious nature, the feeling of the sacred. When Phillip's new stoa is built it will cut off the Altis from the stadium, completely separating the temples from the games. He says it's just a big noisy circus of brawn and extravagance, but that's his opinion. I like them the way they are now: bright, colorful and fun."

"Fun for everybody except the athletes, who must stay in training. Ha, the party last night at the Theban theoroi almost got out of hand. The drunken fools tore the tent down. I had only one cup of well-watered wine."

"There will be enough parties after the games to satiate any need for wine-bibbing."

"Speaking of training, I'd better get on down to bed. The games start tomorrow and I don't want to miss anything." Herakleitos and I took a last look at the splendid sight and walked down the hill of Kronos.

The sun entered the olive, pine, and oak groves with proper magnificence on the opening day of the one hundred and eleventh Olympiad, bathing the dawn clouds with hues of purple and pink. Already the air was a hazy blue with the smoke of campfires and the light breeze tasty with the scent of cooking. Round about, many tents of bright linen canvas provided housing for the thousands of Hellenes gathered to watch the games. Tethered lambs, oxen, horses and sheep waited for their chosen destiny on sacrificial altars.

It was a busy camp. Men carried precious water from the Alpheus river and from the wells in painted urns, and gathered firewood from the pebbled dry river bed. Several drunk horsemen raced their mares through the groves upsetting tents and cooking pots, loud shouts following them. Men sitting on tree stumps or low stools were having their hair cut and beards trimmed, and if they were well off, their slaves carefully rummaged through chests of wood, each looking for his master's best himation and jewels. Perfumed with costly oils, their hair curled and braided, and finely dressed, the men of Hellas prepared for the day.

It is said that Hellas is not a state of being, but a state of mind, and though we might come from the farthest corners of the world we were all Hellenes, unified by Hellenic ideals of order, beauty, freedom and sportsmanship, all gathered at this holy place to praise the gods and the accomplishments of mortals. So I wrote on my papyrus that early morning, watching, thinking, trying to quickly catch my impressions before they slipped from my mind. My reveries were broken when Damon rode up, his piebald mare snorting and pawing the dusty ground. He was laughing and talking with other boys who rode with him, bragging on how they had mischievously scattered the camp. "You'd better hurry, Damon. The processional won't wait for a gang of jockeys." Damon jumped down as the other boys rode off. He was scratching his ass and swatting flies. "This bare-assed, bare-back riding is rubbing me raw." Damon, nearly sixteen, was losing his baby fat and his boyishness.

In the distance we heard the shrill blasts of trumpets and the voice of the herald calling everyone to the opening day ceremonies. "We'd better go. At least athletes don't have to dress up," Damon said. He rubbed his teeth with his finger, gargled and spit the water out. I put my scroll away and we started off, answering the trumpets' call.

The Hellanodikai gathered on the roadway coming in from Elis. They stood greeting high officials and priests who would lead the procession of athletes to the oath-taking. A thousand naked athletes, men and boys, gathered in behind the Eleans. Though the real number of athletes was now small, we were joined by fathers, brothers, former Olympians and hangers-on. Behind us, the fancy chariots rumbled into place, and somewhere behind them the horses and riders would come along. What a day! Madness, frivolity and nonsense ruled at Olympia as we jostled along, rubbing the hot stones from our bare feet and wiping the sweat from our brows.

The road was lined with happy, cheering men. A wall provided a perch for spectators as we marched by on our way to the temple of Zeus Horkios, where according to ancient tradition we would take our sacred vows. The strong morning sunlight poured into the room as the athletes entered, jostling for a position in front to watch the ceremonies. Catching the sunlight at the far end of the big room the bronze image of mighty Zeus sat enthroned; each upraised brazen hand

154

held a golden thunderbolt, a threat to any man or boy who would break their vows. Before the image a marble altar waited as priests prepared a wild boar for sacrifice.

The usually noisy athletes were silent as the priests quickly slashed the boar's throat, then after the death thrashing ceased the boar's hairy genitals were severed and placed on a gold plate. The bloody priest raised the plate, and said with solemn tones, "Those athletes who have trained diligently and persevered may stay, those who have been shoddy and careless may leave." No one stirred. We made our vows before the divine image to fight fairly, to keep the rules, and to abide by the decisions of the umpires. The judges and umpires took vows to judge fairly, and one by one we filed by to place our hands on the bloody mire, sealing our words with holy action.

It was a relief to get outside. Black flies, gorged on the blood of the slaughtered boar, filled the air with their droning. It was rumored that a special sacrifice made to Zeus, Averter of Flies, had in olden times made the annoying and pesky bugs go away, but the sacrifice had somehow lost its power. After we had each registered our name, city, and event with the judges, we crowded into the Altis to watch the ceremony of Kallistephanos, the making of beautiful crowns. According to tradition a boy with both parents living would gather the olive branches used to fashion the coveted wreaths. A boy of about twelve, a pair of golden shears in hand, scampered monkey-like up the gnarled branches of the ancient tree, carefully cutting and gathering the branches of life. The multitude then followed him the short ways to the temple of Hera, where he placed the branches on a gold and ivory table. Later, tied with gold, the branches would be placed on the heads of victors.

The final event of the opening day ceremonies was the choosing of the official trumpeter and herald for the games. The only qualification was loudness. It would be the herald's task to announce the contestants and the events in the stadium. The sound of the golden horn and the voice of the herald would have to carry over the shouts of noisy spectators as the athletes came onto the field.

Returning to the bouleuterion I read the schedule of events and the names of the contestants. My event, the pankration was to be held on the fourth and final day. Damon would race on the third day, and tomorrow the boys' events would be held. I read my name painted on the white-washed board: Pantarkes of Thebes, pankration. Someone had scratched out Thebes and written in Sparta. I guess they were still proud of me though I would fight for Thebes.

I found Charmis milling around in the crowd and we headed off to the palaestra and bathhouse. The baths were heated, a great luxury. They also had a swimming pool and a sweatbath, because sweating draws off the bad humors of the body and cures bad breath.

Walking through the palaestra to the bathhouse presented its usual problems. A crowd gathered around one particularly odd magician, who, it was said, had the good luck to predict Phillip's death the night when the heavens seemed to explode. Men pressed coins into his hands as other magicians looked on with envy. This magician had come from a faraway place called India and was a holyman of their religion. He was strange. Most of the time he sat on a bed of nails, with bronze needles stuck through his lips and body. His long gray hair, matted with dust and mud, hung to his feet. His naked body was covered with curious designs tattooed into his skin. No one had ever seen him eat or sleep and most of the time he sat on his nails in a trance. No one could quite figure him out but now, with his reputation made, he was the center of attention.

I got the urge to have my fortune read and joined the line. After some wait I finally stood looking down at him, and kneeling down I gave him a coin I'd borrowed from Charmis. His hand, like the paw of a monkey, reached out, and he looked at me with a toothless smile, his forehead marked with a sign resembling a trident. Everyone knows magicians are frauds, but our curiosity about ourselves and our future makes some of them very rich.

"Eh," he grunted. "What do you want?" His speech was halting.

"Will the olive crown be mine?"

Wrinkling his nose and wiping it with his tongue, he gave me a hard look, and then bent down, drawing mysterious signs into the ground. He cast some strangely cut sticks. "Shiva, Kali, Vishnu, Kali, Vishnu," he chanted. "Kali. You know of Kali? There are forces here I do not understand. Conflict between opposites, life and death. Achilles? What does that mean? Someone is falling, shouting a curse. A curse of death. But there is victory. I see it. But other things, other things I understand not." The holy man erased his markings.

"Does that mean I'll win?"

"Yes, a crown of olive will be yours at the end of your day." He grinned and gave me the coin back. "I've had enough for the day. Soon there will be another to pay and he's more demanding."

"Charmis, the holy man says I'll win." I stood up.

"He talked for a long time, what did he say?"

"I don't know. Mumblings. Magicians try to mystify you to earn their coins, part of the business. Come on." We headed off to the baths.

Two men, one a handsome youth, the other a bearded older man, stood arguing. The sunburnt youth pounded his finger into the older man's chest.

"Shit! I'll never make it. You've trained me wrong. My joints are stiff and my muscles sore. I shouldn't have trusted you. My father said not to trust you. The pentathlon is tomorrow and I can barely move my legs."

"You're in fine shape. These things are in your mind. You blame your faults on me. Your training the last month has been the best, now your mind makes you tense, doubtful of your abilities."

"Orthon looks at me like I'm nothing. Shit, I know he'll win."

"Don't you see what he's doing? He's making you think you're weak and not fit for the pentathlon. You're stupid to pay any attention to him."

"I'm going to run away."

"You'll be fined and can never come again."

"I don't care."

"Yes, you do. You've come across half the world to be here. Listen, Demetrios, I can train your muscles, teach you the proper methods of sport, but it's up to you. You have a bad case of cold feet, that's all. Get your head on straight, and don't blame your problems on me. Shape up." The older man gave the youth a hard look and walked away.

Charmis rubbed my shoulders and we listened to the conversation, as it was impossible to ignore the loud voices. I was sitting on the marbled edge of the hot bath, dangling my feet in the soothing water, and the young man sat down beside me. He looked dejected, watching the steam rise from the water. "I heard what your trainer said to you. It's true, you know, a worried psyche can hurt your performance. Where are you from?"

"Pergamum. It's a big city in Asia Minor, on the other side of the Aegean sea. You?"

"Sparta."

"Spartans are good soldiers."

"They like to think so. You're entered in the Pentathlon?" The Pentathlon is difficult, consisting of five events: running, jumping, discus, javelin, and wrestling. To compete, one should be good in all of them, and must win in three events, the triakter.

157

"Unfortunately, I'm a runner and jumper, not bad at throwing, but awful at wrestling. I'm not as big as you. I bet you're a wrestler."

"A pankratiast."

"Brutal. Is this your first Olympiad?"

"Yes, I took the laurel crown at Delphi."

"It's my first. I won a lot of victories in Pergamum. I started as a boy competitor. My father had been a successful athlete and wanted the same for me. The big Panhellenic games are different from the small-time stuff, more tension and grief. It's all been easy until now. Are you scared?"

"Everybody is. But you can't let it get you down. Even if you don't take the crown you've placed in the finals, and there's honor in that."

"Ha, very little. Winning is the only thing that counts. Gods, my belly is churning in knots. I just don't think I can take it anymore."

"The greatest disgrace is to run away, to show cowardice." I looked at the young man. I could feel his anxiety as his hands gripped the edge of the stone, his knuckles bled white, shaking. He seemed like a horse about to bolt from the starting line. "Ah, you'll forget all about your knots when you get into the stadium. Let's get some steam and then we'll have a match outside the palaestra. Wrestling is easy, just balance and leverage. Boxing, now, that's hard," I said, not knowing quite what to say to ease his fears. After drying off we went into the sun to practice. Demetrios, while not the best wrestler, wasn't all that bad, and I let him throw me. We departed good friends and I promised to watch his contest the third day.

Dawn of the second day, the first day of games, finally arrived. Already the vast stadium was filled with spectators awaiting the entrance of the ranking Hellanodikai. Soon they appeared, and in a slow measured step, each carrying a palm branch, they walked to the grandstand. Following the Eleans came the lone woman, dressed in veils of purple and holding a shaft of wheat, the symbol of her city, Eleusis. She crossed the stadium to take her honored place opposite the grandstand. After the ceremonies the day would be taken up with boys' games, and the stadium was filled with happy fathers and male relatives. The young lads entered as trumpets and heralds announced their names. Here were the future athletes of Hellas, but now they were like young colts, frisky, awkward, but filled with a hard drive. The day belonged to the men who had brought them and they stood with wet eyes watching their sons and brothers compete in running, jumping, wrestling and the rest. The heat of the day would be great and to spend the day watching adolescent boys throw each other

158

around had little appeal for me. I took my blanket off the dry, sticky grass, and wandered off to sit near the cool river.

Damon was strangely quiet that evening as we sat around the campfire roasting meat. "Tomorrow is your big day. Scared?" I asked.

"Naw, being scared is for cowards. The mare is in good shape and she cannot lose." He looked up at the trees and the stars. "Anyway, just being here is so great."

"You look like you've been having fun, racing the horses and all."

"Yes. I want to come again. I was thinking of entering the Nemean games next year. It's all been so exciting, and the men are really great. It's just like with my buddies back at Sparta, camping out, racing around, stirring up a little dust, raising a little hell, you know."

"I think you've got the fever, a well-known disease, an addiction to entering games. Some men never do anything else."

"Yes, that's it. If I could win and establish my horses as winners, think of it, they'd flock to Sparta to buy my steeds. It's business. You could make money hand over fist. I was talking with some men from Syracuse, they're rich. . . . I still owe you for paying my fines. That was a lot of money."

"I want you to forget about that."

"It's a debt I owe you. Do you want to enter the Nemean games next year?"

"I don't know, it's a long way off. We'll see how things go. I want you to win tomorrow, Damon. I'll be out there cheering for you." Damon was growing up.

Before dawn the great hippodrome was filled with jostling thousands, gathered on the third day of the Olympiad to watch the chariot and horseracing. The glittering gold and bronze chariots rumbled up to take their places. It was a sport for the very rich: governors, princes, even a few kings, borne in costly litters, watched their hired charioteers take the field. Stablemasters guided them into the starting gates. The horses, snorting the air, gradually took their places in the giant triangle.

The starting gate, resembling the four hundred foot prow of a great ship, an ingenious system of levers and ropes, was set into motion. At the tip of the gate a dolphin of bronze stood on a long pole. As the machine started, the pole lowered, and at the base of it an eagle rose up, releasing the ropes stretched in front of the stalls.

The horses started out in a hot blaze of dust and fury. The first race, the tethrippon for four-horse chariots, began its dangerous course.

The skill of each driver was tested as his whip sang through the air. With thundering hooves and flying manes, the tethered beasts hit top speed. Soon came the dreaded turning post, each taut driver staying as close as possible to the fence. The drivers tried to slow just enough to take the turn. Pressed in on either side by furious men and horses, sparks flying off the metal wheel hubs, the chariots were bunched at the turn in a cloud of bellowing dust. The casualties began as the cars meshed, sending the hapless men, overturned chariots, and snorting horses into the baked earth. The thundering hooves showed no mercy as they hit the downed men.

Too soon came the second turn, and on and on the swift chariots flew while the carnage continued. The eighth, the ninth, and at last, the tenth turn was done and a lone chariot came out of the dust, flying to the finishing line. The crowd pressed in to see the winner, who with hands wrapped in tight leather, wiped sweat away from his dust-caked eyes and mouth. Trumpets called out and the herald announced the winner, the wealthy owner of the chariot: Demades of Athens.

The crown of olive was given to the richly dressed man, who floated in a perfumed cloud among the cheers of many. Surgeons rushed in to bandage the driver's hands as he limped down off the car. Some men looked away, disgruntled at having lost their bets on the race. It's said that entire fortunes are made or lost in a single day as gold, slaves, merchant ships, even towns go up for grabs in ferocious betting.

The hippodrome was cleared for the next race. The foals and mares took their places for the various races as the morning drew to a close. At one time, so I heard, there was a race for mule-drawn carts, but the animals were so stubborn that the race was dropped.

Finally the keles was announced. I watched proudly as Damon took his place. Looking neither left nor right he clenched the reins tightly, his knees dug into the hard-breathing ribs of his mare. He shifted his weight onto the backbone of the animal, lifted his genitals out of the way and wiped his nose as he waited for the rope to drop. The eagle rose up on its pole and my sunburnt brother, leaning forward, his body tense, flew off from his post for the first of the six circuits. He took an early lead, staying near the fence. The other jockeys, though hard pressed to keep their mounts on the sweaty backs of their mares, soon gained in a dusty cloud. By the third circuit, the race seemed evenly matched. Cheering for my brother, I could almost feel the tight grip, the biting dust and dirt, the digging knees, and his jostled body as he sat in close to the mare's head, bearing the brunt of the pounding hooves as they bit into the ground. One jockey lost his mount and plunged in a mangled heap to the ground as the race drew to an end.

"Damon! Damon!" I shouted, hoping my cheers would help. Out of the dust cloud a lone rider shot toward the finish line. From the distance I couldn't see the face.

"Ankeres of Syracuse." The name of the winner was announced as I saw my brother come in a hard-riding second. He watched as the winner was lifted to the shoulders of his supporters and carried around, the crown of olive firmly in place around his head. I could feel Damon's hurt and rushed to him. Others had come up to him, slapping his back, shaking his hand. Damon beamed a broad smile. I had expected the sad look of defeat.

"We've won," Damon said, leading his mare. "We're rich."

"You lost. You came in second."

"Syracuse paid me to lose. I placed my bets on Ankeres, a certain winner."

"You threw the game? That's dishonest!"

"Don't be a fool, dear brother. I've not entered these silly games just to win a worthless crown of wild olive. I'm out to make money. I have enough time left in my life to win plenty of games. By the time Syracuse and the bettors pay me off I'll have enough to buy the best breeding stock in Hellas." Damon, surrounded by his friends from Syracuse, gave me a smirk and walked off. The morning races were over and the hippodrome emptied.

A little after high sun the crowd returned to that stadium to watch the pentathlon, the five-event contest that so harshly tests the well-rounded athlete. I thought about Demetrios of Pergamum. Perhaps he had bolted, unable to stand the strain, but he was a fine athlete and I hoped to cheer him on during the long afternoon.

The stadium was filling with tired and irascible men, munching on black olives and cakes, drinking wine or water from leather bags and calling for the contest to begin, as shimmers of raw heat rose from the field.

I'd brought a skin of water and a blanket, and I sat near the grand-stand for a better view, looking around for Herakleitos. I knew he was anxious to watch the matches and soon I saw him come over the embankment. I got up to wave at him and, spotting me, he threaded his way through the discontented spectators. He smiled and sat down beside me.

"What a morning! The physicians are busy patching up the

161

charioteers. Some of them were a mess, nothing could be done. I saw your brother, his hands were cut from the reins. I thought he lost, but he looked happy."

"I guess he was happy to even finish the games. He wants to enter the Nemean games next year. Are his hands all right?"

"Nothing serious. Look, the trumpeters." With a shrill blast and the loud yell of the herald, the pentathlon was announced. Quickly the mob quieted down, and the names of the contestants and their sponsoring cities were cried out.

"I was talking with a young man from Pergamum, he was so scared of entering the pentathlon that he wanted to run away. I hope he shows up."

"I know how it is. It's worse for some athletes than others. How about you, Pantarkes. Scared? Tomorrow is your big day."

"Everybody is scared, but I think I've got the pankration in the bag. Except for Arrichion, that bastard. If I draw him I'm in real trouble. He has muscles out to here and he's strong as an ox."

"Yes, he is a formidable opponent, very sullen and mean."

"Ugly, too."

"A veritable gorgon, a male Medusa, I think. He tried to seduce me one time when we were working out, but he's not my type."

"He's got the hots for everything with a cock."

"Don't worry about him. Just remember all I've taught. You're in top form."

"Hey, they've just called out Demetrios' name. There he is." The man from Pergamum ran out of the dark, arched entrance as his fellows cheered him on. Some of the magnificently built men had a wiry runner's build, others had the heavier body of a wrestler. The wrestlers would find it difficult to run and jump, but the lean men would find wrestling difficult, as they would be pitted against a more powerful body. Sweat ran in rivulets down their tanned bodies as they took numbered lots from a silver bowl. The lordly Hellanodikai settled back into their stone chairs, and the quiet crowd waited for the first event: the long jump.

The skamma, a fifty foot pit of loosened earth, smoothed with a roller so the landing foot prints of the jumpers would clearly show, lay open and ready for the first jump. The men limbered up, shaking their legs, stretching, and several heaved the crescent-shaped haltares. These six-pound weights, sometimes used to build muscles, would now help the jumpers attain greater lengths in the long jump. With the blast of a trumpet the pentathlon began.

To the high-piping auletes, a man prepared for the first jump by walking some feet away, swinging the haltares. Then he turned, his feet dug into the hot ground and he took off in a fast run until his flying feet hit the leaping point and he sailed into the empty air. He held the weights in front and at the apex of the jump his arms and legs were nearly parallel as he flew across the skamma. Near the end of the jump he dropped the weights and his feet drove into the soft earth, his prints clearly visible. Judges carefully measured the jump and announced the length with great ceremony.

"Only twenty-three feet. Not a very good jump. Last year a jumper took the full fifty feet; he landed on the hard earth and broke his leg. That's not common; he took the crown," Herakleitos said, drinking from his skin of water. "I hope your friend can do better."

"He said this was his best event." We watched as Demetrios took his run-up, his face knit with concentration. He leaped smoothly into the air, and after a brief moment of graceful flight his feet hit the earth with a muscle-tearing jolt. The measurement was taken: thirty-nine feet. Demetrios raised his arms and strutted before the exedra, and the Hellanodikai gave him a round of hand-clapping. "He's good, really good. He made the rest of the jumpers look like crippled storks." Some of the jumpers had dropped the haltares in mid-air, or had stumbled to the earth in a heap of flying limbs. The judges, unable to get an exact measurement in these cases, let them try again. Finally the event ended.

"I don't think Demetrios will do so well in the discus. I tried to throw one of the damn things once and it flew out of my hand, nearly killing everyone around. They're difficult to learn."

The Olympic discus, a round plate of bronze engraved with the eagle of Zeus, about thirteen inches across and weighing fifteen pounds, was removed from its special wooden box and given to the first athlete. Swinging the bronze plate in the palm of his hand, he walked to the far end of the stadium and took his place in the balbis, the throwing point, from which he faced the full length of the six-hundred-foot stadium. All heads turned to watch as the athlete began his throw, bringing his arms, legs and torso into perfect rhythm and coordination. Swinging his arm back and forth, he touched the rim of the disc and began to whirl around and around, finally heaving the plate into the air. With a soft swoosh the bronze took off and all eyes turned to the bright heavens as it sailed high overhead. Moments later it landed with a soft thud in a small cloud of hot dust. Its position was marked with a wooden peg and the throw was measured.

"Not bad, though far short of the record of ninety-five feet," Herakleitos said. One by one the athletes took their turns, the crowd watching with strained necks as the measurements were announced. At last Demetrios took his turn. He seemed to be in trouble, for the bronze plate fell several times from his sweating hand. He put it down and rubbed a handful of dirt in his hands to get a better grip on the smooth bronze. As the disc flew away Demetrios toppled back slightly, almost falling from the force of the swing.

"Only seventy-six feet, he'll never make it," Herakleitos remarked as the next contender, a powerfully-built man, walked forward. He seemed to be talking to the bronze, kissing it, like he was making love. Raising it high overhead, his superb body drenched with sweat, his hard muscles gleaming in the sun, he prepared for the throw. He turned rapidly, his fast-flying feet digging a hole, gaining momentum until, with a loud yell he heaved the plate into the sky. It seemed that it must have flown out over the Altis, landing somewhere in the river, so long was it in the air. The judges watched for the impact, their eyes straining, and with a sudden yell one judge flung himself out of the way as the discus hit the earth a short way away. This throw of ninety feet was the longest of the afternoon.

The pentathlon went on. Some spectators grew faint with heat prostration and were carried off the brown dry grass into the shade. Others had passed out from too much wine, and still others wandered away looking for relief from the blistering heat. The athletes, weary and sore, but still not finished, slumped to the ground, bathing their dry lips with water and toweling the sweat from their bodies.

Soon the third event, the stade, was announced. This sprint, running the six-hundred-foot length of the stadium, would severely tax the athletes' tired bodies. Grudgingly the first set of four runners, chosen by lot, walked to the grooved marble starting line. The judges took their places at either end of the marble to make certain there were no false starts. The four runners dug their toes into the cut grooves. When all was ready the umpire gave a shout and with flying arms and feet the four men made a dash to the other end of the stadium. The sprint was judged a dead heat and had to be run again. Herakleitos and I, having emptied our water skins and needing to take a piss, went off, soon returning with water and some sausages bought from a vendor.

When we returned to our place the final heat of the stade had begun. Only two men remained, Demetrios and another runner. I hoped my friend would win as they dashed off. I knew both men must be exhausted, but Demetrios seemed to find new strength as he neared the finish line. With a high head, his powerful chest pushed out, he pulled out and away, winning the stade. He sank to his knees, his tense face managing a smile of victory, and we ran over to lift him to his feet.

"Demetrios, you've won two events, only the javelin and wrestling remain. It's almost over."

"I'm too tired, . . . I'll never win," the exhausted man mumbled, his arms thrown around our shoulders. His body slumped as the javelin event was announced. The afternoon sun was casting long shadows of purple and mauve across the stadium, and a cool breeze came from the river as we went back to our blankets. Demetrios and the athletes took the long pointed poles. The apotomeus javelin used in these contests is lighter than those used by warriors and a leather thong is tied mid-point for throwing. One by one each athlete took the leather loop in his two fingers, testing for the center of balance, then started the run-up and with a strong mighty heave sent the javelin into the air. The winner took the event with a tremendous throw of four hundred fifty feet. He and Demetrios with two wins each remained on the field while the others left. Only wrestling remained; the winner of that event would take the crown of wild olive.

A layer of soft sand was spread before the exedra while the remaining spectators gathered to watch. The day was growing late and if a winner had not emerged by darkness the bout would be declared a draw and the crown would be offered to the god, with no winner.

Demetrios stood nervously as he was oiled and dusted. He feared the match, but seemed to have recovered from his exhaustion. His gymnastes checked carefully to see that the oil was spread evenly, and tried to cheer up Demetrios. The trainer's skill would also now be tested; his word had been law for the previous month and his methods would be put to the test. The two contestants were of the same build and it would only be a question of stamina. Who would find the strength to take the three falls?

I knew Demetrios was scared and that might work against him. The athletes wet their lips, then rinsed their dry mouths with water. Demetrios coughed and seemed to gag, his belly wrenched, and whatever food remained there came up. He looked around, his eyes wild. His trainer read his thoughts. "It's better to die at Olympia than to withdraw," I heard the trainer say, patting Demetrios on the back, kneading his tight neck muscles. Demetrios ran his hands through his short brown hair. The sun bathed his lean, finely muscled body in a reddish glow. Somewhere in his inner depths he would have to find a new fire, a new courage to face the match. Time was growing short, but both men had come too far to have the day end in a forced draw.

The two men quickly took their stances and moved in. Demetrios took the first fall. The umpires moved in around the sand pit, which angered the spectators as it blocked their view. Several men ran in, striking at the umpires and soon the police came to tear the men apart with slashing whips. The fighting outside the pit was now the center of attention and I could see the two wrestlers standing there, hands on hips, waiting. The excited spectators were driven back or pushed out of the stadium and the match went on.

The tired Hellanodikai looked at the dying sun and I saw they were talking heatedly, trying to decide whether to call the match. By the time their discussion had ended, Demetrios had taken the second fall. I looked over at the wreath of wild olive placed on a small golden table. It had wilted and dried up in the great heat of the day.

The two contestants cast long shadows across the stadium as they took the final stance. Demetrios was close to victory, but both were visibly wearing down. Their short hair, matted with sweat and oil, clung to their skulls; their shoulders sagged. The noisy crowd hushed and even the buzzing of the black flies ceased. There was a chill and there in the shadows it seemed I could see all of the thousands of men who had grappled here, hovering in silence as they waited for victory or defeat.

Demetrios moved in quickly. He knocked away his opponent's out-stretched arms, going for a backhold. Tightly clenching his hands together behind the man's back, squatting slightly, Demetrios dug in. The other man pounded his shoulders, trying to break the hard grip, pushing mightily against the arms that held him tight. The fibers of muscle stretched rope-like in his arms, but finally he could stand the grip of pain no more, and wearily he raised his arm in defeat. Not realizing his victory, Demetrios refused to break his hold until the two men were pulled apart. Dazed and choking, his nose bloodied, Demetrios sank to his knees as an Elean picked up the wild olive. Its dark green leaves fell away in a dusty pile and Demetrios was crowned with a withered branch. Barely alive, the happy athlete was carried around the darkening stadium on the joyous shoulders of his fellow athletes. I cheered him on and hoped he would cheer my victory tomorrow as I competed in the pankration.

Herakleitos and I lay together looking up at the bright silver moon, listening to the river and the screeching of night birds. He looked up at me, his beautiful face bathed in pale moonlight, his white teeth brilliant as he spoke. "Tomorrow is the last day of contests. Soon it will be all over. You'll be returning to Sparta?"

"Yes, my brother and I have a small farm. He wants to breed race horses. You'll be returning to Elis, won't you?"

"Yes. My father wants me to marry and settle down. It's all arranged for me, but I want to continue to train athletes. Ah, it's all too good to end. I've liked being with you, Pantarkes. I'll hold our moments together in my heart forever. And tomorrow, the time of the full moon and the holiest day of all, the time of the great hecatomb. The altars of Zeus will run crimson with the blood of a hundred oxen, and we'll see the final events: running, wrestling, boxing, the pankration, and the race in armor, and then we can all get drunk.

"Be careful, all the rich food after a strict diet can wreak hell on your belly. The last time, the parties went on for nearly a week before everyone finally left. Olympia will settle down until the next Olympiad. The priests will take over in their eternal service to the Thunderer and the white-armed Hera. Tourists will arrive to make sacrifices and to pray. So much in so short a time. We Hellenes make too much of the Olympiad. Our entire lives center around the place. We deprive ourselves, face hard, grueling contests, drive our minds and bodies to the breaking point, cross angry oceans, sleep in strange places far away from our homes, spend vast sums of money, all to watch a bunch of mad, sweating men and boys try to win a few leaves of olive. It's insane. I wonder why we do it."

"For victory. To prove ourselves and to be the best.... and with good luck, to be supported by our cities for the rest of our lives. An Olympian is respected, his legends are passed down from generation to generation. Who has not heard of Theagenes of Thasos, the pankratiast? He toured various cities and was said to have received 1,400 crowns. There's that story about his statue which was raised by the Thasians after his death. A man he had defeated came at night to flog it, but it fell over and killed him. The statue was charged with murder and thrown into the sea and soon a great drought came to the land. Fearing they'd angered a god the Thasians sent a delegation to Delphi. The Pythia told them to restore the statue and the drought ended. Theagenes is worshipped as a healing spirit in Thasos, or so I've heard."

"A wild story I think. How about the great Milo of Kroton? He carried a full grown heifer around the stadium to prove his superhuman strength. He was a second Herakles, it's said. He came to a bad end trying to prove his strength; he became trapped pulling a tree apart and was eaten by wolves."

"I read a splendid ode by Pindar, composed for the boxer Diagoras of Rhodes. His mother was said to have conceived the great man after a night with the swift-footed Hermes, the son of a god. He's called euthymaches, the fair-fighter."

"There's also Polydamas of Scotussa. His big statue stands in the Altis. He won the pankration in the ninety-third Olympiad. He was said to be the tallest man ever to live. He killed lions, tore a hind foot from a bull and stopped a chariot that was going at full speed. He came to a bad death when he and his friends entered a cave for shade. The roof started to fall in and Polydamas held it up long enough for his friends to escape, but he was crushed to death when he tried to leave. Everyone knows the stories, though you have to take them with a grain of salt."

"Yes, I suppose. Olympians are remembered and if the tales become a little embroidered with fiction, who's to know?"

"Do you think you'll enter again, Pantarkes?"

"Yes, many more times. But like the mighty Milo I can't go on forever. I suppose I must some day face defeat by a younger, stronger man, but by then I'll be rich, and with luck men a thousand years from now will be here, lying arm in arm, telling my story."

"That is, if you win. I can't think of one story about anyone who's lost."

"To win is the only thing that matters."

The final day of contests began with celebrations on a scale I'd never seen before. This sacred day would bring with the sacrifice of a hundred fine oxen, a gift by the Eleans to mighty Zeus, the thunderer. Kings, princes, governors, and dictators gathered, each bringing beasts, offerings of fine gold and silver, costly gems, amphora of oil and wine and baskets of grains, all gifts to enrich the coffers of Olympia and dedicated to the god of this place, the great Zeus.

Damon and I bought two piglets to sacrifice, even though we had to pay ten times their actual value. From the gymnasium, the processional set out along the high enclosing wall and then entered the temple with shouts of exuberance. Ahead the gold-ornamented oxen trodded to their fate, led along by priests. The grunting, bellowing animals almost drowned out the blasts of trumpets, and those of us in the rear found it difficult to avoid stepping in the wet dung.

In the Altis we could see the gleaming marble pile of the great altar of Zeus. The love life of the god is well known and it would seem that half of Hellas claimed to be his offspring by mortal women. His amorous advances to girls and handsome boys formed the theme of the place of sacrifice. Robed priests stood before the sacred fire and the throats of the expensive oxen were slit. Their thighs were burned and the rest of each animal was divided up. After a long while the bellowing stopped; the air was pungent with the smell of burning flesh as the offerings were sent to Mount Olympus, home of the gods. After the Elean sacrifice, the other missions presented their sacrifices to Zeus. The many altars soon smoked with burning flesh. It was time for Damon and me to offer our sacrifices, our squirming piglets. I took my pig to the altar of Hermes Agon, protector of wrestlers. I took my small knife from its scabbard and quickly drew it across the pink throat of the piglet. The blood splattered my tunic and arms. Damon took his pig to the altar of the fearsome god of the hippodrome, Taraxippos, whose mysterious powers are said to disturb horses rounding the dangerous turn.

I watched as the all-consuming flames ate through the pieces of flesh, sending my prayers for victory to Hermes. The sacrifices made, we left the Altis and its smoking fires to the gods and priests, and after a rest and lunch we made our way to the stadium for the final event of this Olympiad.

Damon wished me good luck as he left for the stadium to watch the contest. With Charmis in tow, I entered the krypte to await my event, passing the time there with the other athletes: lean runners, the heavy wrestlers, the mauled boxers and the other pankratiasts. Nearby, those men who would race in armor tried on their helmets, shields and greaves, pulling and tugging at the leather straps. Theirs would be the final event after the pankration. They looked odd, naked except for the armor fitted to their bodies, as they carefully selected pieces from the pile of bronze arms furnished by the Eleans.

The runners stood in the dark cool passageway, ready to run out as their names were called. Meanwhile they limbered up, pulling at their legs, rubbing their stiff muscles. Some stopped to read the scratched graffiti covering the walls of the krypte, the words of former athletes who had come that way and, while waiting to undress, had used the hard end of the strigil to scratch their name, declare their love for another athlete, or write obscenities about their trainer.

With a blast of trumpets the runners were announced. One by one

169

they ran out to the cheers of the crowd. The heavy-weights moved in to the dressing area. Boxers tied the himantes around their hands, the wrestlers oiled and dusted. I looked at Charmis. He carried my strigil and towels, and had brought a small stool for me to sit on while we waited. As I sat he knelt beside me. Where would I ever find another oiler, duster and masseur? After the games he would go home. He seemed to realize my thoughts, he patted my knee and told me not to worry.

The thunderous shouts of the spectators filled the air as the running events came to an end. Now the heavy events would begin. The wrestlers lined up, and one by one marched into the stadium while the losing runners came back, their lean bodies panting. There were no cheers for them, no palm-branches, no red ribbons as they were booed off the field. Their heads were low and some were sobbing, crushed by defeat. The victors, covered with glory, were carried off the field on the shoulders of their exuberant admirers.

Now the earth seemed to shake as the wrestlers ran out, their ponderous strength to be tested in the sand. Grunting, groaning, sweating, each in turn sought the triakter, the three falls necessary to win the crown of wild olive and the title of Olympian. The time passed slowly until a victor emerged from the burning sand. The physicians took the field to mend the battered and bloodied losers.

Next it was the boxers' turn. Soon their hard pummelling began. Pounded and slugged, their faces and bodies pulverized into blood pulp, noses broken, eyes blackened, they fought on.

I grew tense as the time for the pankration approached. My competition, the twelve pankratiasts, stood waiting. Ladas, Pythokles, Sodamos, Dion, Satyros and Arrichion, men whom I'd trained with this past month, were the finalists in the hard pankration. We stood, waiting for our moment of truth. After a polite nod, each man gathered with his oiler or talked with Herakleitos, who watched for signs of weakness, fright or anger, anything that would upset the balance of the athlete. He would now see the testing of his wisdom as a trainer. Had he trained a man too hard? Too easy? Had he carved that block of marble into a gleaming pillar of strength and perfection?

I had to win and prove myself to the lofty Eleans. They still resented my victory over Agias, their prized pankratiast! How sweet it would be to stand crowned before them now, I thought smiling to myself. I wanted to win for Thebes, the city that had given me a home so long ago, and I wanted to win for Sparta, that stubborn city that threw away a chance for an Olympian victory for an old grudge fight. I wanted to win for Damon, though I was still angry at him for selling his victory to Syracuse. I wanted to win for Charmis, who sat beside me. It would give him something to remember for the rest of his days. And I wanted to win for myself. Pantarkes, Olympian. It had a good ring to it, and my mind repeated the words as we waited for the boxers to take their victories. The crowd let out a tumultuous roar as the winner was announced: Mys of Taras. The old boxer had proven his skill once more. Looking more dead than alive the defeated boxers staggered off the field of battle, some held up or dragged in by their trainers and physicians, and wiping their blood with cool water.

The pankration was announced. I waited. "Pantarkes of Thebes." I walked from the dark krypte into the bright sunlight and we lined up before the noble Hellanodikai to draw lots.

The two "Alpha" men were paired with each other, the two "Beta" men, and so one, as in the preliminary bouts. We moved to the skamma where the soft sand, rolled and smoothed out, waited for the pankratiasts to disturb its placid whiteness.

My first match with Seleukos of Megara began. Quickly I landed a fist to his belly and with a hard kick he sprawled back to the ground. I flew at him, hoping to get the first pin, but his foot caught me in the chest and I fell to the sand. Rolling, twisting, his fists pounded me, but I managed to seize his arm and wrench it upwards. He howled in pain; one throw for me. Seleukos lay defeated as I took the triakter, then won the next preliminary match. Soon only Arrichion of Croton and I remained. The Crotons prided themselves on athletic prowess, in contrast to the softness of Sybaris, a nearby city whose people despise exercise and devote themselves to making money. The heifer-bearing Milo had been from Croton.

Arrichion looked at me with hard, narrowed eyes, running his hands over his bald head, rinsing the dryness from his mouth and blood from his nose. The swarthy Italian was of massive build, though shorter than me, and quiet in nature. We had never talked much during training; now, our wins had brought us together on the sand. My worst fears were realized. Alone of all the pankratiasts, the Croton had never lost. During training he had rarely left the palaestra or the punching bag, and he was always distant in his thoughts, unbending, pushing himself to the limits of endurance. I faced a formidable opponent. He had doted on Herakleitos, following the trainer's every word. He had seemed like a cooking pot about to boil over as he watched the beautiful Herakleitos and me leave the palaestra after each day of training.

This would be the final match before the race in armor concluded the Olympiad. Tomorrow, after I had taken the Italian to task, I could relax, break training and get drunk to celebrate my victory. What feasting there would be! And then home to Sparta and Damon's horses. But first, I had this one last fight.

We took the stance. Arrichion seemed unsure of his moves, dancing around, jabbing the air. Was there fear in those narrow eyes? I hoped so. The restless crowd began to hiss and boo at the lack of action.

"Scared, Arrichion?"

"Shit, no. Stop dancing around. Let's get on with it."

"Your ugly face will be like a battered punching bag when I get through."

"Shit. They'll toss you on the funeral pyre like a thighbone. Herakleitos will have a dead lover. Pity. Then he'll take *me* down to the river bank for a little cocksucking. Let's go!"

"Jealous asshole. You're too ugly for him. Get with it."

Arrichion came to me with fists held high. I dodged, then landed with my fist on his jaw. He grabbed my hand and spun me around, wrenching my arm upwards, kicking my ribs with brutal feet. His other arm grabbed my throat, pinning me against his sweating chest. I could feel his coarse hairs against my back as I bent over, trying to toss him off me. He jumped up, wrapping his muscular legs around my middle while he made good his hold around my throat. Throttled by his hard arm, gasping for air, I dug my elbows into his ribs, trying to cause him whatever pain I could.

I could feel the blood throbbing through the veins in my head. My windpipe seemed ready to burst as I struggled to breathe. My mind was numbed by the stranglehold. Now Arrichion dug the heel of his foot into my balls, crushing them against my groin. Throwing my weight to my left leg, I caught his lower leg and foot between my thighs, trapping them, then deliberately I fell forward into the soft sand. The pressure against my windpipe kept up; I knew he had me, but I would try one last time. My hand traveled down my flanks until I had hold of his foot. If I could twist it enough the pain would cause him to surrender or to break his grip. With one hand, for the other was pinned beneath me, I felt his toes, his heel, and my fingers closed over it. With every last fiber of my strength I twisted. There was no air

172

now, my eyes were blinded by the sand, and I tasted blood in my mouth, but I could hear Arrichion howling with unbearable pain. I smiled, lifting my face out of the sand. I gave a final twist; the foot left its socket and dangled grotesquely from the leg. With a dreadful scream, his eyes streaming tears, Arrichion raised his hand in surrender. I had won the crown.

I raised my head a little. The bright sunlight filled my eyes, then it drifted away into darkness.

❧ Epilog

Pantarkes, dear brother. How proud you'd be today to see your fine statue here in the Altis of Olympia, a gift of Thebes and Sparta. The sunlight catches your face. Though of hard bronze you look almost lifelike, so skillfully has the sculptor caught your features. Your beautiful body, your muscles, gleam in golden metal. See, I've brought flowers to place at the base of your statue. Others have done the same, and the entire base is covered over with their sweet fragrance. Has it really been four years since your noble death and victory there in the sand? I wonder if you ever knew you'd won. I wrote it that way when I finished your story. What a hush fell over the crowd when they saw you were dead. Herakleitos placed the crown on your head with tearful eyes. But you could never know that.

Now it's time for another Olympiad. You'd be proud of me. I too have won victories and now all of Hellas goes to Sparta to buy my horses. I know you disapproved of my throwing the last games, but this time, dear Pantarkes, I'll not let you down.

OTHER ALYSON BOOKS YOU WILL ENJOY

Don't miss our free book offer at the end of this section!

QUATREFOIL
by James Barr
introduction by Samuel M. Steward; $6.95

Phillip Froelich is in trouble. The year is 1946, and he's traveling to Seattle where he will face a court-martial for acting insubordinate to a lazy officer in the closing days of World War II. On the way to Seattle he meets Tim Danelaw, and soon the court-martial is among the least of Phillip's concerns....

So begins *Quatrefoil*, a novel originally published in 1950. It marked a milestone in gay writing, with two of the first nonstereotyped gay characters to appear in American fiction. For readers of the Fifties, it was a rare chance to counteract the negative imagery that surrounded them.

Now we have reissued *Quatrefoil*. Readers today will find that it provides a vivid picture of what is was like to be gay in our recent past; on top of that, it's still a entertaining and well-crafted novel.

QUATREFOIL

a novel by James Barr
introduction by Samuel M. Steward

YOUNG, GAY AND PROUD!
edited by Sasha Alyson; $2.95

One high school student in ten is gay. Here is the first book ever to address the problems and needs of that often-invisible minority. It helps young people deal with questions like: Am I really gay? What would my friends think if I told them? Should I tell my parents? Does anybody else feel the way I do?

REFLECTIONS OF A ROCK LOBSTER
A story about growing up gay
by Aaron Fricke; $4.95

No one in Cumberland, Rhode Island was surprised when Aaron Fricke showed up at his high school prom with a male date; he had sued his school for the right to do so, and the papers had been full of the news ever since. Magazines like *People* and *Newsweek* reported on the case, and Aaron appeared on Phil Donahue and countless other talk shows.

Yet until his senior year, there would have been nothing to distinguish Aaron Fricke from anyone else his age. You'd never have guessed he was gay — and Aaron did his best to keep it that way. He created a shell around himself as protection against a world that he knew would reject him if it knew the truth. But finally his anger became too great, and he decided to make a stand.

Now, in *Reflections of a Rock Lobster*, you can read Fricke's moving story about growing up gay — about coming to terms with being different, and a lesson in what gay pride can really mean in a small New England town.

THE AGE TABOO
Gay male sexuality, power and consent
edited by Daniel Tsang, $5.95

Man/boy love is one of the most controversial issues ever to split the gay community. Here are a number of perspectives on the subject of intergenerational sex. The writers raise such broad-reaching questions as: What constitutes true consent? When does the "protection" of young people (or any other group) turn into their oppression? How do power differences affect personal relationships? ❧ It rapidly becomes clear from these essays that an understanding of the age taboo helps shed light on a great many aspects of human sexuality.

THE MEN WITH THE PINK TRIANGLE
by Heinz Heger, $4.95

As the long-hidden history of gay people slowly comes to light, one of the most terrifying chapters of that history concerns the  thousands of homosexuals who were thrown into Nazi concentration camps during World War II. *The Men With the Pink Triangle* is the true story of one man's ordeal in those camps.

Heger's account begins in Austria, in 1939. The author was a young medical student, in love with the son of a Nazi officer. In March of that year the Gestapo abruptly arrested him for homosexuality, and he spent the next six years in concentration camps. Like thousands of other homosexuals, he was forced to wear a pink triangle on his shirt so he could be readily identified for special abuses.

Heger's book provides the most vivid description we have of what those horrible years were like. Richard Hall, book columnist for *The Advocate*, praised it as "One of the ten best books of the year" and the *Gay Community News* warns that "You may find yourself riveted to your seat" by Heger's narrative.

THE ADVOCATE GUIDE TO GAY HEALTH
R.D. Fenwick; $6.95

You'd expect a good gay health book to cover a wide range of information, and this one does. What you wouldn't expect is that it could be so enjoyable to read! ༔ Here you'll find the expected information about sexually-transmitted diseases; you'll also learn about such things as what you should know before going into sex therapy; how some lesbians and gay men have handled their fears about aging; and the important lessons of the holistic health movement.

COMING OUT RIGHT
A handbook for the gay male
by Wes Muchmore and William Hanson, $5.95

Any gay man will have no trouble remembering the first time he stepped inside a gay bar. It's a frightening and difficult step, often representing the transition from a life of secrecy and isolation into a world of unknowns.

That step will be easier for gay men who have read *Coming Out Right*. Here, the many facets of gay life are spelled out for the newcomer: how to meet other gay people; what to expect when going home with a gay man; medical problems you could face; employment opportunities and discrimination; getting insurance for gay couples; what to expect at bars, baths and cruising spots; the unique problems faced by men coming out when they're under 18 or over 30. . . . in short, here in one book is information you would otherwise spend years learning the hard way.

Get a free copy of Young, Gay and Proud!

When you order at least three other books from us at the regular price, we'll send you a *free* copy of our book **Young, Gay and Proud!** Just be sure to ask for this free book when you place your order. (See order form on next page.)

To c

For more copies of this book, or other books described on the preceding pages, please ask at the bookstore where you bought this copy. We especially encourage you to shop at small, independent bookstores; it is their willingness to carry good but little-known titles that makes it possible to publish books such as this one.

You can also order directly from us by mail. Please enclose full payment, and add $.75 postage when ordering just one book; when you order two or more books, we'll pay postage. Add $1.00 for rush or overseas orders.

Bookstores: Standard trade terms apply. Details on request.

Send orders to: **Alyson Publications, Inc.**
PO Box 2783, Dept. B-20
Boston, MA 02208

— — — — — — — — — — — — — — — —

Please send me the following books:

☐ The Advocate Guide to Gay Health ($6.95)
☐ The Age Taboo ($5.95)
☐ Coming Out Right ($5.95)
☐ The Men With the Pink Triangle ($4.95)
☐ Quatrefoil ($6.95)
☐ Reflections of a Rock Lobster ($4.95)
☐ Young, Gay and Proud! ($2.95)

____Send a free copy of *Young, Gay and Proud!* as offered on the preceding page. I have ordered at least three other books.

Enclosed is my check or money order for $_____.

name: _____

address: _____

city:_____state:_____zip:_____

(Order on your own stationery if you prefer not to cut up this book.)